"How can you not f...
her own plane, combust...
and has a weakness fo...

PRAISE FOR
Charmed & Ready

STACKS

"Havens's writing is snappy, instantly engaging and downright charming."   —*Romantic Times*

"From demon-hunting and club-hopping to boyfriend-minding and shoe-shopping, this book has it all."   —Romancedivas.com

"I'm thoroughly charmed and ready for book number three. If only the networks could figure out how to make their new comedies as delightful as Candy Havens's books."
—Susan Young, *Oakland Tribune*

"A delightful ride from the first page to the last . . . the action is immediate and lightning-fast."   —*Romance Reviews Today*

"Wonderfully witty . . . Readers are sure to enjoy this second book in the Charmed series; it's magically delicious."
—*Paranormal Romance Reviews*

continued . . .

PRAISE FOR
Charmed & Dangerous

"Simply bewitching!" —*New York Times* bestselling
author Jodi Thomas

"From assassination attempts to steamy sex scenes to the summoning of magical powers, Havens covers a lot of ground. Weaving together political intrigue, romance, and fantasy is definitely tricky, but Havens makes it work in this quick-paced, engaging story with unique and likable characters." —*Booklist*

"Mix the mystique of all three Charlie's Angels, Buffy's brass and scrappy wit, add the globe-trotting smarts of Sydney Bristow, and you might come up with enough cool to fill Bronwyn's little witchy finger." —*Britta Coleman,
author of *Potter Springs*

"Smart, sexy, and sinfully wicked."

—*USA Today* bestselling
author Ronda Thompson

"A funny, imaginative take on what it would be like being a young, single, powerful witch." —Fresh Fiction.com

"This is a refreshing, fast-paced entry for Havens, who pulls out all the stops to put the world to rights with humor, some good old-fashioned street-fighting—witch style—and some well-deserved romance." —*Romantic Times*

Charmed & Deadly

Candace Havens

BERKLEY BOOKS, NEW YORK

THE BERKLEY PUBLISHING GROUP
Published by the Penguin Group
Penguin Group (USA) Inc.
375 Hudson Street, New York, New York 10014, USA
Penguin Group (Canada), 90 Eglinton Avenue East, Suite 700, Toronto, Ontario M4P 2Y3, Canada
(a division of Pearson Penguin Canada Inc.)
Penguin Books Ltd., 80 Strand, London WC2R 0RL, England
Penguin Group Ireland, 25 St. Stephen's Green, Dublin 2, Ireland (a division of Penguin Books Ltd.)
Penguin Group (Australia), 250 Camberwell Road, Camberwell, Victoria 3124, Australia
(a division of Pearson Australia Group Pty. Ltd.)
Penguin Books India Pvt. Ltd., 11 Community Centre, Panchsheel Park, New Delhi—110 017, India
Penguin Group (NZ), 67 Apollo Drive, Mairangi Bay, Auckland 1311, New Zealand
(a division of Pearson New Zealand Ltd.)
Penguin Books (South Africa) (Pty.) Ltd., 24 Sturdee Avenue, Rosebank, Johannesburg 2196,
South Africa

Penguin Books Ltd., Registered Offices: 80 Strand, London WC2R 0RL, England

PRINTING HISTORY
Berkley trade paperback edition / June 2007

Library of Congress Cataloging-in-Publication Data

Havens, Candace, 1963–
    Charmed and deadly / Candace Havens.—Berkley trade pbk. ed.
        p. cm.
    ISBN-13: 978-0-425-21525-8 (alk. paper)
    1. Witches—Fiction. I. Title.

PS3608.A878C48 2007
813'.6—dc22   2006021773

PRINTED IN THE UNITED STATES OF AMERICA

10   9   8   7   6   5   4   3   2   1

This book is dedicated to my Divas, who totally rock!

Acknowledgments

A special thanks to Leslie Gelbman, Susan Allison, Anne Sowards, and the gang at Berkley for letting me tell this story and for believing in me. Sha-Shana Crichton, you are the woman. I'm so grateful to the readers of the Charmed & Dangerous series who keep asking for more, and to my fellow writers who help me hone my craft. I'm very lucky to have the friends I do, and I want you all to know how much I appreciate you and that you inspire me every day. David Blackstock, thank you for making me feel beautiful. Curtis S., your kindness and generosity are what make you so amazing. To my family, you are all so supportive and I'm so happy you are a part of my world and are with me on this journey.

Musical inspiration for this story was provided by U2, Joss Stone, the Wreckers, Bob Marley, Fern Knight, the Killers, Nelly Furtado, Evanscence and everyone else on my iPod.

"What the hell is that?" A distorted male voice cut through the fog. I tried to open my eyes. They wouldn't budge. Something cold and wet covered my body.

I'm dreaming. My last thought had been to send myself out to search for the missing men using astral projection, while I tried to sleep in the stupid tree. The safest place to doze in the jungle, Kaz, my guide, had told me. This after a run-in with a leopard that made me feel like a T-bone on a platter. I can't believe I actually fell asleep with those eerie cat eyes staring at me all night.

"Jesus! It's Bronwyn." That voice I knew. Sam was in my dream. No surprises there. I'd been tramping through this godforsaken African jungle for days trying to find my hunka burnin' love.

"Is she alive?" That was Azir, my favorite sheik. I could almost smell his sandalwood scent. It all seemed so real. "Where did *she* come from?"

Two fingers brushed my neck and a hand pushed the hair from my forehead. "Her pulse is weak, but her breathing is steady." Sam again. "Bronwyn, can you hear me?"

Wow. This might be a really good dream. Sam and the sheik.

It was weird, though—I couldn't take control of my dream like I usually did. I wanted to talk with them, to tell them I was on my way, but my mouth wouldn't work.

"Bronwyn. It's Dad. I need you to try and open your eyes." Um, yuck. What was my dad doing in the middle of my sexy dream? "Come on, honey, you can do it." My dad had his doctor voice on. Stern but kind.

I took a deep breath and the effort caused me to cough.

"There's fluid in her lungs." That came from my dork-faced brother. I hadn't seen him in two years, and he sounded older, worried, and as annoying as ever. "Turn her onto her side."

Bite a big one, Brett. Dad had been a top-notch surgeon before Brett had been a zygote. Leave it to my brother to get all bossy. I sure as hell didn't understand why he would be in my dream.

They turned me over, and that was when I realized it wasn't a dream. Their hands poked and prodded. I was with them, but I had no idea how I'd done it. Had I accidentally astrally projected my body? No, I couldn't have; I didn't have that power yet. My brain felt like it had been sucked through some kind of vacuum and I couldn't get my thoughts to gel.

Then I sensed an evil presence, strong and malevolent. The stench of sulfur filled my nose. *Crap.* I had to wake up. I had to protect them. I reached out and connected with Sam's strong arm. I'd know those hard biceps anywhere.

"Talk to me, Bron." He squeezed my hand. "She's fading, how the hell is she doing that? Baby, say something." I heard the worry in his voice. He loved me so much.

Straining to speak caused something weird to happen inside my head. As I slid back into darkness, I whispered, "Evil's coming."

One

Friday
9 p.m.
Amsterdam
Peeved witches: 1
Dead Guys: 1
Spells: 5

Doesn't matter what kind of job you have, some days suck more than others. My friend Zane is a rock star. Sounds exciting enough, but he goes through months of monotonous rehearsals before the big, exciting show. Simone is a demon slayer, and even *she* gets bored sometimes. Kira's a librarian, and although I know she loves her job, I've caught her "resting her eyes" more than once on a slow Monday.

Me, I'm a witch who protects the British prime minister. Most of the time we sit around in meetings listening to the yammering of one diplomat after another. I read their minds and emotions and then let the PM know which way the wind's blowing. Usually, the toughest thing I have to do is stay awake.

Then there are days like today.

This morning we landed in Amsterdam for a peace conference. As we made our way to the limo from the PM's private jet, a bullet zinged past.

Sniper. Crap. It's going to be one of those kinds of days.

"My word. What was that?" The PM automatically ducked as another whistling bullet pinged into the tarmac inches from where we stood, two feet from the limo.

"Down!" I screamed as I shoved him behind the car. I threw a protective shield around us as I searched for the shooter. My magic can only hold out so long, and I needed to find our assailant fast.

I have the ability to open my mind and send it around the world in seconds. It comes in handy when I'm trying to keep track of my clients, a globetrotting bunch, who always seem to land in trouble.

Unfortunately, the talent isn't foolproof. This assassin was protected by a dark magic and it blocked me, which is one of the reasons I hadn't sensed him when we landed. Bullets riddled the car.

The rest of the PM's security team crouched behind the second limo, pulling their weapons and firing toward the roof.

The PM's nerdy assistant, Miles, talked on his cell phone headset and punched something into a small handheld computer. Clueless as usual.

"Miles get down, you idiot!"

Annoyed, he sneered at me, then there was a look of surprise as he realized what was going on. Before he could jump for cover a bullet hit him from behind, its force propelling him toward me. I pulled down the shield for a second so he wouldn't bounce against it and yanked him inside. A dark red stain spread against his chest.

"*Oafff*," Miles stuttered as he hit the ground.

I ripped off my white blouse and shoved it toward the prime minister, whispering a healing spell as I did. "Sir, I need you to hold this against the wound to stop the bleeding." Miles's pasty skin had gone even paler. *Damn, damn, damn.* I couldn't stand the nerdy jerk, but I didn't want him to die.

"I'll take care of him, Bronwyn. You get that bloody bastard." The PM is good under stress and always has that British stiff-upper-lip thing going for him. I haven't ever seen him lose his cool. Even when he was dying once, he was still quite dignified. The man always looks like he stepped out of *GQ* with his graying temples, chiseled chin, and extremely high fashion-IQ.

I nodded and made my way around the end of the car. We'd landed at Amsterdam's Schiphol Airport. They have incredible security, as people are always trying to smuggle one thing or another out of there. Thanks to some powerful magic, the sniper had made his way to the top of the building undetected.

The gunfire ceased, which meant he or she was on the run. Physically, there was no way I could reach the roof, but I didn't have to.

Dropping the protective shield, I focused on tracing the magic. I found one of the holes where a bullet had hit the car and put my hand on it. Opening my eyes I saw the trail of magic. Tiny wisps of black smoke leading to the roof. The hint of sulfur made the tiny hairs in my nose burn.

I couldn't see the sniper, but the magic was concentrated in one area on the roof. I threw a binding spell and held the assailant with my mind, but I couldn't get into his or hers, which was protected by a powerful warlock or witch.

Airport security personnel in short buses and an ambulance raced onto the tarmac. Holding their guns at the ready, they surrounded us.

My Dutch isn't so good, and I didn't want to freak them out by talking in their heads.

"Prime Minister, tell them the sniper's on the roof and to hurry. I can't hold him much longer."

The PM barked orders and I could see the police speaking into walkie-talkies. Normally, it isn't such a big deal for me to hold someone like this, but the magic protecting him was beyond strong.

"They have him surrounded, Bronwyn." The PM interrupted my concentration.

I let the sniper go and fell to my knees, temporarily drained, but I couldn't rest long. Miles needed me.

I pushed through security. The paramedics already had him on a gurney. The curly-haired, snippy jerk had lost consciousness. *Please, God, let it be because he's a major wuss.*

Someone tossed a blanket around my shoulders and I pulled it around me. I'd forgotten I was half naked. Thank goodness I'd worn a decent bra, one of my new purchases from La Perla.

I moved to the PM's side as they lifted Miles into the ambulance.

"I should go with him." The PM's voice was tinged with anger. He hated that his position put those around him in constant danger, but that's just the way it was. Crazy people always want to take out those in power. It is my job to make sure it doesn't happen.

"Sir, I need to question the gunman, and you need to be there." The PM wasn't traveling without me. Whoever hired the sniper wouldn't be happy about the botched job, and they would try again. Bad guys always have a plan B.

The PM had spent the last ten minutes rolling around on the tarmac, but he didn't look it. His Savile Row suit was no worse for the wear.

Turning to the nearest police officers he said something in Dutch. They nodded and spoke into their walkie-talkies again.

That's when we heard the shot. Everyone ducked, and I landed on top of the PM. My breasts smashed into his face. I heard him muffle words.

"Sorry." I moved so I was by his side.

"Bronwyn, we're fine," the PM said while he tried quite hard to avoid staring directly at my breasts, which were still only inches from his face. "I can hear what they are saying over the radio. The suspect committed suicide. That's the shot we heard." He sat up, brushing imaginary dirt from his sleeves.

I pulled the blanket around me again. "Huh. Guess we've had a change of plans. Let's go see how the twer—er—Miles is holding up."

The pilots, who had stayed inside the plane through all of this, brought out our bags. We stuffed the luggage in a limo and took off for the hospital.

Five hours later, Miles was out of any immediate danger and the doctors told us he was doing better than expected. I couldn't decide if I was happy about that news or not. Miles really does get on my nerves.

The PM thanked me. The healing spells had worked their magic.

* * *

We finally made it to the Dylan hotel, which is located on the Keizersgracht, one of the city's most famous canals. It looks like a big mansion on the outside, but it's modern, chic, and small, making it easier to protect the PM. He'd postponed his meetings for the evening, and for that I was grateful. My energy had been drained and I needed to sleep in order to recharge.

Usually his security staff stays with him, and I take a room nearby. This time I stayed in one of the extra rooms in the suite. I put protection wards on every door and window and swept the area with my mind. Seeing no immediate threat, I decided to get some rest.

I walked into my room. It was an explosion of color. Raspberry and cream stripes covered the comforter and canopy. Red lacquered boxes sat at the foot of the bed, and deep, rich mahogany tables sat on either side. A bit Cirque du Soleil for me, but the cushy-looking mattress beckoned me.

I had to sleep, but something niggled at my brain. You know how when you pack for a long trip and you can't think of what you might've left behind? That's how it felt. I'd missed something important over the last few hours, but I couldn't think of what it might be.

Climbing under the covers, my thoughts floated to Lulu's fried chicken back home. I'd been traveling with the PM, who has a penchant for grilled chicken and vegetables, for too long. It had been a while since I'd had a real meal and forever since I'd been to Lulu's café in my hometown of Sweet, Texas.

I turned my thoughts to home and Dr. Sam. We hadn't seen much of each other in the past month and I missed him so much. Depending on the time zone difference I'd call him when I woke up.

Mmmm. The last night we'd been together we'd discovered new

ways to enjoy apple pie. My mind wandered back to that sexy night. He'd made me "Bronwyn a la mode." I snuggled deeper into the pillow and my body relaxed.

That's when the thought that had bothered me for hours finally exploded in my head. Damn, if someone hadn't screwed with my head.

Two

Amsterdam

Saturday

3 a.m.

Thoroughly perturbed witches: 1

Spells: 2

Potions: 2

Makes me mad when someone else's magic gets the best of me, but that's exactly what happened.

Someone had spelled me with black magic so my mind had been muddled. The harder I tried to think, the worse it was. When I finally relaxed—*whammo!*—thoughts ran through my brain like rats on speed.

Once my synapses kicked in, it dawned on me. The magic. I might not be able to get into the dead gunman's head to find out why he'd attacked, but we could trace back the magic in much the same way as I had done with the black wisps at the airport.

Argh! The longer I waited, the harder it would be.

I shoved the covers away and sat on the side of the bed. Using one of the new crystals I'd bought in New York last month, I did a clarifying spell to clear my mind. I popped open my bag of tricks and found a bottle of blue juice. The special concoction is a potion I made up to heal most anything, even the darkest magic.

I checked my aura in the mirror and noticed its pinky glow was emerging from a gray mist. I couldn't believe I'd let someone do this to me.

Threw cold water on my face, put my mess of curls into a pony-tail, and tossed on jeans and a T-shirt. Grabbing my boots and jacket I made my way through the door of the bedroom into the living area.

The PM was talking on the phone and frowned when he saw me.

I waited for him to finish and then explained what must be done.

"I need to get to the morgue, or whatever they call it in Amsterdam." I headed toward the door.

"Could we have his things sent here? Do you need to see the body?" I turned to see the PM's hand was paused over the phone.

I thought for a moment. "No, the clothes would be enough."

"I'll take care of it. We'll have them within the hour. Why don't you get something to eat while we wait?" He pointed to a room service cart.

Food sounded good. I found what looked like a tuna sandwich. I'm not really big on fish, but who knew tuna could be so yummy? They'd mixed it with a wasabi mayonnaise and the flavors were spicy but not too hot. I opened a Diet Coke and let the caffeine clear the tired from my brain.

By the time the gunman's clothes arrived, I'd somewhat revived. I had the police officer place the items in the center of the dining table.

"Sir," I faced the PM. "I'm not sure what to expect with this. You may want to go in the other room."

He raised an eyebrow. "I think not."

I shrugged and turned my attention to the sniper's belongings.

The black clothing didn't look ominous, but I knew better. I circled the bag with salt and said a protection spell.

> *Goddess of Light I call thee,*
> *Protect us from the evil within the circle;*
> *Give us guidance on this night,*
> *Help us trace the darkness to its beginning;*
> *As I will,*
> *So mote it be.*

To counteract any backlash magic, I placed four blue crystals around the bag.

Lifting the ends of the bag, I opened it and slid the dark sweater and pants onto the table with a pair of tongs I borrowed from the salad bowl. There were no other items except a white-gold Rolex. *A well-paid gunman, to be certain.*

Taking a deep breath I held my hands over the items and cleared my brain. A dark magic protected this man, and it held tight, taking me absolutely nowhere. Tiny black wisps spun off it, but nothing to trace. There was something about it, though. Something familiar.

I shivered. Yes, I knew that magic. The smell alone would have done, but I'd also seen those evil black wisps before.

It belonged to my college sweetheart, Jason Asshole Gladstone.
I should have killed the jerk when I had the chance.

Sunday
8 a.m.
Somewhere between Amsterdam and London on the P.M.'s private jet
Tired witches: I

I want to go home. I want to have wild and crazy sex with my
boyfriend, Sam. I want to sit in my living room with my new plasma
television and watch *Live with Regis and Kelly*, and those chicks
from *The View* argue about nothing. I want to stuff my face full of
Lulu's chicken-fried steak, mashed potatoes, and top the whole
thing off with chocolate cake. I want to hang out with my friends
Kira, Caleb, and Margie and talk about who's cheatin' on who at
the Piggly Wiggly.

I want to do all of those things, but it's not happening today.

My first stop is getting the prime minister and Miles settled into
their London digs. Cole, a chief inspector with the International
Magic Police, flew in yesterday to travel with us. He's saved my butt
more than once so he's on the friend list, but he can be annoyingly
bossy at times.

I called him immediately after I realized Jason was behind the
hit on the PM and myself in Amsterdam.

"Cole, how did that bastard get out?" I screamed into my cell.

"Hello, Bronwyn, rough day?" Cole stayed calm, which only
made me angrier. "The weather here in Manhattan is beautiful."

"I'm not in the mood for your crap. Jason Gladstone tried to kill
us today, and I want to know why you idiots let him out of spook
prison."

Cole sighed. "I have no idea what you're talking about, but let me see. This Jason guy, is he someone you know from the past?"

"Duh! College sweetheart who tried to kill me." I paced back and forth on the soft carpet of the living area in our suite. I glanced over at the PM who was trying to look busy while listening intently at the same time.

"Wow! You really know how to pick them." I heard him typing on a keyboard. "What was the last name again? Gladstone?"

"Yes." I bit out the word.

"Okay. He was released two years ago to the Smith-Hawke Institute for Reformation."

That's where they take a bad warlock and totally wipe out his memories and powers, with the hopes of making him good again.

"I can't believe it. Well, their idiotic mumbo jumbo, sure the hell didn't work. His magic was all over this sniper who tried to kill us at Schiphol today."

"Huh. It says here that he's still at the Institute. Are you sure it was him?"

Yes. No. I don't know. I'd been wrong before, but I didn't think I was this time. "When someone tries to kill you with magic, you remember it Cole. You know that. It's something that stays with you long afterward. I know his magic. I realize there isn't anything scientific about that, but I just know it." I told him what I picked up when I took a look at the assassin's personal belongings.

He grunted. "Your instincts are seldom off. I'll check into it. If he's left the institute we'll track him. I'm sending someone to pick up the clothing so our people can get a better lead."

I stared at the pile on the table. "It's really dark magic. I tried."

"We have resources that can help us break down those wards.

Don't worry—if it's him, we'll find him." The spook squad was capable of tracing magic like a fingerprint, no matter how impenetrable it might seem. Of course it could take a month. I needed to find him a lot faster than that. I didn't want to give him another chance to kill me.

We disconnected and I told the PM everything Cole had said. He wasn't happy about the news. Every time magic is involved in an assassination attempt things get very complicated.

It also put the threat solely on my shoulders. The gunman hadn't been trying to kill the PM. He was most likely after me. Lovely.

The great thing about the PM is he never points the blame finger. His job puts us all in danger, too, so he gets it. Doesn't really make me feel any better that he is so understanding, but it helps me keep my job when crap like this goes down.

Later that night, Cole called with the news.

"Gladstone's been out for six months." Frustration was evident in Cole's voice. "His records indicate he was totally reformed, but he wasn't ever supposed to leave the institute. Someone screwed up in a major way."

"God. The man tried to kill me. How could they let him go?" On the upside, if he *was* loose, then I could kill him.

"I don't know, Bron, but I'm headed there to find out. You don't need the advice, because you're used to angry warlocks trying to obliterate you from the planet, but be careful. I don't think it'd be a bad idea for you to head back to Sweet as soon as possible."

I would if I could.

The PM decided he'd feel better on his home turf, too, so he arranged for us to get out of Amsterdam as soon as Miles was able to travel.

The namby-pamby Brit is holding up well considering he'd been hit in the shoulder with a bullet. He hasn't whined once, which may have something to do with the heavy sedation. The big question is if he will be able to use his arm again. A doctor and two nurses are traveling with us on the PM's private jet, but so far the trip has been uneventful.

Cole's been talking with the PM for the past hour. He wants to add some mystical support to the security staff, besides me—two or three people who can be with the PM full time. Basically, they're cops with powers, but nothing too strong. Their presence will give me a much-needed break.

I need to get home and recharge. All of this traveling makes me feel frazzled. I need to be at my best when I face Jason.

London
1 p.m.
Everyone is settled in at the PM's London estate. Miles has his own set of rooms and medical staff to look after him. We've beefed up the security force and I've done a quick sweep of everyone. I don't see anything dark lurking here.

We've had more than one security breach the past few months, so I have to keep a constant check on everyone who works on the PM's staff. Even when I'm in Sweet I do daily checks.

Cole's staying on for a few days to make the changes he'd talked about with the PM. I'm in a limo on my way to Heathrow. I'm heading to New York in a few hours and then on to Sweet.

Earlier today I called Sam to tell him that I was finally coming home.

"I can't wait, baby." His sexy voice melted over me like hot butter on a freshly baked roll.

"You need to rest up, because I'm so jumping your bones when I walk in the door."

He laughed. "I'll make sure to have my bones jumping ready. What do you want from Lulu's?"

"Hmmm. Everything. Tell the girls to surprise me." Ms. Helen and Ms. Johnnie are two hot chicks in their seventies who can cook better than anyone has a right to. I've never had anything bad at Lulu's—ever.

"I'll tell them and make sure they have some extra apple pie for us." His voice dipped just the tiniest bit when he said it and I had to cross my legs.

Our apple pie experiment had been extremely successful.

"Yes," I cleared my throat. "Apple pie should definitely be on the menu."

He laughed again. I loved the sound. The last six months had been tough for us. A stupid warlock, Blackstock, had tried to kill us. We'd survived but it hadn't been easy. We'd also had to work out some difficult issues, mostly about trust, but things were going along well these days.

"Bron?"

"Yeah?"

"I'm glad you're okay." That was his code for "thank God you didn't die—again." Every time I left home that was a possibility.

I told him everything about Jason's sniper attack.

He blew out a breath, making a soft motorboat sound with his lips. "But you're okay?"

"Yes. I feel weird. I don't know how to explain it. I thought I would never have to mess with that guy again." I hated that we had to deal with another badass warlock.

"You know we can handle it, Bron. We've been through worse."

True.

"Have I mentioned how much I love you?" I couldn't keep myself from smiling. Sam was one incredible man.

"You know I feel exactly the same way. Oh, before I forget. Kira told me to mention that she and Caleb decided to buy the house down the street, so they'll be your permanent neighbors."

The local librarian, Kira, had become one of my dearest friends. Caleb, a hot-shot investigative reporter, was appointed by my brother Brett to sort of look after me while Brett's in Africa saving the world. I don't know what Kira sees in him. He reminds me a little too much of my stinky brother. But I guess Caleb's an okay guy.

"Well, at least I don't have to worry whether or not they'll fix the place up. I bet Caleb can't wait to get his hands on that house." In between writing articles, Caleb had helped me fix up my abode, and had done a darn good job. He had his merits.

"Yes, we've been invited to a housewarming next weekend. The invitation says wear the oldest clothes you own."

"Sounds like we'll be painting." I laughed. It was the least I could do; Kira and Caleb had done so much for me.

"The car is pulling up in front of the airport. I'll get there as soon as I can." I blew a kiss in the phone.

"I'll warm up the apple pie."

Oh, that man. He gets me every time.

Three

Cfter taking a commercial flight in from London, I rested for a few hours at the Meridian this morning. I'm making a quick stop by Garnout's shop to pick up supplies. He's my favorite wizard and I think I may be the daughter he never had. I know he's been having a tough time keeping the peace between some of the local covens. Corporations are now using magic to protect their investments, and you know what happens when money and magic mix, it all goes to hell.

It's Garnout's job as a wizard, one of the most powerful beings on the planet, to keep things in the magical community in an even balance. It isn't easy in a place like Manhattan, where witches and warlocks thrive on the energy. There are more covens there than anywhere else in the world.

The last few times I've talked with Garnout, he's sounded tired. I'll stop by and see how things are going, and use the supplies as an excuse.

If I were a good daughter I'd also stop by my mom and dad's brownstone, but I'm not. Oh, I love my parents beyond belief, but if I walk into that house my mom will want to talk for hours and she'll try to give me six pairs of designer shoes or something. Well, the shoes aren't such a bad deal. It's all the bonding and guilt that come with it.

I just want to get home to Sweet. (Maybe I've mentioned that, but I feel like I'm in a hamster wheel.) I can see so clearly where I want to go, but I just can't seem to get there.

I'll check on Garnout and then I'm outta here.

Newark Airport

2 p.m.

Garnout doesn't look good. He has always had a big white beard, but he's never seemed old. Today he did, and he wore one of his fancy robes. He only wears the gold one when he's working on something big. I hate it when he won't tell me what's going on. Stubborn wizard.

Since I was there, I decided I might as well do some shopping. I picked up a couple of Doron spheres. They come in handy when channeling power under a full moon. I also needed a new mortar and pestle. My idiot cat, Casper, decided to knock mine off the worktable and now there's a big, long crack in it.

I knew Garnout was in a bad mood because he kept picking on me, which isn't at all normal. Except when he's giving me dire warnings about death ahead, he's a pretty laid-back kind of wizard.

"Have you been updating your Book of Shadows as your power grows?" His long white beard was tossed over his shoulder as he perused some book that looked like it was made from an animal's hide. PETA would love that one.

"Yes." I lied. "Well, it isn't completely updated but I did make some new notes." Pink sticky ones to remind me to write it all down later, but he didn't need to know that.

"Hmmph," he grunted and lifted a hand. Down floated a black stone mortar. Garnout never even looked up.

"Oh, I like this one. Very nice." I smiled.

"Pestle to match on the third shelf to your left."

I found it and put it on the counter with the bowl. I continued to browse, picking up a few more things and watching him out of the corner of my eye.

Garnout's shop is filled from floor to ceiling with oddities for witchcraft and wizardry, almost anything you can imagine, and if he doesn't have it, he can make it appear. The shop is located in the überwealthy Upper West Side, and his apartment faces the tree-lined paths of Riverside Park. A few months ago he'd nursed me back to health there, when I'd almost died for the third time in two months.

Whatever was going on with him, he didn't want to talk about it. Of course, that didn't keep me from trying.

"Garnout, is something wrong?"

He ignored me.

"Garnout?" I crossed my arms.

Finally, he looked up. His blue wizard eyes were hazy at first and then focused in on me. Darn, what kind of book was he reading? Maybe it was wizard porn.

"Bronwyn? Did you find everything you need?" He closed the book and I tried to read the spine, but he moved it. *Argh!*

"Yes. I also wanted to know if everything was okay."

"Nothing I can't handle, and if I do need your help, I'll ask." He punched the old-fashioned cash register with a vigor I didn't think necessary.

Well, okay then. He was right. If he needed my help, he'd ask. We'd always been there for each other. At least since we met five years ago.

"I guess that's about it, then." I handed him the cash for my purchases. "I'm headed home. Can't wait to have some of Lulu's chicken-fried steak."

"Mmmm. A delightful delicacy, as I remember." His expression softened. "Tell those lovely ladies who run the diner I said hello."

"I will." I paused by the door with the tiny bell that chimed whenever a customer entered the store. Closing my eyes I sent him a quick comfort spell to ease his worry.

He shook his head. "Save your strength, young woman. You never know when you may need it most. I'm an old man with a lot on my mind, but don't worry yourself. I'm fine." Then he smiled, a real Garnout smile, and I felt better.

"Garnout, you can tell me anything."

He shooed me away with his hands. "I know, Bronwyn. Enjoy your time at home and tell your doctor and friends I send my best wishes."

I considered telling him about Jason, but I didn't want to add to his worries.

"I will." I waved good-bye.

Tuesday
2 p.m.
Sweet, Texas

Thoroughly satisfied witches: 1
Fantastically talented boyfriends: 1
Dead guys: 0, but I'm working on it

Have I mentioned lately what a lucky chick I am? When things get dark—and they usually do—I need to remember days like yesterday.

My tall, tanned, and handsome boyfriend, Dr. Sam, met me at the hangar as I guided in the jet. He wore jeans, and a black button-down shirt. He'd been spending a lot of time outdoors and his skin had turned the color of caramel. His black wavy hair had just been trimmed and I could tell, even from the cockpit, that he'd had a professional shave. Mmmm. I couldn't wait to rub my face against his.

I did a quick systems check and opened the door.

"Hey beautiful." He reached up to help me down the steps. I skipped the last two and lunged into his arms, kissing every bit of Dr. Sam's gorgeous mug.

Holding my head still with his hands, he captured my lips in his. Sweetness. I would never grow tired of the man's kisses.

He tasted like peppermint Altoids and—

I backed up. "Hey. Did you eat Lulu's chicken-fried steak without me?"

He shrugged. "Bron, a man has to eat."

I growled. "You didn't have to eat chicken-fried steak. You know I've been craving it for weeks." I put my hands on my hips.

"Babe. How can I make it up to you?" He wiggled his eyebrows in a silly way.

I thought for a moment. "Well, you could, um, help me make the bed in the back of the plane." I pointed toward the tail.

"Really? And why is it messed up? Something you want to tell me?" He pulled back, but grinned.

"It isn't messy yet, but it's going to be." I tugged on his hand and he followed me up.

He did that thing where he makes me stand still and he undresses me. Then he slides his hand from the middle of my breasts down to the melting parts and I pretty much turn into jelly-knees at that point.

Let's just say, Dr. Sam is very, very good with his hands and has a wonderful bedside manner. An hour and a half later I was exhausted and exhilarated at the same time. Making love with him does that to me.

I was also hungry.

Facing me, he drew a finger over my cheeks and down to my lips. I grabbed his sexy finger and bit.

"Ouch! What was that for?"

"For not bringing chicken-fried steak with you." I kissed the boo-boo to make it better. The sheets were tangled around my ankles and I wondered where we'd left my bra.

He grinned. "I thought you forgave me and that's why we're here."

"For total forgiveness you must feed me. Now!" I rolled on top of him. "Or I might have to devour you." I winked.

He chuckled. "That's not a very good threat, Bron. I've been devoured plenty of times by you and it's quite nice."

"Nice?" I smirked.

"Wrong word. Delightful. Quite delightful."

"That's better. So," I said as I jumped off him and reached for my leather bag to change clothes, "while I finish checking out the jet, you call Kira and Caleb and see if they want to meet us at Lulu's. We'll have a good visit. Then you and I are going back to my place. I think you need some practice with this forgiveness thing."

He'd been sliding on his jeans, but stopped to grab my arm and pull me to him.

"Practice? You think *I* need practice?" He whispered the words into my ear and then followed by tracing the outside of the lobe with this tongue.

I shivered with pleasure. "Mmmmm," I moaned. "Practice makes perfect, Sam." I whispered the words back to him.

"Oh, I'm going to practice on you all night." His voice was deep and hungry.

"I can't wait." I kissed him.

Dinner was delayed a little longer.

Four

Eventually *we* made it to Lulu's about a half hour past the time *we*'d told Caleb and Kira.

They waited for us in the back booth and I waved as I walked in. First I had to say hello to my favorite chefs.

"Well, I declare our girl's finally come home, Johnnie!" Ms. Helen yelled as she pulled me into a big hug. "Now, let me look at you. Hmmm. Those are some pink cheeks you have there. Looks like you've been getting some exercise." She winked at me.

Sam rolled his eyes and walked toward our friends.

"You could say that. How have you two been doing?" I hugged Ms. Johnnie when she came out of the kitchen.

Today the twins were wearing straight-leg Levis cuffed at the ankle with bright red Keds and men's shirts. Ms. Helen's was bright yellow; Ms. Johnnie's lime green. These two wild women had lived full lives, and the evidence was in pictures lining the walls of the small diner. Every available space was covered with their history.

"Johnnie has her a new man. Could be husband number six." Helen nodded.

Johnnie swatted the shoulder of her twin. "Don't go jinxing it." She looked at me. "Kira and Caleb told me you were on the way, so I've fixed you a feast. Chicken-fried steak, mashed potatoes, black-eyed peas with jalapeños and three kinds of pie. Hope you're hungry."

That made me laugh and I realized I hadn't done so since I left Sweet. It had been a very long month. "I'm hungry. Get the wheelbarrow out back ready to roll me out of here."

The two older women giggled. "We're going to put some meat back on those bones, girl. Don't you worry," Ms. Johnnie added.

I made my way to the back booth where Sam had joined Kira and Caleb. I hugged them and settled in.

Sam and Caleb were dressed exactly the same way, except Caleb's shirt was white. They could be twins had it not been for Caleb's sandy blond hair highlighted by the sun and the fact that they looked nothing alike.

I turned to Kira. "Give me the juice. Everything. I want to know it all."

The men chuckled.

Kira was bursting with news. I could tell. We call her a "reformed" corporate lawyer. She quit her high-paying job in Atlanta to take over the Sweet library. She still wears the suits and stilettos, but she usually piles her long curly hair on top of her head and wears black-framed glasses she doesn't really need. She still looks like she belongs in a courtroom, but no one's going to tell her that. And she makes a darn fine librarian.

"Bronwyn, you know I don't believe in gossip. I simply relay the facts as I see them." She pretended to be offended. Then she raised an eyebrow. "I think Margie and Billy are getting married," she whispered. Sweet's a small town with very big ears.

I gasped and accidentally spit tea through my nose. That's why they call me the graceful witch. Sam handed me a napkin and pretended like it wasn't odd I'd just snorted tea through my nostrils.

Kira laughed. "I know, right?"

"Did Margie tell you?" I dabbed my nose.

"Um." She looked uncomfortable.

"*They* told her," Caleb interjected.

Kira, along with being a lawyer/librarian, is also psychic, something she discovered a few months ago when dead people began talking to her. She's still not happy about the idea but accepts it more each day.

To his credit, Caleb doesn't seem to mind at all. He thinks it's far better to be a psychic than a witch. At least it's safer.

"Are *they* a reliable source?" I buttered one of the soft rolls Ms. Helen had left on the table.

Kira nodded. "Oh, yes. It's Mrs. Henry who used to own the five-and-dime. She knows everything about everyone. None of her family is alive for her to look after, so she's pretty much in everyone's business. Anyway, she saw Billy stuff a ring in his sock drawer."

"I wonder what Margie will say?" Margie's another friend of ours. She works at the nursing home where Sam's on call a few days a week. She and Billy have been dating for a couple of months, but it seemed kind of soon for an engagement.

I didn't say that out loud, though. Kira and Caleb's relationship had been moving at a pretty fast pace, too. Who was I to judge? Sam and I had been through so many bumps and potholes on the road of love, some days I couldn't believe we were still together.

Ms. Johnnie wasn't lying about the feast, and of course I felt like I had to eat everything because I didn't want to disappoint her. By the time we made it out to Sam's SUV, I could barely breathe.

Lulu's is on the town square, which is populated by Gothic-styled buildings. And it's one more reason I like this place so much. It looks like a small European town, but it's set in the middle of the West Texas plains.

"Hey, Bron. Can I talk to you for a minute?" Caleb followed me out. Kira was still in the ladies' room, and Sam was having boxes of leftovers wrapped for us.

"Sure. What's up?"

"Have you talked to your friend Garnout lately?"

The question kind of threw me off guard. Caleb knew Garnout, but they didn't run in the same circles. "Yes, this morning. Why?"

"There's some heavy-duty corporate action taking place; looks like maybe some insider trading, you know, that sort of thing. There have also been rumors of magic being involved."

While we don't keep our magic a secret from the regular folks, we don't like any kind of press. I wondered if this might be the problem Garnout faced. Perhaps the warring covens had taken things too far.

"He didn't say anything about it to me." I shrugged. That was the truth.

"Well, I wondered if maybe you thought it'd be okay if I talked to him. I'm covering the story for the magazine, and flying up tomorrow."

"I don't know. He doesn't like talking to the press any more than I do."

"Oh, it's nothing like that. I've been doing some research and I think I have a couple of different leads. I don't want a quote from him, I just want to run a few things past him." The investigative part of Caleb's brain seldom slept. If there were a story there, I wouldn't keep him from it.

"I don't see the harm in asking him, but don't expect much." I wrote down the address of the shop and Garnout's phone number. I looked up at him. "Be careful, Caleb. Whenever there's money and magic involved, things can go bad fast."

I watched as Sam and Kira walked out. She would never forgive me if anything happened to Caleb. As he moved toward his truck I threw a protection spell at him. I'd do my best to keep him safe.

Wednesday

10 a.m.

Witches wanting to murder a sexy sheik: 1

I'm going to kill Sheik Azir. I mean it. The next time I see him, he has a big, fiery ball with his name on it. Stupid man.

I swear, he must have my schedule somewhere and is purposefully trying to keep Sam and me apart. Arrogant jerk. Azir, not Sam.

Last night we were *practicing* some more and it was all very lovely until Sam's cell phone rang. It played some high-pitched song that sounded like something you'd hear on the streets of New Delhi.

We'd just come back from a rather arousing shower together, when Sam reached for the phone.

"You are not going to answer that!" I tried to sound stern, but it's difficult when your body is humming from incredible lovemaking.

"Sorry, Bron. It's important." He pushed the button.

"Hello? Yes." He picked up his watch and grimaced. "What time will it be here? . . . No, I'll be ready."

He hung up and couldn't hide the guilt from his face.

"I've got to go." He took my hands in his. "I promise I wouldn't leave if it weren't absolutely necessary, but this is something that can't wait."

"That was Azir, wasn't it?" The sudden urgency meant only one thing: the sheik needed help—again.

"Yes." He sighed.

"He needs you on one of his saving-the-world trips, right?"

"Yes."

I could have pitched a fit, whined, and done any number of unattractive things, but I didn't. Azir was known for going into third-world countries and saving women and children from horrible atrocities. It was one of the ways he used his incredible wealth to make the world a better place, but I selfishly wished it didn't involve my boyfriend.

Azir was a client of mine and I still checked on him now and then. There was a time when I wasn't sure if maybe I might be in love with him, and he'd told me once that he loved me. One day I just decided Sam was the dude for me and I sent Azir on his way. It wasn't as easy as I make it sound and I still wonder sometimes if I'm over the sheik.

I knew if he called Sam, it meant the people they had to save had an obvious medical crisis.

"Okay." I sighed again. "Do I have time to put a couple of protection charms together for you?"

He smiled. "I love you."

I rolled my eyes. "I love you, too. Just come back in one piece."

Then I hugged him. He's said those same words to me more times than I can count.

I put together the charms while Sam gathered his things.

"Sorry about the rush, but I need to run home and pack. He said this one might be awhile."

I bit my lip. I swear, I will *kill* Azir next time I see him. There are hundreds of doctors he could call. Why did he have to call Sam? I knew the answer. Sam was discreet and talented. There wasn't anyone more qualified for the job, and Azir always wanted the best.

We kissed good-bye and I handed him the charms. "I'm not terribly happy with him right now, but give the extra one to Azir."

Sam kissed me again, and I drank in as much of him as I could, from his patchouli scent to the warmth of his strong arms.

1 p.m.

I called Peggy, who is the head of the local coven. The coven is what keeps Sweet the special place that it is. No evil is allowed in, and they can spot it fast if it does drop by for a visit. They've helped me out so many times over the past few months it isn't funny. They don't seem to mind that evil is attracted to me, but they do like a warning now and then if possible.

We went through all the niceties. Then I had to give it to her straight.

"Here's the deal." I cleared my throat. "There's a warlock who is involved in some dark magic."

She clucked her tongue. "Let me guess, he's been trying to kill you?"

I was glad she couldn't see my eyes roll.

"Yes. He's someone from my past and he's nasty. We haven't

been able to trace the magic back to its source, but we are fairly certain it's him."

"Hmmm. I guess we'd better prepare for the worst." She didn't sound angry. It was all very matter-of-fact.

"That's probably not a bad idea. If you see anything at all suspicious, you definitely want to check it out."

"We always do, dear. I suppose the coven will be glad to have something to do. It's been rather quiet while you've been out of town."

There was the tiny dagger in my side. I'd wondered when she'd get in a dig. The funny thing is, she's also one of my mom's best friends from college and they are so much alike in that way. It must have something to do with being a mother.

"We're meeting next week, and would love for you to join us." That was a nice way of saying, "Young lady, the least you could do is come help us strengthen our protection spell."

"If I'm still in town, consider me there." I turned the oven timer so it would go off. It buzzed on cue. "Oh, there goes the buzzer. Have to run, but thank you. I'll see you soon."

After we hung up, I headed to the laundry room off the kitchen and sorted out the dry cleaning from the stuff that could be washed. I loaded the first washer full of clothes, then headed for the workroom.

Talking to Peggy made me think. It wasn't just my life at stake if Jason found me here. The whole town could be in danger. I'd pulled out my Book of Shadows when the phone rang.

Darn, doubling up on the protection would have to wait a few more minutes.

Five

Sweet, Texas
Wednesday
9 p.m.
Witches with crazy mothers: 1
Dead guys: 0, but the night is young

There are days when you shouldn't answer the phone. Really.

"We haven't heard from Brett in more than three weeks."
Mom was at O'Hare. She and Dad had been at a medical conference in Chicago. A surgical specialist, Dad had given the keynote speech at the dinner the night before. Mom's a really powerful witch who turned from the 'craft to teach literature. She prefers the magic of prose to throwing fireballs.

I headed out to the garden. It's usually better for me to be pounding dirt around my herbs when I'm talking to my mom. I mean, we get along great, but she's my mother. She drives me crazy. Everything was green, which meant Sam and Caleb had been looking after my place. They are such good guys.

"Bronwyn?"

Oops. I hadn't been paying attention. "Sorry, Mom. The connection's weak out here in the conservatory." Big lie, but she was so concerned with my butthead brother that she didn't notice. "Communication in the jungle is tough, you know that. You and Dad were just there a little over a year ago working with Brett. Sometimes he goes weeks without a shower. I wouldn't worry that he hasn't sent an e-mail."

Hmmm. Time to re-pot the rosemary.

"You don't understand. I'm his mother and I feel like something isn't right." She sounded very unlike *my* mother, a little hysterical. She's usually so Zen, with a side order of bossy. Some people call it passive-aggressive, but she's never hysterical.

"What do you want me to do, Mom?" That sounded mean. "I don't mean that the way it sounds. I'm just trying to figure out what it is you need from me."

"Search for him, Bronwyn. You are one of the most talented witches on the planet. Open up that brilliant mind of yours and look for him." The hysterics were gone. The *Bronwyn-clean-your-room-now!* Mom was on the other end of the line.

"I can try, but he's good with the shields. He always has been. He never lets me in. But I'll try."

Taking a deep breath, I shut my eyes. It took a few seconds, but I saw him in the jungle arguing with a man. It'd been years since I'd seen him in anything but khakis and a T-shirt, and he didn't disappoint. There was something different about him. He seemed thinner than I'd ever seen him. He looked to the sky as if he could see me and shook his head. Then his shields slammed down and I lost him.

"He's fine, Mom. Still playing king doctor of the jungle." I left out the part about him looking like crap. I didn't want her to worry any more than she already had. Maybe I should send him a care package of Ho Hos and Zingers, or a freezer full of steaks.

"That's a relief. Something came over me here in the airport. Anxiety about him. I can't explain it, except it was the same kind of thing I feel every time someone tries to kill you."

I didn't want to go down that path. My mom understands why I have to be a high witch. It's the way I'm made. But she doesn't like the "daughter in peril" game I play on a daily basis. What sane mother would?

"So, how was Dad's speech?"

"Don't try to change the subject, dear, but it went well. Oh, by the way—Peggy e-mailed and said you had dinner with Kira and Caleb last night, how are they?" Remember what I said about the big ears? The coven may keep the positive energy flowing in Sweet, but unfortunately for my sake, they also help the gossip flow freely.

"They're fine."

"Good, good. Oh, they're calling our flight."

Thank you, Goddess of the phone. Okay, so there's no *real* Goddess of the phone, but I was grateful just the same.

"Be safe. I love you guys and tell Dad I said hello."

"I will, darling."

I gently banged the phone against my head several times. I had to learn to check the caller ID before I picked up. Minutes later I was lost in my herbs. It had been a long, hot summer, but we'd all made it through just fine. Not just the plants; Sam and I had survived, too.

A little over a month ago we had both died and been brought back to life. The incident would have torn most couples apart, especially since I was the one who had to kill him, but it hadn't. He and I were closer than ever and had reached a certain comfort level with our relationship. We no longer freaked when the other one was gone, which was a very good thing. Of course, that didn't keep me from missing him. He'd only been gone a day and I already ached for him.

To get my mind off him, I called Kira and asked if she had dinner plans.

"Darn. I have to play piano for the ice cream party at the nursing home. I promised Margie. You could come and hang out with us. The old folks are so much fun."

Kira's idea of fun and mine were a little different. "Well, that does sound interesting, but I think I need to make myself work on some potions here at home." I was very low on everything so it wasn't a real lie.

"Oh, Bron. I'm sorry. Is it still too soon?"

For what? Ohhhh. "No, please don't feel bad. I wasn't even thinking of Mr. G., honest. I just realized I have a lot of work to do tonight. How about we have an enchilada celebration tomorrow?" I knew that would change the subject fast, and it did.

We settled on a time, and Kira and Margie are coming over to party. We'll drink too much tequila, eat too much food, and have too much fun. I love my chicks. They, along with Sam, have made Sweet the best place I've ever lived. There are people who don't understand my connection to this West Texas town, but it doesn't matter. I know why I'm here.

I wanted to concentrate on my Book of Shadows, but I couldn't focus. I did make potions and I thought about Mr. Gunther. He's an old guy I met in the nursing home. I helped solve his short-term memory problems long enough for him to log his life story in a bunch of leather journals.

I learned so much from him about life, love, and just doing what makes you happy. He's the one who gave me the courage to go after Sam. He left the journals to me, but I haven't been able to read them yet. Someday.

Whew! Look at me being all melancholy. Maybe I should grab a glass of Jack Daniel's and throw on some Patsy Cline. Hey, that's not a bad idea.

Thursday, 9 a.m.
Witches with sexy boyfriends who leave great text messages: 1
Sam can be so clever when he wants to be. It took him four tries, but this is what he sent this morning on my cell phone:

Crazy. Busy. Be home to prctic (I'm thinking he meant practice.) Wed. Need whp crm. Lots.

Isn't he just the most adorable thing ever? He doesn't like Azir listening to his phone calls when he's talking to me, so he started text messaging. I suck at it, but I try. I sent him back one word— *Yum*. When I go to the Piggly Wiggly for the Spanish rice this afternoon, I'm *so* picking up a couple of large tubs of Cool Whip.

I've decided to make this a day of doing all of those little things that drive me crazy. I've made a list and I'm sticking to it. I'm going to update my Book of Shadows, since I didn't do it yesterday, dust and vacuum the house, call the contractor to finish my master bath (I've decided we need to expand the shower and put two nozzles in there for double the fun), and go to the grocery store to stock up.

Sam's been doing the shopping lately and there's not a single Snowball cupcake in the house.

There's a lot to do before the girls get here at seven.

Thursday
6:30 p.m.

What the hell is wrong with me? I spent all day on the couch watching television. I swear that thing sucks me in and I lose track of time. It's all Regis and Kelly's fault. They were talking to my friend Zane. He's using his concert tour to raise money for the starving children in Africa. He's one of my favorite people in the world, but a stranger guy you'll never meet.

Then he was on *The View*, so I had to watch. You know, to show my support. Then Oprah was doing her book-club thing and I realized I hadn't read anything besides magic books in months. So I grabbed my laptop and ordered buckets of books online. Argh.

By the time I was done, I barely had time to run to the store to get what we need for tonight. I stopped at Lulu's for a light snack of fried chicken and blueberry pie, then I had to vacuum and dust, so my friends wouldn't discover what I slob I am, and find something cute to wear. I've decided on white shorts and this cute red top I found in London a couple of weeks ago. Oh, which reminds me—the prime minister called to tell me that Miles was already back at work, and he wondered if we'd had any luck tracking down the warlock behind the shootings.

I'm the world's biggest dork. Seriously. With everything else, I sort of pushed that whole thing with Jason out of my head. I didn't really *forget*, more like procrastinated. Since I landed back in Sweet

I've been concentrating on growing my power. It sort of happens naturally here, but I've been saving it up.

I did another quick search with my mind on the off chance he might have his shields down. Then I could sizzle his brain from the comfort of my own living room, but I couldn't find him.

While I was picking up the house, I made some calls and checked in with Cole.

"Bron, looks like your ex hexed his way out of the institute, but he didn't act alone," Cole informed me. "The magic he used was powerful stuff."

My stomach felt queasy. "Did his family help him?" I'd heard rumors they'd put hits out on me for ruining their son. Some people just didn't get it.

"Not as far as we can tell. When I say powerful, I'm talking wizard or sorceress strong," Cole said.

"What? That's impossible. There aren't that many around, and the ones who are wouldn't help a scumbag like Jason. They'd see right through him." I plopped down on the couch feeling weaker by the minute.

Wizards are the most powerful magical beings alive, and the work they do is for the good of the universe. The same with sorceresses except they have a tendency to turn to the dark side.

"That's what I would have thought a few hours ago, but I'm looking at the magic now. I've already called Garnout to get his opinion. He should be here in a few seconds. But you need to be more cautious than ever." Cole sounded nervous.

There was honking out in my driveway and I jumped up to look out the window. Margie and Kira had arrived. I told Cole to call if there was any more news.

My lovely night with the girls was ruined. I put my party face on. No need to make everyone else miserable.

Midnight

It was totally useless to try and hide my worries.

About fifteen minutes after Kira and Margie walked in with covered dishes they cornered me in the kitchen.

"We hear there's another bad guy after you." Kira pointed at me accusingly.

"There are always warlocks trying to kill me. Nothing new." I'd curse her ghostly gossip line but it wouldn't do any good.

"I'm told this one is particularly nasty and that you used to date him. So spill." She and Margie stared at me.

"Fine, but can I at least have a glass of sangria before I tell you my life story?"

"Of course. I'll even pour." Margie pulled the pitcher out of the fridge and grabbed the glasses down from the cabinet. A few sips later I was in heaven. I love sangria. The mix of wine and fruit tastes reminds me of berry pie as it slides down.

"Short version of the story is, I dated this guy Jason my senior year in college. Drop-dead gorgeous with blond curls and a swimmer's body that wouldn't stop. I met him in my History of Magic class, and we bonded. We were the only two real magical people in the class. Of course no one except our professor knew that. We started as study partners and then, well, things progressed."

Kira's eyebrow shot up. She knows what can happen when a warlock and a witch sleep together. Sam's a warlock, but he blocks his power. He's one of many warlocks who turn away from the craft.

Jason didn't.

"So, the first time we sleep together, it's pretty amazing. Our auras mix and I have the first real orgasm of my life. I fell for him big-time after that." I'd finished off the first glass of sangria and could feel my shoulders ease.

Margie poured me another glass.

I needed it for the next part of the story. It was embarrassing to tell my friends how stupid I was back then. "The next day he ignored me in class. For days after, every time I approached him, he'd say he was busy. I was crushed. Then two weeks later, he called. Told me he was sorry, that our lovemaking had sort of freaked him out. He'd never experienced anything like it.

"He offered to take me out for a real meal. You know how it is in school, anything better than Taco Bell and you'll go out with the Hunchback of Notre Dame if you have to."

They both laughed and nodded in agreement.

"He went all-out. We ate sirloin at this nice restaurant in town, had wine and crème brulee. I felt so grown-up, and by the end of the meal, all was forgiven. I was happy and exhausted at the same time. I mean, I was actually embarrassed because I had trouble keeping my eyes open."

"The bastard *drugged* you." Margie bit out the word.

I paused. I hadn't thought about this in so long, but the hurt felt like it happened yesterday. It nestled low in my belly. A swirling mass of pain.

"Yes. He took me to his place because it was closer. I was tired and he said I could rest. No strings. He was so sweet. I remember—"

Kira stood up and put her arms around me. "I'm sorry, Bron. I had no idea it was so bad. You don't have to tell us any more. Really." There were tears in her eyes and that was my undoing.

I let out a small sob and then pulled myself together. I swore long ago, that I'd never let that asshole hurt me again.

I shook my head. "I'm okay. I want to finish it."

Kira moved back to her chair, worry in her beautiful blue eyes.

"When I woke up I was chained to a wall, naked. He'd drawn symbols all over my body. His plan was to drain me of my powers, but something had gone wrong. Whatever he was doing was making me stronger, not weaker. That was the first time I tossed a fireball. It was small, but it flew from my fingertips and set his jeans on fire.

"He stood there staring for a minute in disbelief. In that moment I saw him for the evil he really was, and it made me angry that I hadn't noticed it before.

"The flames grew and triggered the fire alarms. At first I hadn't realized where we were, but then it dawned on me: we were below the gym near the lockers in a storeroom. He rolled around on the ground trying to put out the flames, and I remember thinking I wished he would scream louder. He wasn't hurting enough.

"The police and firefighters showed up in minutes. That was one of the great things about having them on campus. They took off the chains and wrapped me in blankets. Then the spook squad showed up and rolled Jason up in some bag. He was still alive but had burns over a good part of his body.

"I never had to see him again. I had forgotten about him until I felt his dark magic on that gunman's clothes in Amsterdam." I shook my head.

Kira and Margie both took one of my hands. "Tell us what we can do to help." Kira squeezed my hand.

Margie's hair swung as she nodded. "You know, Bronwyn, there's not a woman in the world who hasn't had to deal with a jerk or two in her life, but you sure do get more than your share. Hell, girl, you've got a homing device for assholes."

That made me laugh.

"You know, you're right, Margie. That's why it's good to have girlfriends like you. I think it's time to leave this morbid subject behind and eat some enchiladas."

We even broke out the tequila. I didn't drink any. The sangria had been enough for me. The night wasn't a total loss. Margie had finally had enough tequila to tell us she and Billy had been talking about marriage.

"So far he doesn't seem real keen on the idea, but I don't care." Margie frowned, and pushed her straight auburn hair behind her ears. It was a new color, and I really liked it on her. "Well, I do care, but I'm trying so hard to act like I don't." She slapped a hand against her mouth as if she'd said too much.

Kira and I looked at each other over Margie's head and smiled.

"You don't worry about it." Kira patted her arm. "These things usually work out the way they are supposed to."

She was right. After Jason, I never thought I could care about another warlock, but I was wrong. Sam was the love of my life. A year ago I wouldn't have ever believed that possible. Love's funny like that. You never know when it's going to slap you upside the head and invite itself in.

Six

Sweet, Texas
Friday
Noon
Prozac-worthy witches: 1

I really, really don't like it when I feel this way. I woke up in a bit of a panic, but I don't know why. Nervous, antsy, that skin-crawling, mind-niggling feeling that something wasn't right washed over me. *Dread*. That's the word I'm trying to think of and I hate it when that happens.

Immediately I sent my mind out to all the usual suspects: Sam, Kira, Caleb, the PM, all of them. Nothing. Everyone was fine.

Then my favorite demon-slaying best friend, Simone, called.

"What's wrong?" I didn't even give her a chance to say hello.

"Geez, Bron, take a Xanax." Simone is never one to mince words.

"Sorry. I've got one of my icky feelings." I apologized. "That always makes me a little crazy."

She snorted. "Well, it's not me. At least I hope not. I'm in San Fran tracking some idiot Chelon demons who have strayed a bit far from home."

"What the hell's a Chelon?" I know a lot of demons but hadn't heard of those.

"Dumbshit horse-looking things. Used mostly for manual labor. Pulling semis out of the dirt, that sort of thing. They usually hang out in the Mojave so I'm up here trying to figure out who's using them. Then I'll kill them all." The words were said so nonchalantly it made me laugh. Like she was doing laundry or something.

Simone is tall, dark, and exotic, and has a penchant for leather and slaying all things demonic. She's been my friend since college and there are few people in the world I trust more than her, even though she once tried to get Sam into bed. Of course, it was all for the greater good, in her way of thinking. It was the only way she could tell if he was good enough for me. He turned her down flat, and now she thinks he's the world's greatest guy. That's how Simone works.

"Do you need some help? Spells, potions, anything?" I found a ponytail holder and pulled my errant curls into it.

"No, I didn't call for help. Just wanted to check and see how things were going."

She never called for small talk. Great. She knew about Jason the nasty warlock. "Who told you?" I knew it was probably my mother. Peggy probably told Mom, who couldn't wait to rally the troops. I know my mother is only trying to save me, but it drives me crazy when she goes behind my back like this.

There was a long pause. "I keep my sources confidential, you know that." Simone laughed. "Is he out of spook prison? The asshole? Please say yes; then I can kill him." Simone was one of the few people who knew most of the gory details about my past. Jason was just one of many idiots I'd had to deal with over the years.

"Get in line, chick. I should have done it years ago." I grumbled.

"Any leads?" It sounded like she was moving clothes on a rack. I could hear the scraping sound of hangers against metal.

"Not yet. Cole's on it. Are you shopping?"

She grunted. "Looking for new leather. Damn Blarth demon shredded my favorite jacket last night. Pissed me off so bad I left him in a pile of dust, and then hunted down his brothers."

Gotta love her.

"You heading to New York in a couple of days?" Her question surprised me.

"Wasn't planning on it, why?"

"Figured you'd be out there helping Garnout with the coven wars. In the last twenty-four hours things have gone bad fast. It's going to be an all-out war in the next couple of days."

This is why I never like it when I get that icky feeling. "I knew it was bad, but how did you hear about it?"

"Garnout called. When I finish up here I'm headed east to assist. Seems a flood of demons has hit town. Those bastards are drawn to evil and they are out of control."

My favorite wizard called Simone before he called me? That was so wrong.

"Bron?"

"I think I'll take a Manhattan run tomorrow and see what's up. Maybe do a little shopping. Maybe stop in to see why a stubborn wizard has asked everyone but me for help."

Simone laughed. "Don't get your panties in a knot, he thinks you have your hands full with this Jason problem. He just didn't want to add to your troubles."

Crap. I knew I should have told him about Jason. He'd found out from someone else and now he was trying to protect me. First my mother and now the wizard. Whatever.

"Can you meet me at the airport in Dallas tomorrow around noon? Then I can fly us both in." I reached for my pilot's log and made some notes.

"Hmmm. Depends on the numbers. If I find the Chelon nest tonight, we should be good to go." In addition to being a kickass demon slayer, Simone is a brilliant statistician. She uses her awesome math skills to locate the demons and then obliterates them.

After we hung up, I packed. Kira was next on my list. I felt bad about missing her housewarming party, but when I called she said the event was on hold until Caleb made it back. I sent another protection spell to him, just in case he was in the middle of the trouble.

I e-mailed my mom and asked if she could stop calling my friends and telling them my business. I didn't trust myself to use the phone—my anger was still too close.

I loaded two bags full of potions, and then wondered if I should go on ahead and fly up right away.

I decided to meditate and gather my strength. I've learned in the past few months to store it like tiny boxes on a shelf I can pull out whenever I need. I still get drained when I'm in the middle of something big, but not like I used to. I'm also learning how to draw power even faster from what's around me.

Hmmm. Yes. That's the plan. Meditate. Then I'll go to Manhattan and kick some warlock and witch ass. Now there's a fun weekend for you.

Manhattan
Friday
8 p.m.
Dead guys: 2
Pumped witches with crazy demon-slaying friend: 1

Simone and I have taken over my parents' prewar brownstone. Mom and Dad are traveling again, this time to Denver for another conference. We dumped our bags in the foyer and then headed to Garnout's store, which is just a few blocks away.

While he wasn't surprised to see Simone, he did raise an eyebrow when I walked in behind her.

"Hi." I waved.

"Good evening, witch. And to what do I owe this honor?"

I smirked and crossed my arms.

"Oh." He smiled at Simone. "It seems I've offended Bronwyn."

Simone chuckled. "Yep. She's jealous you called me."

Laughing, he motioned us toward the counter. "Well, I'm glad you are *both* here. I have something interesting to show you." He pointed at me. "I spoke with your reporter friend, Caleb, and he's helped me make some notes on our situation. Bright young fellow."

It was good Caleb had been an asset to the wizard. I wasn't at all certain what Garnout would think of a reporter nosing into his business.

Garnout had several papers and magazines on the glass-and-wood countertop. "I've been tracking these corporate takeovers, and I think I've found a link. I was hoping, Simone, you could help with the numbers, before you hunt your demons."

"They aren't my demons, old man, but you know I love to crunch a number. Let's see what you have here."

She thumbed through the articles he'd torn out and looked at the chart he'd made. "Who owns Kelsen Enterprises? Ah. Well, what do you know? Nox Krasmirs. Never met a deal he couldn't take advantage of, and you think he's using magic to get insider info?"

Garnout nodded. "I know he is. His sister is in charge of the coven gathering the information. It's illegal on many levels. But that isn't the biggest problem." He pulled out a notebook with several photographs pasted inside. "One of the other covens is competing with the Krasmirs. It's escalated out of control. They've taken to the streets like an old-fashioned gang war. Absolutely ridiculous."

I sat on a stool for a few minutes watching them work. Garnout was so cute trying to figure out corporate takeovers and making charts. I couldn't stay miffed that he wanted to leave me out of the fun, to "protect" me.

He's one of the most powerful wizards in the universe. He could just make everything right with a flip of the hand, but he wouldn't. Well, not unless absolutely necessary. He believed in using magic as a last resort. The past few weeks had been rough on him, and the worry was heavy around his eyes. Keeping the magic in balance couldn't have been easy with warring covens running around.

"So, what if we get the two heads of the covens together and just show them reason?" I picked up a small book about finance he had laying on the counter.

Garnout looked up from his paper. "Splendid idea, young witch, if they didn't murder each other on sight."

"No need to get snarky." I shrugged.

An orb beside him began glowing red. "Oh, my. I believe we're needed." He touched Simone's arm. "Do you mind coming with me?"

She smiled. "Are there demons involved?"

Garnout nodded. He threw a large ring of keys at me. "Be a dear and lock up, I'll get the keys when I bring Simone home."

And—*poof*—they were gone. I could grumble and whine, but there was no one there to listen. It's not like I'm not one of the most powerful witches on the planet. My mom just said so the other day.

Okay, that was petty, but I don't like being left out of the action. It isn't fair.

I checked the back door and turned the light off in his office. There are so many cool things back there from orbs, otherworldly vessels, and a bunch of stuff I didn't recognize. I didn't want to snoop. Well, I did, but I wouldn't.

It was early September and still warm in the city. On the way to my parents' home I stopped by Fabrelli's, a cool place for pizza, and brought the box home.

I'd just moved the three pieces I'd left for Simone on a plate into the fridge when the front door banged open.

Before I could send my mind to see who it was, Simone yelled. "Bronwyn!"

I ran.

There she stood covered in blood. That didn't surprise me. The fact she had Garnout slung over her right shoulder did.

I'd never seen her look so worried.

She took a deep breath. "I think he's dead."

Seven

*G*arnout is alive, but just barely.

It took about five seconds for me to move through the shock, but then the take-control bitch inside me stopped by for a visit.

"Put him on the bed in here." I threw open the door to my parents' master suite. I ripped the comforter off the bed, less to save my mother's misty blue and bronze Contessa bedding and more for Garnout's comfort.

While she did what I asked, I grabbed my bags of potions and goodies.

"Tell me what happened." I dumped the contents of two healing spells made of cedar, chamomile, angelica, St. John's wort, and some rosemary oil down his throat. His body shuddered but his breathing wasn't as shallow.

"When we left his shop he plopped us down in the front of Macy's. Three Nork demons were terrorizing the customers in the store. They weren't hurting anyone, just running around knocking things over. I had the three of them cornered—"

"Simone! Not you. What happened to Garnout? I need to know fast."

She held up her hands in surrender. "I'm trying to tell you that I don't know. I was busy gathering up demons. I heard Garnout talking to someone, but I didn't see or hear whom it was. The next thing I know he's on the ground. The last words he said were, 'Tell witch Shadow learns.' Then he passed out."

"What does that mean?" I screamed at her, my fists tight by my side.

Simone shook her head. "I don't know. It was almost like he was confused or something."

He'd been spelled and it could take forever to figure out what someone had done.

Holding my hands over his body I sought out the spell, poison, or whatever the hell it was that had taken him down. I did feel a sense of confusion as I tried to enter his mind. His thoughts were so jumbled they made no sense.

The visions I see when I'm delving into minds are usually pictures. It's not always a straight-on kind of thing. But this was different. Someone had screwed with his mind. All I saw were blasts of red and yellow. There were no voices, words, or pictures. His mind was like a Jackson Pollock painting on crack.

I sent another healing spell through his body, and then another for clarity. Nothing worked.

I didn't find any poison, so it had to be a spell. Confusion mixed with something else, and it had to have come from a massively strong warlock or witch. No. If someone like that had done it I would be able to undo it.

Another wizard. *Holy crap*.

I lifted my hands and turned to Simone.

"Come here."

I've never seen that particular look in her eyes. It was almost like fear. She must have thought I might hurt her. As if.

"I just want to take a look in your brain and rewind a bit. I might see something you wouldn't be able to." I could do it without touching her, but the vision would be clearer with contact.

I grabbed her wrist and focused.

Men and women were running out of Macy's, their eyes wide with fear. Simone and Garnout pushed through the mob. The Nork demons, fuzzy, horned beasts with three eyes, ran around on the counters pushing displays of cosmetics and perfume over.

When the demons caught sight of Simone they paused. Everything seemed to happen at once. The three of them jumped toward her. She already had her trusty Bowie knife in her hand, and thrust upward into the jugular of the first demon to reach her. Another came at her from the side and she kicked a booted foot into his chest, sending him flying across the room.

I made myself step back from the action and I heard Garnout bellow, "You are not welcome here!" He was furious and his voice radiated power. Whatever it was, he was trying to vanquish it.

I didn't hear a reply, but when Simone turned to fight the third demon I saw something. Garnout faced a shadowy figure, more like mist formed in an outline. Power radiated from it and Garnout held out a hand as if to block it. I understood why Simone didn't see much. The demon she fought was a little smarter than the others. When she kicked, he moved to the left and ran for the escalator.

Sirens rang in the background. She jumped and caught the demon by the leg, sending them both into a tumble. His big paw slammed into her face, but her head didn't even move. She felt the pain, but ignored it as she shoved the base of her hand into the middle of his three eyes. Her other hand used the knife to pierce his heart.

Leaping up, she turned, and that's when she saw Garnout sprawled on the floor. His robe pooled around him in golden waves.

"Crap! Bronwyn's going to kill me if the old man is dead." I heard her thoughts, but I also experienced the emotion. She cared for Garnout and she didn't want him to die.

She scooped him up, not even bothering to check his vitals, and put him over her shoulder. Then she ran through the crowd and the twenty-five blocks it took to get here.

I let go of her wrist and hugged her. She didn't return the embrace, keeping her hands at her side, but she didn't push me away.

"I'm sorry." I squeezed her tight.

She let me hold her a few seconds and then stepped back. "Stop with the mushy stuff and fix the old geezer." Simone shook her head. "I thought you couldn't kill a wizard."

"You're right. He's not dead. He's in suspended animation. What I can't tell is if he put himself there or if someone did it to him. One thing I know for sure: the whole thing was a setup.

"Whoever brought those demons to Macy's didn't count on him bringing you. He wasn't as distracted as they wanted, and I think he was able to block part of whatever was thrown at him. All I can find is a confusion spell, but I can't undo it."

I walked back over to check his pulse. It was low. If he were a regular guy I would know he was dying. But he wasn't. Wizards weren't made like the rest of us. Their basic physical makeup is the same, but they have to be able to jump back and forth between dimensions and do, well, all the cool stuff wizards do. Wizards have complete control over their bodies and can change them to adapt to any situation. They can shape-shift, turn into rocks or any other object, and teleport to different planes of existence in a matter of seconds.

I would have bet money he knew this was going to happen. Wizards are privy to upcoming events but they don't necessarily know the end result. He could have at least given me some kind of heads-up.

A simple "Bronwyn, someone may put me down, perhaps you could help me out when that happens," would have been nice.

Then it dawned on me. If I could rewind Simone's brain, why not Garnout's? He was confused now, but not when this all began.

I placed a hand on his white head, and closed my eyes.

Thoughts rushed through me in a swirling mass but everything moved too fast for me to see. I tried to slow it down, but it didn't work. Other than flashes of color every now and then, I couldn't make out a thing.

A searing pain burned into my brain. I knew I should let go, but I couldn't. It was if I'd been attached to a big magnet, and pulling away was impossible.

"Stop it!" I heard Simone's yell, but couldn't respond.

A stabbing pain began in my shoulder. Someone had nearly pulled my arm out of its socket. The pain ended and I stared into Simone's eyes. I must have had my evil eye on, because she blanched.

"Don't you dare yell at me!" She shoved me into the chair in the corner. "You were in pain. I could see it on your face and then your color drained. Your lily white ass was getting paler by the minute."

I took a deep breath.

"I'm not mad. I think you may have saved my life. What was that? I couldn't let go." My body ached like I had the flu and I was shaky with chills. "I need my bag."

Simone brought it from the bed and sat it in my lap. I swallowed the new healing potion, the same kind I'd given Garnout. Almost instantly a surge of energy moved through my body, warming me.

Excellent.

I looked at Garnout. His skin had deepened in color. His breathing was stronger. Then it dawned on me. His body had been drawing power from *me*. I knew he hadn't meant to hurt me; it was an automatic response. You can't kill a wizard, but you can drain his power and leave him in a giant hole of nothingness.

That's what had happened. The shadow, whatever it was, had drained most of his power. Garnout's quick action in blocking whatever was thrown at him had allowed him to hold on to some of his life force.

I needed a way to give him power without killing myself.

Only I had to find a way to get rid of the confusion spell before that happened. Giving a confused wizard back his powers could be a very bad thing. Accidentally destroying the world: bad. Argh!

I ran for the door. "Stay with him and yell if anything changes. I need to make some phone calls."

"Wait a minute. At least tell me what just happened," Simone said.

I explained, and laughed as she backed away from the bed. "Simone, he can't drain *your* powers. It was because I connected mentally. You don't have to worry about it."

She nodded. "Okay. I know you're trying to save his life and all, but I could use a shower and some food. Um, you might want to change clothes, too." She pointed to my T-shirt.

For the first time since she arrived with Garnout I took a real look at her. Demon goo was in her hair and she was covered in blood.

I glanced down at my shirt and rolled my eyes. I'm not sure, but I think a piece of demon brain was stuck to my chest. Lovely.

"Okay. New plan. I'm going to grab a shirt and my cell phone and I'll be back in a second."

I ran upstairs to the room I used when I was here and grabbed a clean black T-shirt. I kind of wanted to jump in the shower, but there wasn't time. It was just the tiniest bit of brain, but it still grossed me out. Running the taps, I wiped my chest with a washcloth. I threw the soiled shirt in the trash and put on the other one. I found my cell phone on the nightstand.

There was one person who could help me with all of this and actually do something about it.

I punched the number.

Cole answered. "Hey, Bronwyn, what's up?"

"Where are you?"

"Virginia. Why?" I could hear the ding of a car door.

"I need you in New York now. Someone tried to take out Garnout. And he's bad, Cole, really bad. They threw nasty crap at him, and I can't fix him." I was mad at myself because tears had started to fall. I didn't give in, though. I pushed them away with my hand.

"I'll be there in an hour." He'd gone into Cop Cole mode, his voice serious. "Whatever is going on, we'll get to the bottom of it. I promise."

I made my way back downstairs to relieve Simone so she could shower.

"I called Cole and he's on the way."

She grunted. For some reason, she'd never liked him. It's weird because Simone likes all men. I'd asked her once, and she told me she felt like she owed him something for saving my life, but I don't think that's it. Like I said, weird.

I realized I hadn't left her much pizza, and I made a quick call to Fabrelli's to order three more pies. She would eat a whole one on her own, and who knew if Cole had eaten yet.

I checked on Garnout and he was exactly as I'd left him. I straightened his robes around him and took off his boots. That's when I noticed he had jeans on under the robes. I laughed. I had always thought of him as being so old-fashioned.

I'd known Garnout for more than six years and he was the one who had helped me get my career going. I owed him so much. I found a cashmere blanket in the closet and placed it over him. He probably didn't feel heat or cold, but it seemed the right thing to do.

Simone had moved the big fluffy armchair from the corner over by the bed, and I sat down in it. There were a few more calls to make, but I needed a moment to think.

Garnout had said something about learning from the shadows. I'd ask Cole about it, because I honestly didn't have a clue what he was talking about.

I did know all of this had something to do with those stupid warring covens. I didn't care what kind of business deals they were trying to wheel and deal. They'd screwed around with the wrong witch this time.

You can mess with me, but don't dick with my friends. If you do, you die. Simple.

Eight

Tomorrow was supposed to be Cool Whip-on-Bronwyn night. I'm really pissed off that I'm going to miss it. Of course, I'd be Cool Whipping myself because Sam is stuck wherever it is he and Azir have gone to save the world. Whatever is going on is keeping them busy; Sam was supposed to be back days ago.

I'm still in Manhattan, and to add to the craziness that is my life, I've become a relationship therapist and am doing my own bit to save the world at the same time.

Ack!

It's been insane. Let me hit the highlights. Once Cole arrived, Simone went off on a demon-slaying binge. I'm fairly certain there isn't a demon alive in Manhattan, and if there is, it won't be around long. The slayer's on a roll.

Cole has called in a team of medical spook experts to help Garnout. There's just one problem: no one has really had to take care of a wizard before. There aren't that many of them in the universe, they are immune to all diseases, and they never die. So we keep dumping the health potion down his throat, and the spook brigade is working on unlocking the confusion spell he's under.

Not being one who can just sit around and wait for the fun stuff to happen, I've recently kidnapped the heads of the warring covens, bound their powers, and stuck them in my parents' basement where they can't get out. Technically, I didn't do the actual kidnapping. Cole helped a little. Being a big honcho in the international spook brigade has its advantages. The first thing he did when he arrived was ask how he could help so I told him.

"I want those son-of-a-bitch coven leaders in this house by tomorrow morning at eight a.m. sharp, or I'm going to kill them." I think I scared him the tiniest bit because I said it all in a very calm voice, while I sat in the big fluffy chair next to Garnout.

"Okay." He walked out of the room but I could hear him on the phone. Eventually I fell asleep in the chair. I'd been up for forty-eight hours straight.

Around five a.m., Cole woke me up. "The items you requested will be here at eight. Where would you like me to put them?"

I didn't even question how he'd managed to kidnap the most powerful witch and warlock in the city. I was just grateful. When Cole and I first met he thought I might be one of the bad guys—something about the death and destruction that seems to follow me around. But after hanging out with me for a few months, he's discovered I'm on the good guy's side. We've been able to help each other out of a couple of tight jams.

"Put them in the basement." I spent the next three hours putting wards around the house, making it invisible to the magical eye. No need to have their covens ruin our fun.

In the basement the spook crew helped me get everything that could be used as a weapon out. All that was left was a table and two chairs. Oh, and the washer and dryer.

My mom keeps everything tidy, even in the basement. There are only boxes and a couple of wardrobes filled with clothes and shoes. I swear she had half of Neiman Marcus stuffed in there. I didn't think her Michael Kors sweaters would make much of a weapon, but the Manolos with the spiked heels could be dangerous.

I did all of this and some major research before they arrived. I'd discovered that none of this had anything to do with money or hostile corporate takeovers. It was a centuries-old feud that had started over land in Bulgaria, though the specifics of the disagreement were never disclosed. The Dragomirs and the Krasimirs had been fighting since 1708. Funny thing is, both of the family names mean "beautiful peace" in English. Bunch of idiots who never once, in all of those years, tried to sit down and talk to one another.

Argh! That was about to change. I decided Constantine Dragomirs and Lilyana Krasimirs would solve their differences, or die trying.

They had black cloth sacks over their heads and their hands were handcuffed behind their backs. They'd been yanked out of their beds. Constantine wore a blue robe over Elvis pjs and I bet he wasn't expecting to be kidnapped first thing in the morning. Lilyana wore a red silk robe over a little shortie set of the same material.

This was going to be so much fun. Nothing like a little peace conference to take my mind off Garnout.

I bound their powers again before the pair stepped over the threshold of the door. The only magic in this house would be done by me. No one from the outside would be able to locate them, and they wouldn't be able to get past the wards. They also couldn't physically hurt one another by strangling, breaking necks, or any of that fun stuff.

The "investigators" (Cole begged me to stop calling them the spook squad) moved Constantine and Lilyana down the stairs to the basement. The cops had also installed cameras and microphones so we could keep track of what was going on.

The witch and warlock were shoved into chairs, and the bags were yanked off their heads. As their eyes came into focus they both jumped up and backed away from each other. Their mouths were covered with duct tape.

I slid into calm bitch mode.

"Okay, kiddies. Here's how this is going to work. You will sit down and discuss your differences in a calm and nonviolent fashion. I don't care how long it takes. You aren't leaving here until there's some kind of truce." I motioned for them to sit again.

Lilyana was pretty with her black hair and milky white skin, but she wasn't about to take orders from anyone. She gave me a look that could stop global warming.

Constantine had dark brown hair with graying tips. It almost looked frosted. He was tall, at least six-three, and he wasn't interested in playing my game.

"Tell you what. You sit down, and I'll rip that tape off your mouth." I winked at Lilyana. She gave me another arctic stare.

I shrugged. "Doesn't matter to me." I walked toward the door and motioned for the two investigators in the room to come with me.

Lilyana grunted. It was the best she could do under the circumstances. Then she sat down.

"Same offer goes for you." I pointed to Constantine. Even with tape on his mouth, he was kind of cute.

He sat down, too. "See, it's all about compromise."

Reaching out I grabbed the tape on both of their mouths and ripped.

"Mother of god! Are you insane?" Lilyana screamed. "Do you have any idea who I am? You will die for this treachery!"

I snorted. I love playing with bad witches. "Doubt it. Yes, I know who *you* are. And if you think about it, you know who *I* am. You also realize that it would bring me nothing but joy to kill you both where you sit." I sighed. "But I'm going to try the diplomatic approach first. If that doesn't work . . . well, we'll see."

Constantine had been oddly quiet. He studied the situation, looking for exits around the room. There were none. It was a concrete box surrounded by my magic, but I wasn't about to tell him that. Let him discover it for himself.

"For now, until I'm sure you two will play nice, I'm leaving your hands tied. Kiss and make up, and you two can go home. Or I can kill you for harming my friend Garnout." I shrugged. "I'm good either way."

When I mentioned Garnout, they both let out gasps. "Can the surprise, you guys. One of you conjured something that has drained a good bit of my favorite wizard's powers, and now you are both going to pay." I didn't bother keeping the hatred from my voice. If they were afraid, maybe they'd move faster toward a solution.

They both looked to opposite corners of the room.

"Have it your way." I walked out and the investigators followed. Cole had set up a monitor in Garnout's room for my viewing pleasure.

Cole and the other officers were stationed around the house in case someone did find us or if one of our guests downstairs managed to escape the basement.

Nothing happened for a long time. They didn't talk or move. Didn't even shift in their seats.

I spoke to Garnout. I didn't know if he could hear me or understand even if he did. "This might be better than going to the movies. Maybe I should microwave some popcorn. Yes, and eat some Junior Mints. Now that sounds like a plan."

Garnout's condition remained the same, and I could only hope he was on the road to recovery. Perhaps the confusion spell would eventually wear off, or if I could find the source and destroy it, it would be broken.

I watched the witch and the warlock downstairs. Lilyana's posture and beauty reminded me more of a supermodel than the CEO of a company. Finally, she stretched her arms up behind her, her wrists still in the handcuffs.

Gazing at the ceiling she cocked her head. Then she set her eyes on Constantine. "Why did you lie to me?"

The shock on his face told me he hadn't expected this. "We will not discuss this here." He said the words through gritted teeth.

She raised an eyebrow. "We aren't discussing it anywhere else, so why not here?"

He stuck his jaw out. "You know they're watching us. I will not discuss our personal business in front of them."

'Personal business'? So they weren't strangers after all. Huh.

They went on in silence for several minutes. She pretended to be intensely interested in the wood grain of the tabletop, but I noticed her stealing a look now and then when she was sure he wasn't looking.

I thought about probing their minds for more information, but realized I'd soon have the answers.

"And I didn't lie. I've always used an assumed name. It's easier to avoid your family that way. You may remember that you didn't use *your* real name, either."

What the heck? This was fun.

She sighed. "For the same reason. Had we been honest from the beginning, we would have had to kill each other on sight."

He grunted. "Nothing has changed."

"True. You're still an idiot." She bit her lip, and I could see the tears well. Taking a calming breath, she stuffed the emotions back down. "Are you the one who called the demon to drain the wizard?"

Anger fell over his face. He shoved his chair back. "I am an honorable man. I would not use a demon from hell to do my bidding, and I happened to like the meddling wizard. Can you say the same?"

She didn't say anything.

Hmmmm. I didn't know of any demons that could hurt a wizard. I'd have to check with Simone to see if she knew of any who had the intelligence and power to do such a thing.

"Did you call the demon?" Constantine paced back and forth in front of the table.

"No. I don't like the troublesome wizard, but I had no wish for his death. I had nothing to do with it. Stop that, you are like a *rat* in a cage." She emphasized the word *rat*.

He grunted again. The man really needed to work on his communication skills, but he did sit down.

"Did you send the Stuark demon to kill me that night?" Her eyes were closed now.

She didn't see the second look of shock on his face, and the pain.

"A Stuark tried to kill you?" There was concern in his voice. I could see him check himself. When he spoke again, it was with little emotion. "I told you, I do not use demon spawn to do my dirty work."

"Is that what I was, Con, dirty work?" This time she stood and paced. "It explains so much. Was the big plan to screw the little witch and then kill her? So many nights you could have gone through with your plan. Why did you wait?"

Wow! This was better than *Footballers Wives* on BBC America, and I love that show.

I didn't think it possible but he stuck his chiseled chin out even farther. Still, he made no comment.

That made Lilyana even angrier. "You are a coward. It does you no harm to admit the truth now. Yet you sit there in silence."

He kicked the chair across the room. "I am no coward, witch." He growled the words. "If I had wanted you dead I could have done it a hundred times over. So you tell me, Lil, why would I not kill someone who I discovered is my sworn enemy? Tell me." The anger came off him in waves.

He wouldn't hurt her. He loved her. Though she was too dense to see it. Oh my god. This whole mess between the covens was over a lovers quarrel. The family feud had been going on for years, but had never crossed the Atlantic until these two. Pathetic. Countless lives had been taken and many others ruined because of this ridiculous spat.

I should kill them both for their idiotic selfishness and stupidity.

Lilyana backed against the wall. "My brother told me the truth.

He explained all of it to me. You and your coven had planned to use me as a sacrifice. That night the demon was in your apartment, you pretended to be ill, knowing I would come to care for you." She grew more hysterical by the minute.

He chuckled, but it wasn't a happy sound.

"Think about what you are saying. Why would I send a demon to kill you if I needed you as a sacrifice? These are lies from that worthless brother of yours. Nox is the one who sent the demon to kill you that night, not me. He couldn't stand the fact that his lovely and powerful sister had a thing for the enemy."

Backing closer to the wall she screamed at him. "My brother loves me. He would never do such a thing. I will kill you for saying such filth."

Constantine shook his head. "Your brother loves power. Look at the lives he's ruined over the past few months. So many in both of our covens have died. And for what?

"I love you, Lil, I always have, and I would give my life for you. Can you say the same for your brother? Would he sacrifice his life for you?"

Something must have clicked in her brain, as realization dawned on her face. She slid down the wall. I clicked my fingers and the handcuffs fell off them both. Constantine caught her before she hit the floor.

My, my. Looked like I'd locked up the wrong people. Oh, I wasn't about to let them go—they still had things to work out. Meanwhile, I thought I might go visit this Nox guy.

I hope he tried to kill me. I'd been itching to blow someone up all day.

Nine

Manhattan
Fired-up witches: 1
Dead guys: 1

Well, that was entertaining. Nox turned out to be one nasty, festering soul who really hates chicks. Especially witchy chicks. Yay, me!

Thanks to Lilyana's connection to him, it only took me a few minutes to locate him. I could see him in a SoHo loft, sound asleep. Evidently he didn't know his sister had been kidnapped.

After a few words to the investigators asking that they look after Garnout, I grabbed a taxi. I could have requested one of them give me a ride, but I didn't really want anyone in my way. I lied and told them I had to run an errand. Cole was busy on the phone, so I didn't have to explain anything to him.

I snuck into Nox's building, shielding myself from security, and made my way up the elevator. Then I used magic to break into his apartment. I know, I know, but this guy had most likely been the one to hurt Garnout, and as I've mentioned, all bets are off when you mess with my friends. There were several wards on his door, all of them easy to break. He hadn't bothered to lock the door itself; I'm sure he thought the wards would be enough. In a matter of seconds, I was inside.

The floors of the apartment were painted black concrete, the walls and furniture white. I'm sure it was *trés* chic, but it was boring. No personality at all.

Luckily for me, he was still in bed. I love waking up evil warlocks.

I stood at the end of his bed, which was on a short platform. Played his mind in fast-forward for clues. It didn't take long. I saw flashes of him torturing women. I could have killed him for that alone, but there was so much more. He had conspired with demons many times. His goal was to take over the coven from his sister, and then Constantine's coven. And he'd done whatever it took to make it happen.

I could hear him talking to the person who tried to murder Garnout, but I couldn't see the evil being. It had been smart enough to shield itself, but Nox had used the evil to go after my favorite wizard.

I'd seen enough.

"Wake up, asshole!" I yanked the white fur blanket off the bed and threw it on the floor. "Ewww. This is real. What did you do, kill a polar bear? That's just sick."

He sat straight up in bed, hands flying out to throw something, but I stopped him.

"Who the fuck are you?" He didn't have any eyebrows or hair. But he did have a six-pack. *Good waste of abs, if you ask me.*

I laughed. It felt good. "I'm the chick who is going to kick your ass." I tossed him out of the bed with magical force up against the wall. Then I let go.

"Bitch!"

I snorted. "You have no idea just how big of a bitch I can be, but I'm totally anxious for you to find out." I motioned to him to come toward me. "Okay, big, bad warlock." I deepened my tone with my best sexy voice. "Come and get me."

The evil and anger surrounding him grew. His aura was almost black. The world wouldn't miss this guy. Oh, his sister might, for a few moments, until she discovered the truth about her nasty brother. Even Lilyana had her limits. After watching her with Constantine, I knew she was basically a good witch, but she'd been steered down the wrong path by this jerk.

"So when were you planning to kill your sister? Today? Tomorrow? Or were you waiting for her to get caught up in one of the street wars?"

He watched me, but he didn't move. "You are insane, witch. I love my sister."

"Oh, I seriously doubt you love anyone but yourself, Nox. I think you would use anyone to gain power, including your sister."

"Who are you?" He was still against the wall. Boring. I was ready for a good, old-fashioned battle.

I rolled my eyes. "You already asked that, and it's none of your damn business. I know about you conspiring with the demons and everything you did to poor Lilyana. I know everything, Nox."

He growled and jumped for me. Yippee.

I ducked and threw a warty spell at him. Yes, it was a petty little spell, but it was fun watching his face as bulbous skin bumps popped out all over his body. This warlock clearly took great pride in his appearance and couldn't stand imperfection.

Then it dawned on me. "*That's* why you wanted Lilyana dead. She'd consorted with the enemy. Tainted, she wasn't fit to lead a coven. Right?"

He sneered and then mumbled something. I threw up a shield, so whatever he tried to throw at me would bounce off and hit him.

The spell must have been nasty. It put him flat on his back and turned him green. His body spazzed and twitched for a bit, then his mouth foamed. I heard him whisper a healing spell, but it was too late.

Twitching, he raised a hand as if to throw something and then it fell to the ground. Dead.

What an idiot. He'd just killed himself.

"You killed him already?"

Simone's voice made me jump and I twirled around.

The demon slayer stood in the doorway, her long hair pulled into a ponytail. The legs of her leather pants were in shreds and it looked like she'd been bathing in demon blood. Kind of smelled like it, too. A coppery scent flooded the room.

She moved toward me. "Damn, Bron, I wanted to kill him. Rip him apart."

"Sorry, the idiot already killed himself by accident." I told her what happened.

That's about the time Cole walked in.

"Jesus, Bron, you could have told someone." He bent down and looked at Nox, without touching him.

"How'd you get here so fast?"

He chuckled. "Had you followed. I was already on the way, once they told me you were outside this building."

"Did you know about Nox?"

"Nah, but it explains a lot. So, he did this to himself?"

"Yes, the idiot." It's awful but I wanted to kick Nox in the nads. I didn't, but I really wanted to. "He ruined everything."

"We'll clean it up. Why don't you go back to the house and check on Garnout? Are you going to tell the sister?"

Argh! Lilyana would have to know. It's never easy telling someone about ultimate betrayal, but it had to be done. "Yep. I'll tell her."

Monday
9 a.m.
What a night.

When I came back, Lilyana had recovered from fainting earlier. I'd wondered if maybe we should feed her something before telling her the truth.

I hadn't absolved her of all guilt; it was under her leadership that the coven had broken the rules and attacked other covens. But I'd seen in Nox's mind how he had manipulated her. She'd trusted the wrong man. I've done that more times than I care to remember.

I checked on Garnout, hoping that since Nox was gone, the confusion spell would be banished. No such luck. I hate feeling helpless, but that's exactly how I felt. I'm supposed to be one of the most powerful witches on the planet and I have no idea how to help one of my dearest friends.

I called and ordered coffee and sandwiches from Zabar's and had the food taken down to the basement. I watched. At first they tried to ignore the meal, but it didn't take long. Lilyana wrapped her hands around a coffee mug and held it tight.

I gave them another hour, and then I went downstairs.

They hadn't spoken a word while they ate, and Lilyana eyed me suspiciously. The investigators informed me that the couple had continued to argue once Lilyana woke up. Nothing had been settled.

I sat down on the table between them. "Okay. You two still have things to work out, but there's something you both need to know. I think the easiest way to do this is to show you what happened." I shifted further back on the table and crossed my legs. I'd informed Cole, who had followed me into the room, of what I had planned to do.

"I need you to move your chairs where you can each hold one of my hands. No funny stuff. I'm only showing you memories, and trust me, you both need to see this."

Constantine gave me a look that could have frozen a penguin on the spot. I sent him a mental message. *"You need to be here for her."* He gave a slight nod and moved his chair in front of me.

Lilyana followed him.

I stretched out my arms. "Take my hands." I wondered if perhaps I should give Lilyana some kind of warning of what she was about to see, but I decided I'd pull back as Nox threw that last spell.

I grabbed their hands. Cole stood behind them both. We had no idea how either of them would react.

Rewinding the memories I'd borrowed from Nox, I let them all play out. Lilyana gasped when she saw him talking with the demon who had attacked her, but she didn't let go.

Then she saw all of her brother's manipulations roll out in front of her, one nasty deed after another. It made me physically ill to watch how he'd tortured witches and other women, so I could only imagine how she felt. At the end I began to pull away, but she held on, squeezing my hand tight.

"No, show me." She whispered the words. I could hear the sorrow.

I didn't want to do it, but I did.

To her credit, she didn't collapse. I think I would have, had I discovered the depth of a brother's betrayal the way she did. I let go of both of their hands.

Lilyana jumped up and ran for the corner. Leaning her hands against the wall she stood with her head down. It looked as though she was trying to catch her breath. I knew she was trying hard not to sob.

"You've both been used. How you decide to move forward after this is up to you. But you *will* take your family feud off the streets of Manhattan, and you will find a way to heal my wizard." My voice was calm, but firm.

Constantine nodded. Then he walked to Lilyana and put his arms around her. "We will make it right." She didn't push him away.

"Like I said, that's up to you, but the violence stops today." I scooted off the table.

"Yes. It stops today." Lilyana had obviously steadied her nerves. "How much longer will you keep us here?" She raised her head and faced me. "My coven will work to heal your wizard. Tell me what was done, exactly, and we will help make it right."

"We will work with them," Constantine added.

Lilyana held out a hand. "You have no reason to trust us. You can keep my powers bound if you wish. I will make a solemn oath to harm none. One punishable by death if I break it."

"Lil!" Constantine admonished her.

She moved away from the comfort of his arms. "No. I will do

this. Bind me, witch. I will do whatever you want." I saw the contrition in her face and the need for redemption. Her brother's crimes would weigh heavy on her for years to come.

I knew it wasn't necessary, but I did what she asked. More for her sake, than anything. She'd been corrupted by evil, and she knew it. The binding would work as a safeguard against hurting anyone else. The only time it wouldn't kill her is if she were fighting back in self-defense.

Constantine's eyes narrowed as I said the spell, but he didn't stop me. When we finished he took Lilyana's hand.

"Now bind the spell to me. If anything happens to her I have no reason to be here." He bowed his head to her.

"Con, no!" Lilyana cried. "You can't do this. You know what my brother has done. Someone will have to pay for his crimes and it will be me."

"You don't understand, Lil. The people who would want retribution are my family. If we bind ourselves, then the war ends today. They won't risk killing you because it would also end my life."

She sobbed, and I have to admit it was pretty damn touching. But I had things to do and I needed to move this along.

"Okay, Romeo and Juliet. Make up your minds. We've got a wizard to save."

Ten

Totally weirded-out witches: 1
Spells: 10

Saving Garnout is going to be way tougher than I ever imagined. After Lilyana and Constantine made nice, they called in their covens to work on my wizard friend.

We'd all gathered around Garnout's bed. There were a ton of people in my parents' bedroom: the most powerful members from both covens, Cole's team, and even Simone and Caleb, who finally showed up a few hours before. Caleb hadn't known I was in town until he'd heard about Nox's death. I'd forgotten he was even in New York, but was happy to see he'd survived the coven wars.

We chanted healing spells. I could see Garnout's color was pinker and his breathing on track.

Then all of a sudden a big wind hit in the middle of everything, like one of those West Texas dust devils. There was this crazy wind and papers flew everywhere, all of it taking place in the middle of the bed. At the time I thought maybe it was Garnout's way of healing himself. Then someone shouted, "Come to me, darling!"

Suddenly the wind went away, and so did Garnout. He just disappeared.

Cole and his investigators are working on it, but it looks like some magical being whisked him up. I've tried every spell I know to find him, but nothing works.

It's so weird. I've failed him and I don't even know what happened.

On top of everything I had to make a quick trip to London to help the PM with some meetings. The world's gone crazy and everyone wants to talk peace when that happens. The top dudes and dudettes of the world are setting up a series of minisummits to keep the conversations going.

There's also an enormous birthday party for Zane's soon-to-be six-year-old niece, Zoë. She called me personally to invite me, and I couldn't tell her no. The cute little moppet holds my heartstrings in her hands, and she knows it.

Mom and Dad must have shown up right as I left. Cole called and said they didn't seem surprised at all to find a load of strangers in their house. In fact, Mom is helping with the search for Garnout. They have become great friends over the last few years. She backed away from the craft years ago, but she still has amazing powers.

After ridding Manhattan of its demon population, Simone is headed back to Los Angeles. Cole's staying around to see if he can figure out what happened to Garnout, and to make certain the two feuding families keep the peace. There will also be legal and magical inquiries into the business dealings of the covens and the companies they run. Glad I'm not in the middle of that.

I still haven't heard from Sam. I've left a couple of voice mails and text messages and told him about everything that happened in New York. I even tried to send my mind out to him, but he has me blocked.

I'm not worried, yet, though I am tempted to call Maridad. She's Sheik Azir's right-hand woman. When it comes to these rescue missions, she usually doesn't know much more than I do, but she is good at keeping up with Azir. If I don't hear from Sam tomorrow, I'll definitely give her a call.

I've been checking e-mail and catching up with the business side of life, paying bills and all that other fun stuff I haven't been able to do for a while.

I really miss Sam. You know how you have those crazy thoughts and wishes that are totally unreasonable, but you wish for them anyway? I wish Sam were here with a big tub of Cool Whip.

Hmmmm.

London
4 a.m.

My mother and father are insane. Mom just called and said Dad is on his way to Africa.

"The camp where your brother's been working was attacked by guerilla fighters and we think he's been kidnapped." (I think that's what she said through the sobs.) She was genuinely scared and I felt bad for her.

My brother can take care of himself, and I didn't understand why my mother was in a sudden panic about him. I sent out my mind while we spoke, but my brother had me blocked. He was still on planet Earth, though. I might not be able to see him, but I could feel he was there.

"Brett's a big boy and he handles this kind of stuff all the time, Mom. Last time he was kidnapped they needed antibiotics, and the time before they held him for ransom so they could get money for a new hospital. It's just the way they do business in that country."

Mom sniffled. "I'm telling you, this is serious. The nurse, Tiana, who works with him, says these rebels are vicious. I'm having one of my feelings again. This time I know I'm right. Something is terribly, terribly wrong."

It was too early in the morning for me to be my normally compassionate self, but I tried. "I can't see him Mom, but I know he's alive. He's blocking me. If he were really in danger, he'd open up his shields and beg me to come save him." *As if.* "But he hasn't, so I know he's okay."

"Do me a favor and keep tabs on your dad, too. I worry that I should have gone with him."

I yawned and stretched. I'd only been asleep for about an hour and a half when she called. I'd be knocking back the herbs today to stay awake. "I promise, I'll check on Dad every few hours. He'll be fine. Everybody loves him."

My dad has contacts everywhere, and I really wasn't worried. If my brother was in trouble, he'd find him.

11 a.m.

I'd sell my cat, Casper, to the highest bidder for a Diet Coke right now. (Okay, the cat's not worth much, but I really do need a Diet Coke.) I've been trying to stay away from the hard stuff, but I give up. I'm running on an hour and a half of sleep.

This day has been beyond weird.

When I'm home in Sweet, Kira and Margie play this game with me. Usually it's after a few shots of tequila. It goes like this: one of us starts with the phrase "There was this one time when . . ." and then we tell some totally whacked but true story. After about an hour we are all on the floor laughing so hard we can barely breathe.

I have a new story to add.

There was this one time . . . when the prime minister walked in my room and I was naked.

Argh! I'm not sure I've ever been more humiliated. Well, at least in the past twenty-four hours.

Anyhoo, I was just about to step into the shower when I realized I'd forgotten my razor. I'd hit that point with the underarms where it simply had to be done, or else I might be mistaken for Joe the Gorilla's new girlfriend. And the stubble on my legs could have been used to sandpaper off ten coats of varnish.

I ran back out to my room just as the PM opened the door. I screamed—that girlie kind of "Oh!" that we do when someone surprises us naked.

His hand flew to his eyes and he jerked his head back as if he'd seen something so horrible he might become ill. I mean it. Then he said, "Oh . . . oh, my," and slammed the door.

It kind of hurt my feelings. I mean on the one hand, *gross*—the British prime minister just saw me naked. *Mondo* embarrassing. But couldn't he have at least ogled for a split-second?

I'm no troll, but you wouldn't know it when it comes to the PM. Whatever. Well, it *would* be whatever, except now he can't meet my eyes. When he talks to me he either looks over my left shoulder or stares down at some files.

Was I so horrendous that the memory has been burned into his brain?

God. Why do I care? He's like, the stuffiest man on the planet. Probably hasn't a seen a real naked woman in years. I think he had the hots for someone on his security staff a while back, but she turned out to be a spy who wanted to kill him, so it didn't work out.

I'm looking forward to tonight. It's Zoë's birthday, and I know we're going to have a blast. She's going to be a powerful witch one day. Her parents were killed in a tragic accident and now Zane's her caregiver. She's been on tour with him, but she wanted to come back to London for her birthday and for school.

It will be good to see Zane, too. He's a terrible flirt, but he always makes me feel good. It will be nice to hang out with someone who doesn't think I'm a total troll.

Eleven

London
Wednesday
4 p.m.
Partying witches with rockin' new outfits and wicked
fine shoes: 1
Hunky, hot boyfriends: 1

When you are hanging out with one of the most popular rock stars in the world, you kind of have to go with the flow. This is something I've learned in the last few months after becoming friends with Zane.

After the meetings this morning, I had a chance to catch a quick nap. It's a good thing. Hanging out with Zane is tiring enough, but when you throw his precocious niece, Zoë, in the game, it's even wackier.

My lovely nap was interrupted by the latter's tiny voice.

"Bronwitch, wake up." She stood beside the bed dressed in the cutest red jumper and white blouse. Her black hair had been trimmed into a bob, and her bright, cornflower blue eyes were as big as ever.

"Well, hello there, Miss Zoë." I sat up in bed and stretched. "I thought we were having dinner tonight. Did I oversleep?"

Lifting two shopping bags, she put them on the side of the bed. "Uncle Zane says everyone gets presents today."

I touched her cheek. I'm not overly fond of children, but this one had found a place in my heart a few months ago when Zane had been worried about her safety.

She smiled. "Your presents are in the bag. I helped pick them out."

I made a funny fish-mouth and wiggled my eyebrows. "Is it a red jumper like yours? I really like it."

She shook her head.

"Is it a giant jar of Gummi Bears? I could use something sweet."

She laughed. "No, but tonight we are going to have the biggest cake my brain can imagine. That's what Uncle said. And candy and cookies, and we can eat all of it."

Someone will need a trip to the dentist when this night is over. I was glad I wouldn't be the one peeling her off the ceiling. Poor Nanny Bee probably would have that job. "That sounds soooo good. I'm starving."

"Mr. Cook says he'll bring in tea when I ring, but I want you to open your presents first." She was hopping from foot to foot in excitement.

I made a big show of opening the first bag slowly. It was from one of my favorite stores here in London, Maxi's. It's a funky place with designer clothes from all over the world.

Zoë helped pull the item out of the bag. "I helped Uncle pick it out." She put it on my lap.

I opened the paper and found a delightful dress in red, green, yellow, and white. The wild patterns of the colors were dizzying to the eye. It was a tango-style dress with a ruffled bottom and halter neckline. I loved it on sight.

"Oh, Zoë, it's beautiful. Thank you, honey." I reached over to hug her, and she squeezed me back. She smelled like cotton candy and baby powder, and it was hard for me to let go.

Then she crawled up on the bed beside me, sitting on her knees. "Open the shoes. Oops." Her hand flew to her mouth. "I ruined the surprise."

I waved a hand. "Don't be silly. Shoes?" I wiggled my eyebrows again. "You know how much I love shoes." We opened the bag and found a pair of four-inch red jeweled Rene Caovilla appliqué sandals that matched the red in the dress perfectly. I'd seen them at Bergdorf's a month or so ago, but I just couldn't justify that kind of purchase at the time.

I whistled. "These are amazing."

She clapped her hands. "I saw them and then we went to find the dress to match. I chose well, didn't I, Bronwitch?"

I kissed her rosy cheek. "Yes, you did perfectly. You have really good taste in shoes. Hey, wait a minute."

"What?" She crawled across me to sit on the other side.

I touched her nose with my finger. "I thought it was *your* birthday, not mine."

"It *is* my birthday, silly!" She giggled. "But Uncle Zane says you need serious wardrobe help and we have to do what we can."

I laughed out loud. "Oh, really?" *Toad.* My wardrobe was just fine, thank you. "Where is your uncle?"

"Talking to Uncle Matt about business stuff." She shrugged. "It was boring, so I snuck out with your bags. May we have tea now?"

I scrunched up my nose and pretended to think on it a bit. "Yes. I know how much you love to call Cook, so you do that, and I'll go change. Tell him we'll come down to the kitchen." I patted her head and ran for the bathroom.

Before my nap I'd changed into a big Paul Frank T-shirt sporting Julius the Monkey. Sam gave it to me months ago. I threw some water on my face and thought about him.

I didn't try to find him, but I sent him a mental message just in case he didn't have me blocked. "I love you." I sighed. Then I heard him in my head. *"I love you, too."*

I jumped in excitement. I sent my mind out to him again. "I've been trying to call, is everything okay?"

"We're good, it's much worse though than we thought. The children—well, it's bad. We're in the jungle, and the phones don't work. I miss you, baby, more than you know. Every time I close my eyes I dream of you. Damn. I've gotta go. Love, love, love you." He put up his shields.

I sighed. Sam. Lord, my body ached for the man.

I stared into the mirror. My cheeks were pink. Thinking about him did get the blood to flowing.

Zoë knocked on the door. "Tea's ready, Bronwitch. Cook says to come downstairs."

I laughed. *Impatient little magpie.*

"You go on down and check out the treats, just don't eat them all before I get there."

She giggled. I had a feeling the only thing left would be the watercress sandwiches.

I freshened my makeup and added a little kohl liner around my eyes and a red lipstick to match the dress. I slipped it on and the silky material was marvey against my skin. It fit perfectly. I swear, Zane has a talent for knowing a woman's size. Sheik Azir does, too. Must be a talent of the wealthy and powerful.

Thankfully, my toes were pedi-perfect. I slipped on the Rene Caovillas. They would kill my calves by the end of the night, but they were the most beautiful shoes I'd ever seen.

I did a quick fluff of the hair and called it all good.

Downstairs, Zoë was sitting at the granite breakfast bar doing serious damage to a cream puff.

She pointed to the door leading to the PM's offices. "They need to talk to you," she said with her mouth full. If it hadn't been her birthday, I might have said something.

I grabbed the remaining cream puff and gave her a little wave. "Be back in a sec."

I knocked on the door.

"Come in."

The PM was in a bad mood. I could tell from his tone.

I opened the door.

Zane and the PM were fuming. The world's most popular rock star and the British prime minister are related. Most of the time they get along fine, but not always.

Zane sat in a chair, wearing a vintage Pucci shirt and ripped jeans. His blond curls had grown out and he looked as sexy as ever. Arms crossed, he was in serious pout mode.

Great. What now?

Midnight
Dead Guys: 1
Men can be so utterly ridiculous.

The PM and Zane were at odds over a kitten. Really. The prime minister had bought Zoë a kitten, a cute little black-and-white, mewling piece of fluff.

Zane didn't want him to give it to her. Took me a few minutes to figure out what was going on. The rock star was worried the diplomat's simple gift would trump everything he'd planned for Zoë.

They were bickering back and forth.

I held up a hand in a "stop motion" that was Supremes-worthy. "You two are being idiots." They both looked at me, and the PM quickly averted his eyes.

God, he's lucky I didn't blow him up right then.

"First of all," I said, pointing to the PM, "get over it. You saw me naked. It's not a big deal."

The PM blanched.

Before he could speak, I pointed at Zane. "*You* stop being an asshole. Zoë will love a kitten, but she'll also love the multitude of gifts you have planned. If, at the end of the night you don't feel you have her full adoration, you can try to buy her off with a new pony. One with pretty pink bows or something."

Zane became thoughtful, and I could see the wheels turning. The man was ridiculous. It would be a sure bet that a pony would be the highlight of Zoë's birthday.

"Now both of you get it together. This is her night, her first birthday without her parents. We will make it magical, special, and a party she will never forget. Understood?"

They both nodded.

"Okay. I'm going to go get the birthday girl ready." I turned my glare to Zane. "I assume you've bought her something fab to wear? And by the way, thank you for my outfit."

"Looks bloody brilliant on you." Zane smiled.

I rolled my eyes. "Where's Zoë's party outfit?"

"It's in the car, I'll have Jonathan go get it."

"Fine. Where are Nanny Bee and Georgette?" The latter was Zane's personal assistant. She was the only woman I'd met who could keep him on track.

"They're getting the restaurant ready for the party."

"Okay." I walked toward the door. "You two behave."

As I walked out I heard Zane say, "You saw her naked? Lucky bastard." I laughed. God bless Zane. He made my night.

A half hour later, I had Zoë's hair combed to a shine, complete with a tiny tiara. "I want to look like a fairy princess." Her voice was a soft whisper. We stood at the sink in one of the downstairs bathrooms.

The dress she picked out was a beautiful sapphire blue color with tiny silver appliqué flowers on the long sleeves and on the trim of the neck and skirt.

"You are most definitely princess material, pretty girl." Carefully placing the comb in her hair, I made certain her tiara was snug.

That smile of hers would knock the socks off the boys someday and it even makes *my* grumpy heart do flips. She turned and squeezed me tight.

"I wish you could be my new mommy, but Uncle Zane says you have a boy already. And that you really love me, but he's not really the settling-down type."

I coughed. "Well, yes. He's right. I do have a boy already that I love." Sam probably wouldn't like being called a "boy," but he was definitely mine. "But thank you. I hope if I ever have a little girl she's as wonderful as you. Now, let's go find those guys and get to your party."

That made her squeal.

We were headed out the back of the PM's residence when I felt it; a magical presence.

"Get her in the car and go!" I didn't want to scare Zoë, so I whispered the order in the PM's ear. "Now."

He all but shoved Zane and Zoë in the car and they took off.

Protecting myself with a shield, I waited. Over the past few months I've learned how to triple my protection shields and now they can hold up to massive attacks.

Two warlocks came down the alley. "You are not welcome, witch." The taller of the two men raised his hands.

Oh, boy. This is going to be a blast. I'd been itching for a fight since I arrived. If these two idiots wanted to play, who was I to argue?

"See, now, I think you have your facts wrong. I'm welcome here. You, on the other hand, were not invited." I shrugged. "So from where I stand, it's you who are not welcome."

The fat one reminded me of someone I'd met once. *Oh my god.* "Sphere? Is that you?" I'd met the little basketball of a warlock months ago in Brussels. When the poop hit the fan during one of the summits, he'd vanished from the scene of the crime. Turned out the other warlock in Brussels had been the culprit and I'd forgotten all about the pudgy and often annoying warlock.

I could tell he didn't recognize me at first, but when he did, it was something straight out of a Laurel and Hardy movie. "Ah-hhh!" Sphere shrieked and ran away as fast as his chubby legs would carry him. I'd have to deal with him later.

"I suggest you follow your friend." I did that brushy wave thing people do when they want you to go away.

The warlock stood his ground. Moron. Totally deserved to die. "Are you at least going to tell me why you are here?" As I said the words I wondered if I should just go ahead and kill him. I didn't want him throwing something that might mess up my new dress and shoes.

I could feel some power in him but he had no idea what he was up against. The idiot forgot the first law of magical war: "Know thy opponent." The second law is: "If the other guy is stronger—run." Okay, so I made that one up, but it makes sense.

This guy obviously didn't have any—sense, that is. He didn't bother to explain anything. Throwing out his hands, he tossed a big ball of fire, which I promptly caught and played with in the air.

I sent my mind into his. "You know the little fat guy who ran away? Well, he's seen firsthand what a high witch like me can do."

Struggling mentally, he tried to put up his shields. I could see the stress of trying to push me out of his head as it wrinkled his brow.

Tossing the fireball up in the air, I made it disappear. "This is your last warning, asshole. I have somewhere to be, and I'm really not in the mood to play games with you tonight."

When he didn't move, I rolled my shoulders and cracked my neck. Using my forefinger in a figure eight pattern, I threw a binding spell at him and wrapped it around his ankles. He'd already begun spewing a spell.

I stomped my foot without thinking. The earth shook. That's one of my newer powers and I forget all the time.

With his body bound, he teetered to the right, then the left, and fell to the ground. His brain splattered all over the drive.

Damn. I hadn't really meant to kill him.

I picked up my beaded evening bag where I'd left it in the driveway, called the spook squad on my cell phone, and explained what happened. They were there in less than five minutes and took care of the mess, promising to find Sphere for questioning.

The PM sent his driver to pick me up and I made it just in time to see Zoë blow out the candles on a cake that took two tables to hold. It had been made into a chocolate castle.

The presents were in a mountain behind her. I didn't see a pony, but there was a four-story dollhouse courtesy of Sheik Azir. The rest of the presents would make any toy store envious.

Any other child might turn into a spoiled brat, but that would never happen to Zoë. She was someone special.

"Bronwitch. Look at my cake." She waved her hands over the cake, and I worried she might topple into it.

I winked at her. "It is the biggest cake I've ever seen. Do you think it will taste good?"

She stuck a finger into the icing and put it in her mouth. "Mmmmm."

"Well, I guess that answers that."

The PM and Zane gave me looks, as if to ask if everything was okay. I nodded that it was and tried to enjoy the party.

But all night I kept wondering what Sphere and the other warlock had been up to. Were they after the PM, Zane, or me?

Twelve

*A*h, Paris. The Eiffel tower, Christian Lacroix, cabaret music, and slimy worm warlocks—there's so much here for a girl to see and do.

There are witches who hunt for a living. They track down nasty, evil, magical beings and kill them. Me? All I have to do is stand around and the bad dudes show up to kill *me*. It's been that way ever since I came into my powers at seventeen.

After the altercation with Sphere and his dead buddy, I had Cole investigate the warlock. That's how we ended up in Paris—Sphere came back here to the protection of his coven.

Fat lotta good that did him.

Cole discovered there are three hits out on me right now. That's nothing new. In fact, I was beginning to feel unpopular the last few weeks because Jason seemed to be the only one wanting to kill me. The last five years of my life have been dedicated to ridding the world of evil magic dudes and dudettes, and I've made a few enemies along the way.

One of the hits is courtesy of Jason, I'm certain. Seems he's vanished from his psychiatric prison and is God knows where.

The other two, well I haven't a clue. Honestly, someone is always trying to kill me. It's just a part of life. But I hadn't pissed anyone off in a while, so I was really curious who it was this time.

"We're working on it, Bron." Cole tried to reassure me. We were staying at the Hotel Meurice. The two suites we occupied looked like something from Versailles. A bit too over the top for me, decorated in blue and gold with lots of silk, but who am I to complain? They do treat Americans with civility, which I appreciate. Of course, it could just be because I'm hanging out with Zane.

The rock star insisted on coming with us, and he always stays here. The staff is discreet and doesn't seem to mind that we have people coming and going at all hours of the night.

Tonight we all had dinner downstairs. The dining room has a beautiful dome ceiling, very elegant, and unfortunately, very open.

We'd been sitting down for less than fifteen minutes. It was Zane, his assistant Georgette, Cole, and myself. In the five hours since we'd arrived I'd been able to find a beautiful red dress with a tight-fitting bodice, low back, and flared skirt. It was as if the dress had been made for me and matched my new Rene C.s perfectly. I made protection charms to put in everyone's pockets and warded our rooms with protection spells. No one would get in without warning.

I faced the entrance of the restaurant and we were at a table near the back when I picked up the presence of several magical beings. Two warlocks and three witches. As they came through the entrance, I noticed they were dressed to the nines. Probably out for a great night on the town, except they walked straight toward our table.

I was about to throw up a shield, when one of them held up a hand. "We wish you no harm." Then they all bowed their heads.

Nodding, I stood. "Do you want to speak to me about something?"

The shorter man stepped forward and held out his hand. "I am Abelard." His English carried a heavy French accent. I shook his hand.

"This is Aimee, Esme, and Noel," he said, and pointed to the women, all of whom had long, straight black hair, elegant, classical features, and warm smiles. "And this is Davyn, he is our leader but his English is not so good." Davyn was positively regal in a tuxedo. His hair was gray, and he had that handsome, "I'm incredibly wealthy" air about him. "We wish you welcome to our city. We are of the Dartagnan coven."

Wasn't that one of the three Musketeers? These didn't seem like the kind of people who would be hanging out with slimeball Sphere. Cole had mentioned earlier that the Dartagnan coven was the last one Sphere belonged to. I didn't have any idea what all of this was about, but I readied myself for anything.

I smiled, very friendly-like. "It's nice to meet you." It's not unusual for coven members to introduce themselves to a high witch. We tend to do a lot of damage when we aren't sure about people, and it's always good to make friends first.

"Would you ladies and gents like to join us for dinner?" Zane was staring Aimee down pretty hard, and she was giving it right back to him. The man never stopped with the womanizing.

Georgette elbowed him in the ribs, and whispered, "Down boy. We don't know if they're the good guys."

I laughed. "It just so happens we are on the search for one of your warlocks, a guy named Sphere." At the mention of his name, Davyn began spewing French.

Esme reached a long red-nailed hand out and touched his arm—Davyn shut up instantly.

Though my French is elementary at best, I had an idea of what he was saying from the images in his mind. I was a bit surprised he'd let his shields down.

Cole chuckled behind me. "He called Sphere a fat, insolent pig and wished him dead."

I smiled. "Well, that's something we both have in common."

Abelard told him what I'd said. They both nodded seriously.

"We will help in any way we can." Abelard put a hand on Davyn's shoulder. "It upsets Davyn and our coven that Sphere tries to hide behind our name. He was exiled two years ago for practicing black magic and we've had nothing to do with him since."

So they'd come to make sure I knew they had nothing to do with the hit on me. Smart.

"Do you have any idea where he might be?"

Esme spoke. "The warlocks he works with are hiding him, but we, too, will hunt." She, even more than Davyn, had incredible power. I had a feeling she'd very much like to find Sphere before I did. He must have done something really wicked.

Abelard took his hand from Davyn and motioned to the woman. "Esme's brother was harmed by the warlocks Sphere hides behind. I think she very much wishes to crush his heart."

Esme was going to have to get in line.

"If you know he's with these guys, how come you can't find them?"

"Ah. It is very dark magic that protects them." Abelard added. "We have not seen this kind of magic in many centuries. As soon as we discover their location, they move. It is most upsetting."

I noticed the other diners were giving us curious glances. Davyn must have thought the same. He whispered something to Abelard, who bowed toward us.

"We only wanted to give our intentions, High Witch. We did not wish to keep you from your meal. Good evening to you all." He handed me a small business card. "Please call if you wish to meet with us."

They walked out.

Zane clapped his hands. "Good show, Bronwyn. Bloody brilliant. They are scared to death of you."

I sat down.

Cole poured me a glass of wine and I took a sip.

I honestly would have preferred Jack Daniels, but the wine helped to ease the tension from my shoulders.

I think I had chicken for dinner. I was more concerned with the search for Sphere. Several times during the meal I sent my mind out to see if I could catch the little worm, but had no luck.

By midnight we were all upstairs. Zane and Georgette planned to hit some of the Paris nightlife, Buddha Bar and La Bains to name a few, but I was actually tired. And, well, the last time I went out with Zane it caused big trouble with Sam. The paparazzi had gone crazy and things spiraled out of control.

I told them I had work to do, and left them to their partying.

The lie was a small one, but I did need some rest. Finding Sphere was on the top of my list, but I also had to figure out what happened to Garnout. I couldn't do that while partying till the wee hours of the morning, no matter how much fun it might be.

I would find the wizard, and then I'd kill whoever had stolen him away.

Thirteen

Paris
Saturday
3 a.m.
Dead guys: Too many to count
Spells: 15

I've been feeling weird lately, more tired and irritable than usual. Probably has something to do with not sleeping well since everything happened to Garnout, but I'm not sure. Paris hasn't been exactly restful.

By eleven-fifteen on Friday night, after dinner with Zane and the crew, I'd washed my face and changed into my monkey T-shirt. I was snuggling into the pillows when the phone rang. Thinking it was Zane trying to convince me to go out with him, I answered.

"What?"

"Bronwheeen?"

It was one of the French women, from earlier.

"Yes?"

"It is Esme. I have found the slimy peeeg." Her heavy French accent weighted the word *pig*.

I sat up in bed. "Wow! That was fast. Where are you?"

"Abelard has the car waiting for you outside the hotel."

"Okay. I'll be down in two minutes. Esme, don't kill him until I get there."

"I will try. But hurry."

Cole was in the shower. I thought about leaving, but I didn't want him to go all crazy ape on me later.

"Hey!" I yelled through the steam. "The coven found Sphere."

He stuck his head out of the doorway, his blond hair plastered around his face. He had a gorgeous tan and I wondered where he had gone for vacation. "Two minutes. I need two minutes. Now get out of here so I can get dressed."

Before I could stuff my pockets with potions and charms, he was out of the bathroom, dressed in jeans and carrying his boots and shirt in his hands. "Let's go."

I'd never noticed how ripped he was, but we were in a hurry so I tried not to think about his biceps and that stomach. Hell, he'd give Sam a run for his money and that was really saying something.

Davyn was in the limo with Abelard and as soon as we jumped in, it sped off.

"We found them at the home of one of our former members," Abelard spoke so fast I could barely understand him. "We determine there are at least twenty witches and warlocks inside. It will be a battle to reach him."

Cole punched some numbers on his cell phone, and then began

barking orders. Magical investigators would surround the place very soon.

"I'm not worried about who is protecting them." I sounded bold, and I was. Anyone who tried to protect *"ze fat peeg"* would die tonight. He'd tried to kill me and almost ruined little Zoë's party. All bets were off.

And if these assholes were practicing dark magic, then they should die.

The limo pulled onto a narrow street in a quiet, tree-lined neighborhood. The homes—mansions, really—were magnificent.

We moved down the street. I could see the wards protecting the house, we all could. Giant green and yellow ribbons tied in a series of knots were hard to miss.

I raised my hands and whispered a spell of release.

The knots slipped out and the ribbons fell away.

"Vache sainte." Abelard whispered the words.

"Holy cow is right." Cole shook his head. "Damn, sometimes I forget how powerful you are."

I rolled my eyes. I took out the protection charms I'd slipped in the pockets of my jeans. I shrugged out of my jacket and pulled out a few more.

"Make sure all of you have one. They won't keep you from getting hit with magic, but they will keep you from dying."

Esme, Amiee, and the other woman whose name I couldn't remember walked up. Cole handed them the charms.

"Abelard. I need you to tell everyone to stay behind me for now."

I turned to face Esme. "I'll let you kill Sphere, but I must speak to him first. I have to know who ordered this hit."

She nodded.

"Okay. Let's go play." I smiled as I walked toward the house. I'd been so tired earlier, but now the thought of killing Sphere had me totally energized.

I threw a fireball and blew the two giant wooden doors off their hinges.

Screams filled the night air. "I love this part," I whispered as I ran into the melee on the first floor. They must have been holding a meeting. The warlocks and witches wore hooded black robes, which made it difficult to discern who was who. I set a couple of hems on fire as we made our way to the stairs. The flames made wearing the robes near impossible, so several were immediately tossed to the floor. Naked witches and warlocks ran around like crazy people.

It's absurd, but all my life my mom has told me to wear clean underwear in case I'm in an accident. These people could have benefited from her advice. Some well-placed undergarments beneath the robes might have helped their situation.

I sent my mind out to all who might not have had shields. "You don't have to die. Give me Sphere."

Shouts of "Bitch!" flew through the house.

I was going to have to do this the hard way.

I tossed a binding spell at the biggest warlock I saw.

He couldn't move at all.

"Where is Sphere?"

The hooded figure didn't answer. I flicked my hand and pulled the hood back. His bald head shone in the eerie light.

"Where is Sphere?" I repeated as I shoved my mind into his, screaming the words. I could see his brow wrinkle. He had no idea how bad this was about to get.

The witches and warlocks who had come with me spread out in a straight line. They were chanting in French, but I understood. They were calling out for Sphere.

Blowing a small burn into the brain of the one I held, he screamed in agony. *"Il est en haut."*

"Upstairs we go, then." I pushed the big one down and stopped the brain flame. Cole's gang could deal with him later.

"Oh Sphere," I called. "Better for you to come out now, because if you make me come look for you, it's going to be very, very bad." The words came out of my mouth in a sing-song. "You know how much I like to fry little piggies like you."

We made it to the first landing of the split staircase. From the left came a stream of sludge headed right for us. Esme spat out a spell and the black goo fell to the ground. Then she turned to the perpetrator and said another spell that made his eyes roll back in his head as he tumbled down the stairs.

Well, that was one less warlock to worry about. Chaos surrounded us. Fireballs and sludge flew around but I didn't have to bother with any of it. Esme and the Dartagnan coven members took care of it all. It was kind of nice to have some help for once.

We made our way up the left stairway and through a long hallway of doors. I sent my mind out in search of the idiot warlock, but he was still blocked by something powerful. I couldn't imagine why anyone would bother protecting someone like him. It was ridiculous.

"I can't sense anything," I told the others. "We're going to have to check behind every door. I say we spread out at least two to a door. Watch out for the wards, they're strong." I could see the knots of blue and green woven almost into a braid before all of the doors. Yes, someone was hiding something, and it was time we found out what it was.

Esme and the others ran toward the doors, pausing for my go-ahead. I worked fast to unlock the wards so no one would be harmed by them. It was tough and draining. When I hit the last door, I nodded.

I heard a collective gasp as the doors opened and I made my way down the hall. In one room there were demon bodies piled on the floor. In another, men and women were chained to the walls. All of them had been drained of their blood. If any were alive it would be a miracle.

"What kind of sick, sadistic bastards do we have here?" The sight infuriated me and I could feel my powers rise. If Sphere had anything to do with this I'd string him up by his little porcine toes and leave him to rot.

There was one remaining door that hadn't been opened. I threw a fireball and knocked it down. There stood Sphere mumbling over some book. He was naked and sweating profusely, but he didn't look up. His bulbous body would forever be burned into my brain. *Ick.*

I stood in the doorway and glanced into the room. A nude woman sat on the edge of a large four-poster bed, her eyes glazed over in trance. Sphere must have to put someone under in order to have sex with them. Repulsive.

"Oh, Sphere." I stayed just outside the door.

He continued to chant in Latin.

"He's calling forth a demon," Esme whispered behind me. "We must kill him now." She shoved me into the room and that's when all hell broke loose. At least six Staleg demons with weapons came out of a doorway on the right, ready for battle.

I rolled my eyes. Forget leaving Sphere to rot. I'd rip off his stubby toes one at a time.

"This," I hissed at Esme, "is why I was in no hurry to charge in. I knew he had backup." Too late now to toss the blame around—the demons approached.

"Cole, get your ass in here and anyone else you can find." I chanted another protection spell for myself and Esme.

Stalegs are at least seven feet tall and are born with giant breast-plates that make them difficult to kill. But thanks to my demon-slaying buddy Simone, I had a plan.

I felt Cole and the others behind me. "Crap," Cole laughed. "Those are faces only a mother could love."

Sweeping my eyes across the room, I looked for any more un-wanted visitors. "Yep, you guys keep them busy, shoot low, and take them out at the ankles. Esme and I are going after Sphere. The longer he chants, the worse it's going to get." I could see steam rising in a pot behind Sphere. Whoever he was trying to bring forth was close to materializing. We didn't want that to happen.

"Got it." Cole and the others moved forward as I grabbed Esme's hand and pulled her with me.

"This time follow my lead." We'd almost made it to the left side of the table when one of the Stalegs threw out his paws, slamming one into Esme's shoulder and knocking us both back.

Demons are born of fire, so fireballs are not terribly helpful.

I threw a binding spell at him and then shoved him toward the melee in the middle of the room. He fell over like a big tree.

A forcefield surrounded Sphere like bulletproof glass. I used my mind to carve large holes into it with a psychic knife. With the third hole the entire thing disappeared.

Sphere finally looked up, his beady little eyes in a panic.

I threw another binding spell to hold him where he stood. As I did, his power lessened and the demons disappeared. The warlocks and witches surrounded him.

"Whatcha been doing, Sphere?" I leaned over the book and saw that it was covered in human skin. *Yuck*. I hate black-magic garbage like this. It holds all kinds of negative energy.

I pointed to Esme. "This witch really wants to talk with you, but I have a few questions of my own. Like who sent you to the prime minister's? . . . Hmmm. Still not talking? Let's see. How about if I do this?"

Waving my fingers, I began a slow burn on the end of his big toe. Normally, I would have started with his tiny dick, but I wanted to be polite in front of company.

He shook his head, and then moaned. Nothing like burning feet to get someone to talk.

"Tell me what I want to know, and I'll make it stop." I set my mouth in a thin line.

He toddled a bit and then fell back, as he tried to blow out the flame on his toe.

"Let me kill him," Esme ground the words out.

I gently pushed her aside. "In a minute."

I sighed and took the flame away. "Look, Sphere, you aren't going to make it out of here alive. Even Cole the cop wants you dead after what he saw in those rooms. Don't ya, Cole?"

"Yep." He raised an eyebrow. I almost laughed out loud at his expression. He meant it. Mr. Justice-for-all had no pity for the squirmy worm in front of me.

"You're mixed up in some bad juju, Sphere, and I think it's time to fess up."

That's when he opened his mouth and I saw the gaping open space where his tongue had been. Gross. I heard the others whispering.

I couldn't figure out how he'd been chanting without a tongue.

"So, whoever you're working for ripped out your tongue. Still,"—I pointed to the blonde on the bed—"you obviously had some perks."

He shook his head and I saw the fear in his eyes.

I heard a movement behind me and turned to see the blonde standing with her arms above her head. Her eyes were no longer glazed over. They were a bright yellow. A wind picked up in the room.

"Not today, witch." Her voice was sexy and warm. She flicked a hand toward Sphere. I glanced back to see him disappear. *Whoa.*

The wind grew stronger and a cloud of white encircled her. Then she, too, was gone.

"Holy crapola, what was that?" I was shocked. "Oh my god. I know that voice. She was the one who took Garnout." The leftover magic was so thick I could barely breathe under the weight of it. "That's one powerful chick."

There was a loud rumble and the house shook.

Cole grabbed Esme and me, and he yelled, "Run!"

As we made our way out of the room the entire home shook again. Booking it down the stairs, we dodged falling paintings and priceless antiques.

At the front entry, Cole shoved us to the street and then fell on top of us. The house collapsed.

When the rumbling stopped we all sat up, covered in white dust. Esme coughed and so did I.

Finally, I could speak. "What happened?"

"Vindictive sorceress bitch!" Cole punched numbers into his cell phone.

Sorceress? Wow. I knew they existed, but had never actually seen one. I'm a powerful witch, but multiply me by fifty and you have the power of a sorceress. They were the only magical beings equal to a wizard.

Barking orders into his cell, Cole stood and then reached out a hand to help us.

"Have you ever met a sorceress before?" I asked Esme.

She brushed the dust off her clothes. "No, but I know zat iz a very bad thing that she recognizes us."

"What do you mean?"

Abelard interrupted. "We are all well, and you?"

Esme hugged him. *"Il est plus mauvais que nous avons pense."* It's worse than we thought.

He squeezed her tight. *"Je sais, cher."* I know, dear.

Cole finally closed his cell.

Putting my hands on my hips, I faced Cole. "Can you please explain what the hell happened in there?"

"That, my friend, was Calinda, a sorceress who has been exiled for more than five hundred years. Now she's back." He sighed. "It's a very bad thing that she's here. She thrives on chaos, torture, and murder. Sphere was one of her minions. I'm sure she already has hundreds of them across the planet. It's not good. Not good at all."

Great.

"So how do we catch her?"

Abelard chimed in. "Hmmph. You do not 'catch' a sorceress. She is as powerful as any wizard."

I turned back to Cole. "So what's the plan? I'd bet large sums of money that she's the one who kidnapped Garnout. We have to find her fast."

"I wouldn't take that bet. I agree with you." He shrugged. "The problem is, I don't have a clue where to begin. The investigators are on it. They'll trace her magic, and we'll see what we come up with."

Lovely. No friggin' plan.

"So, what, we just sit around and wait for her to murder a bunch more people? Maybe even the prime minister? She must be the one who sent Sphere to kill him. What if she kills Garnout?"

"We are on it, Bron," Cole said the words through gritted teeth.

I rolled my eyes. "Whatever." He could bring in all the investigators he wanted to. I was going to find the sorceress on my own, if necessary. I wondered if Kira had any books on the subject. In the middle of trying to figure out time zones to see if it was too early to call the librarian, my phone rang. I checked the number. *Geez.*

"Hey, Mom. I'm kind of busy right now. Can I call you back?"

Sniffles.

"Mom?"

"They're both gone." Her voice was scratchy and hollow.

I walked toward the river, away from Cole and the others.

"*Who's* gone?" I turned my attention back to my hysterical mother.

"Your father and your brother. One of the other doctors at the camp called and said they woke up and your father was gone. No one has seen him since last night. I've tried. I've opened up my powers and tried to find him, but I can't." She sobbed again.

As I mentioned before, my mom turned away from the craft before I was even born. For her to use her powers to find my dad—well, it meant she was really worried. "It's okay. Let me get where I can concentrate." I was in the middle of Paris and had just been through hell. But it was my mom. I found a small bench and sat down.

I tried to locate my dad first. I could sense him, but not see him. "He's alive, Mom, I can feel him. I can't exactly tell where he is. I'll look for Brett now."

Once again, I closed my eyes and searched for my annoying

sibling. He'd better be okay or I would kill him for making Mom worry like this.

He let his shields down and I zeroed in on him. "Brett! Where the hell are you?"

He must have been asleep. The grogginess clouded his mind. "Cave. Been drugged."

Crap. "Where are you?"

"Don't know. Can't see anything. Dark. Head hurts."

No telling what kind of drugs they were using. I sent a healing spell to him.

"Is Dad there?"

That woke him up. "What?"

"Dad's missing. He's been searching for you. Someone kidnapped him during the night."

"Hell." I could feel Brett's irritation.

"Listen, I'm on the way. Just don't do anything stupid."

"No!" His voice was so loud it made my head hurt. "It's too dangerous. We'll figure it out. Do not come here."

"Okay, it's a little too late for that, big brother. I'll be there as soon as I can hop a flight."

He sighed. "Be careful. I don't know who these guys are, but they're a nasty bunch."

"You be careful, too. I'm putting a communication spell on you. If you need me, all you have to do is say my name three times."

"Oh, I'm already beginning to feel like Dorothy from *The Wizard of Oz*. Do I need to click my heels? And here I forgot my red shoes." He threw his hand against his forehead in a dramatic fashion.

My brother is against any kind of magic. He has some powers for healing, but only uses the ones that help with intuition for diagnostic purposes. "Just do what I asked, Bozo."

I picked up the phone and told Mom everything.

"I'm coming with you." She'd pulled herself together and was in her "I'm taking charge" mode.

"Better for you to stay there in case the rebels try to contact you. There may be some kind of ransom." Lame, but it was the best I could do in the moment.

"I don't know." She hesitated.

"Look, Mom. I'm going now. If I have to wait for you to get there that's another twelve-hour delay. You know how this kind of stuff works. We have to move fast."

She finally acquiesced.

Cole was standing on the other side of the street waiting for me. He looked as tired as I felt. It'd been a busy couple of days. I'd been mad at him earlier because he's always the guy with the answers, but lately he hadn't been coming through for me.

The whole thing with Jason was a big question mark, and now there was this sorceress. But there was something in Cole's eyes that made me feel kind of sorry for him. He wasn't happy about not having the answers, either—I could tell by the way he looked at me. None of this was his fault and I had to stop pointing the blame and fix the situation.

I rolled my shoulders to ease the tension, and walked toward him.

"So, who do you know in Africa?"

Fourteen

Africa
Tuesday (I think. The time zones are killing me.)
9 p.m.
Witches tired of red tape: 1

The problem with asking for help, especially from government officials, is the crap you have to go through to get anything done. The prime minister has flown with me to Tanzania, which really isn't where I need to be. And I've been stuck here for more than a day, while my father and brother are missing.

Unless they've been here, most people have no idea how big Africa is. You could fit the United States, Argentina, China, Europe, New Zealand, and India into the continent and still have space left over. It's huge. So the fact that I'm in East Africa when I really need to be in the center of the continent is kind of a big deal.

When he heard about my dad being kidnapped, the prime minister insisted we visit his friend Dr. Zocando, who is staying near the Lake Kamanrok reserve. It's one of the valleys and is filled with animals, from crocodiles and elephants to birds I've never seen before. We arrived at the camp and met with the doctor immediately after.

"I am sorry to hear about your news." Dr. Zocando nodded in my direction but did not shake my hand when we arrived. He'd done this before when we first met in New York a few months ago, so I should have known better than to stick my hand out. I'm beginning to think he's a bit of a misogynist. "I will do everything I can to help you."

"Thank you." I smiled at him. There's something about the man that doesn't feel right, but I've never been able to get a read on him. Other than not shaking my hand, he's always friendly, but something is definitely off.

"We appreciate your generosity, Doctor." The prime minister looked from me to the other gentleman and nodded. "We're sorry to have interrupted your holiday."

Zocando waved him away. "It is nothing. I only took a few days to observe the wildlife. The beauty of my country reminds me why I continue to fight for her." He was known for his AIDS initiatives throughout Africa. Traveling the world, he had raised millions for his cause.

He motioned us to a set of chairs out on the veranda. The private lodge was large, but fit perfectly into the landscape. It had a thatched roof, but the interior could have been any five-star hotel. Polished wood gleamed, and the furniture was bright and comfortable.

"Tell me where they last saw your father." He poured water from a pitcher into three glasses and handed them to us.

"He was last seen by the doctors of the camp just outside Mambasa in the Congo. My brother's been working with the doctors there to stop a typhoid fever outbreak, and to promote AIDS education. He was taken a few days ago, and when my father tried to find him . . ." I realized I was rambling. "Anyway, my dad was kidnapped from the camp by rebels demanding money and medicine."

The doctor moved his hands to make a steeple with them, and then leaned back in his chair. "And you do not wish to pay the money?"

In the time it had taken to fly from Paris to London and then off to Africa, the doctors at the camp had received a ransom note.

"Of course, we'll do whatever it takes," the PM interjected. "Bronwyn fears that just giving them the money will not bring her father and brother home. And as you and I know, that might certainly be the case."

Zocando nodded. "You do understand this area is under constant unrest, and there's no way to know which rebels may have taken your father."

I wanted to roll my eyes at his patronizing tone, but I didn't. "Yes. If it would be possible to find me a guide, I believe I can track him."

"You want to go into the jungle alone? But you are a woman."

The PM shifted in his seat and leaned forward. I guessed it was to keep me from punching Dr. Zocando right in the smacker. "She's quite capable of taking care of herself. I've offered to put a team together, but she has refused." He turned a reproving eye on me.

Realizing the conversation was going to get me nowhere, I stood. "I can move faster on my own. Doctor, I do appreciate your help in finding the guide. The prime minister will continue to negotiate with the rebels, and I have given him permission to act on my behalf to do whatever is necessary in the way of funds and medical supplies. My father's hospital has already shipped the items listed on the ransom note."

I stepped away from them. "If you don't mind, I'd like to freshen up before dinner."

I've been waiting twenty-four hours for my guide to show up, so we can fly to the middle of nowhere and find my stinky brother and my dad. I'm not sure, but it feels like Dr. Zocando is stalling. I mean, he's a powerful dude. Why the hell is it taking so long to find one guide who can take me where I need to go?

Wednesday
Mambasa, Democratic Republic of the Congo
5 a.m.
Witches with powerful friends: I

I snuck out of Dr. Zocando's camp last night and I'm now in Mambasa. I left the PM a note to tell him what I was doing, and asked him to avoid the doctor until I was out of the city.

I'd grown tired of waiting. After dinner back at the camp, I called Sheik Azir on his cell phone. I knew he was in Dubai, because Sam had called to tell me he was back in Sweet. They'd been on another trip to the Philippines to take care of orphans.

When I told Sam what had happened, he wanted to come and search with me, but I told him no. I had to move fast, and by the time he could get here I wanted to have already found my dad and brother.

It was around seven my time when Sam called me.

A few minutes into our conversation, I blurted the words. "I'm calling Azir, and I wanted you to know."

He took a moment to answer. "I would do the same, Bron, he has friends everywhere. He'll be able to help. I feel like I should be there with you. It's rough country where you're going. We were there a couple of months ago, and even though it's now a free government, the rebels don't seem to have received the message." Sam coughed. It was croupy and kind of gross.

"Are you sick?"

"Nah. Just a head cold, nothing serious." He sniffled.

"I know you want to come here, but don't. Please. Stay in Sweet and get well. This will be over soon and then I can come home. I miss you so much."

He put up a good fight for another few minutes, but finally said he'd do what I asked.

My call to Azir went about the same way. He wanted to meet me in Mambasa. "Look, I just had this conversation with Sam. Please just let me do this my way. If you want to help, get me the hell out of here tonight and find me a guide."

He made a clicking sound with his tongue and I knew he was thinking. "I will do as you ask. Hold on for a moment." I heard him typing on a computer keyboard. "Call this number in an hour. He'll pick you up and have a plane available to get you into Mambasa. I'll arrange for a guide to meet you there." He gave me the number and then the lecture.

"I know you can handle any situation, Bronwyn, but this place is as dangerous as it is beautiful. You cannot underestimate anyone. Kazandon is someone I would trust with my life and I trust him with yours. Do not trust anyone else."

Ah, look at Azir with all the warm fuzzies. "I promise not to do anything too stupid. Hey, do you know if they have wild animals there?"

He laughed. "It's the African jungle. You will probably run into some wildlife."

See, I know it's kind of stupid, but I hadn't really planned for that.

Animal brains work on a different wavelength than humans' and I can't communicate with them the same way. I've traveled the world a couple of times, but I've never actually had to go through a jungle.

I know lots of people track gorillas in the mountains of Rwanda, which is nearby, but I'm not really what you would call an outdoor enthusiast. That probably seems strange, since I draw most of my power from nature. But creepy crawly things like snakes and critters just aren't my bag. I don't mind watching them on the Discovery Channel, but sleeping in a jungle with them, well that's different.

Azir's friend Kazandon met me about a mile outside of camp. Dr. Zocando's security force is impressive and it had taken several cloaking spells to get through the maze of soldiers with high-powered rifles.

I continued to cloak us until we reached the aircraft. Kazandon, who is close to six-four, would be enormously handsome if it weren't for the web of scars covering the right side of his face. I'd seen the signs of torture before and it was more than evident he'd been through hell.

When I offered to take control of the plane so he could rest, he smiled for the first time on the trip.

"Azir did not tell me you were a pilot." He had a Nigerian accent. He flipped a switch and handed me control of the jet.

"Thank you for doing this." We had just made it to about twenty-one thousand feet and were leveling off. The jet was small, but much nicer than I'd expected. Honestly, I wouldn't have cared if we'd been in a biplane. I just needed to get to my brother and dad.

"I am happy to assist," Kaz (as he asked me to call him) said. "When Azir needs Kaz, I am always there."

I assumed Azir must have saved the man's life or his family. Saving someone's life, well, that's something most folks don't forget. His respect for the sheik was evident.

We flew in silence for two hours. I worked with my mind to search for my brother and father, hoping that as we drew closer I could sense them.

We were over mountains, then suddenly, just as the sun rose, we made our way over a canopy of green trees so tightly woven it looked like you might bounce from one treetop to the other. That's when I heard it, soft as a whisper.

Bronwyn, Bronwyn, Bronwyn. Brett used the communication spell to reach out to me.

I closed my eyes and followed the silver tendril of the spell. It seemed to point east and then slightly north. We were close.

"I sense my brother is near." I kept my eyes closed and tried to focus. "Is there somewhere we can land, in about a fifty-mile radius?

I heard Kaz pull out some maps. "There's an air strip outside Mambasa we are near. I will land there."

That had been our original destination, but I hadn't realized we were so close. The silver thread suddenly vanished like chalk on the underside of an eraser.

Magic. Someone knew Brett had contacted me. I didn't know if he could hear me, but I whispered, "I'll find you." And when I did, I'd have some fun with those kidnappers.

Friday
Midnight
About five miles from Mambasa
Possibly stupid witches: 1

Azir didn't lie. This place is amazing and scary as hell at the same time. I can't believe my brother chooses to work here. He's crazier than I ever imagined.

Once we landed, Kaz introduced me to Ezeoha, a man about my

height, making him "vertically challenged." He's also paper-thin. I keep trying to get him to eat protein bars.

From what Azir said, I thought Kaz would leave me with Ezeoha, but he decided to come with us.

"There is danger where you are going, and Azir has asked that I protect you." Kaz was regal and his voice powerful.

"I appreciate that, but I'm good at protecting myself. I know you must have other work to do." In the short time we'd spent together I'd grown to like him. The words had been few between us, but it was a feeling more than anything. I understood why Azir trusted him.

"You are precious cargo to Azir, and I will assist with what is necessary."

Cargo? I snorted. "Well, okay." I turned to Ezeoha. "What supplies will we need?" I was wearing jeans and a T-shirt, and I had a feeling I might need something a little more lightweight, and some food.

Ezeoha pointed to what looked like a general store. We were actually outside of Mambasa in a small village. The store was old and dusty looking. "We need three days of food and water." His English was accented with French. "You need zee boots."

I laughed. Ezeoha had a point. I didn't think my flip-flops would cut it in the jungle. I'd been in such a hurry when running away from Dr. Zocando's camp that I'd left my Pumas behind. But even those wouldn't keep a snake's fangs from penetrating.

Kaz had scared the hell out of me the last few minutes of our flight with stories about the dangers of creatures in the jungle. If you didn't get your throat slit by a nasty rebel or eaten by a tiger, there was a good chance the snakes would make a meal of you. I didn't plan to be anyone's meal.

A quick trip to the general store and we had full packs, a change of clothes, food, water, several cans of bug spray, (people who live here don't believe in it, but I do—bugs love to chew on me) and I sported some new khakis. Before heading into the jungle, the two men pulled out a map and lay it across Ezeoha's Jeep.

"We drive to here." Ezeoha pointed to a speck on the map. "Den we walk."

Kaz shook his head. "She believes them to be somewhere here." He pointed to a spot dead-center in the jungle.

Ezeoha frowned. "It is three days' walk and very dangerous. The river or the roads would be easier, but the rebels . . ." He pulled his finger across his neck in the universal sign for slitting throats.

Lovely. He and Kaz should be the spokespeople for avoiding the jungle. I'm sure I could have taken care of whatever rebels we encountered, but I didn't want to give whoever was holding my family a heads-up. If sneaking through the jungle gave us the element of surprise, that's what we would do.

"Okay. Well, I choose trekking through the jungle. I like my neck just the way it is. I don't need a bloody necklace."

So here we go into the wild green jungle.

Fifteen

The jungle
Tree-hugging witches: 1
Dead guys: 3 (But I didn't kill them all.)
Spells: 2

I'm not sure I'd recommend the African jungle as a vacation hotspot. That is, unless someone is into real adventure. The creature noise is migraine-inducing and the insects (thank god for repellant) are annoyingly persistent. I'm really glad I'm current on all my shots. Oh, and the lovely sounds of rapid gunfire have been our constant companion the last twenty-four hours.

I know it isn't fair, but right now I'm so angry with Brett for putting us all into this mess. If he didn't have to be the great do-gooder I'd be able to look for Garnout, chase down Jason, or, at the very least, be at home in Sweet eating at Lulu's.

Stupid brother.

Today has been one giant crap pile.

The first bit of fun began when we were still in the Land Rover. About three hours into the interior of the jungle, we came to a roadblock.

A tree had fallen, or at least that's what it looked like. As we slowed, Ezeoha pulled out a rifle from under the seat and handed it to Kaz. Then he pulled out another and gave it to me. I didn't really need a gun, but I held on to it.

"When I stop the vehicle, you must run for the trees to the right," Ezeoha whispered. We slipped on our packs as he pulled to the side of the road.

He reached down again and this time brought up what looked like and old-timey machine gun. Something you might see in a John Wayne war movie or something. When he stopped, we jumped out.

I heard yelling but didn't look back until we hit the trees. Kaz held a finger to his lips. Then he motioned upward.

I raised my eyebrows. He wanted me to climb the tree. *Crap.* The last time I'd climbed a tree I'd been seven. I fell, broke my arm, and Brett wouldn't let me tell Mom because he didn't want to get in trouble. His plan worked until dinner. I'd tried to eat with my left hand with no success, and that's when Mom had noticed. I'd been rushed to the emergency room, and he'd been grounded. He never forgave me and to this day calls me a "wuss."

I couldn't understand what the men looking for us were saying, but they weren't happy about finding the vehicle abandoned. Just for fun they shot off their guns into the greenery. The popping sound made me jump, and that's when I saw something.

At the end of my branch, the leaves moved in an odd fashion and I thought it might be the wind. Then I realized: there was no wind. I was flat on my stomach staring ahead when something black and huge slithered toward me.

The head of the snake was bigger than my hand, and I almost peed myself right then and there. My breath caught. It was two feet away and would have to creep over me to move along.

The Earth Goddess doesn't like it when you blow up her creatures for no reason. This was the snake's domain and I was in the way. Using magic against it wasn't an option. The Earth Goddess is not a chick you want to anger.

Slithering closer, the snake was only a few inches away. My body seemed to have a mind of its own and flung itself out of the tree. I was falling when someone caught my arm. Pain seared into my shoulder. I opened my eyes to see Kaz's dark eyes staring into mine. My arm was sweating, partly from the heat, but more from the confrontation with the snake. I slid out of Kaz's grasp and hit the ground feet first.

The rebels, who wore dark blue uniforms, heard the movement and showered the area with bullets. I threw up a protection shield on both of us. Once I caught my breath, I stood, and I could see them heading my way.

I threw the first fireball at the man in the center. He screamed as his uniform caught fire and the other two turned to see what the commotion was about. They tried to pound the fire out with their hands and then threw the man to the ground and stomped on him. The fire spread quickly, and there was nothing left but a pile of ash in a matter of seconds.

That's when I heard two pops, and I saw the other two men fall forward.

Ezeoha stood up out of the bushes and walked over to the rebels. He kicked one over and then the other, grabbing their guns.

Kaz jumped down out of the tree and shook his head. His brown eyes were huge with surprise. "Azir told me you were a witch. I didn't know you had such great power."

I shrugged. "Sorry. I hadn't really meant to kill him. I have a habit of blowing people up first and asking questions later."

Kaz didn't get the joke. "No. Do not be sorry. It is good they are dead." Kaz moved forward and Ezeoha handed him something. It was a necklace with something on the chain.

Kaz held it up to show me. "These men are animals. They prey on women and children, and they do not deserve your worry. These men believe killing the young gives them power."

The horror and disgust of it rushed over me, and the fury began to build. If I ran across more of these bastards I'd wipe them all off the face of the planet.

"What do we do now?" I took a sip of my bottled water to help settle the rising bile.

"We must move away from the road and into the jungle." Ezeoha grabbed some more water out of the Land Rover and put it in his pack. "The rebels will come looking for these men. We must move quickly."

If I hadn't been in such a hurry to find my dad and brother, I would have stayed and given the rebels a *real* welcome party. But if these were the kind of people who had kidnapped my family, I wanted to find them fast.

We're taking a few moments to rest near a large tree. Now I hear roaring. Kaz and Ezeoha both told me there was nothing to worry about; it was probably just a leopard. Just *a leopard? Gah! Are they insane?*

Judging from the way they both looked at each other when the animal roared again, I wouldn't be surprised if they'd realized they were wrong, too.

Friday
10 p.m.
Dead guys: 11

We've been walking forever, and everything still looks the same. Twisted green trees, mud, snakes, spiders, and really weird monkeys that shriek so loud I almost blew up Kaz, who was standing in front of me the first time I heard them. They made me jump out of my skin. The heat is worse, and there were times when I wasn't sure I could take one more step. I never say a word, but I think Kaz knows I've sort of reached my physical limit.

He suggested we stop for a couple of hours to rest near a small river, more like a creek. About five minutes after we sat down, I must have fallen asleep.

In my dreams I heard Sam and Azir talking. They were coming here, even though I had asked them both to stay home. When I tried to reach them telepathically, Sam put up his shields, and he must have done the same for Azir. He knew I would try to stop them. The last thing I needed was those two getting lost or killed. I was furious in my dream but had no one to scream at.

I woke up with someone's hand over my mouth and I realized I was being dragged away from the river. My first instinct was to blow up whoever had their hands on me, but when I opened my eyes, I saw it was Kaz. He motioned with his head that someone was coming. He let go and I scooted back into the bushes on my own. The green leaves were damp with the last rain, and the branches scratched through my shirt.

Ezeoha was to our right.

I don't know why it took my brain so long to kick into gear, but I finally opened up and tried to sense how many people were on the way. I could see two boats loaded down with soldiers and small children.

The boats moved past us and I heard the children crying. I sent my mind into that of a small boy I could see on one of the boats. The rebels had taken all the children from a village. The tiny boy was frightened and repeated a constant prayer for his mother. I saw her lying on the floor, her throat slit.

Bastards. God only knew what they would do to those poor babies. I couldn't kill the rebels on the boats. The children might drown. I jumped up and grabbed my pack. Following the path of the riverbank, I ran after the boat. I could hear footsteps behind me, so I assumed Kaz and Ezeoha were close.

I didn't really have much of a plan past killing every one of the rebels and saving the children. At about the time my lungs were giving out from running in the heat (maybe I've mentioned I'm not the most fit of witches when it comes to running—yoga is more my speed), the men turned the boats toward the shore.

They tossed the children from the boat and then ushered them forward into the jungle.

Kaz stood behind me and we watched from the safety of the bushes.

"I'm going to kill them," I whispered.

Kaz touched my shoulder. "I will help. Ezeoha has moved to the other side to trap them. We must not let any get away, or we will have a war on our hands."

"Don't worry, Kaz. I don't plan on there being many survivors. I'm going to try to get their attention. You move the children away if at all possible, and don't let them see what I'm about to do."

"I will do as you ask." Before I could thank him, he was gone.

Moving toward the sound of the soldiers, I threw protection spells at the children, Kaz, and Ezeoha. Pulling my shirt out from the waistband of my khakis, I tied it into a knot under my breasts, and unbuttoned all of the buttons. I needed a quick distraction, and boobs are some of the best things a woman can use.

I put two confusion potions in my pockets. I said a protection spell for myself, and then stepped into the clearing.

"Hello?" I waved a hand as if I were greeting a neighbor. "I'm a little lost and I wondered if you could help me?"

All of the men turned and stared open-mouthed at me. I gathered that coming across a half-naked white woman in the middle of the jungle wasn't an everyday occurrence.

Two of the men moved toward me. I tossed the confusion potions at them. They turned and pointed the guns at their comrades.

"Now!" I yelled as I threw two fireballs.

Ezeoha rushed forward, firing at the men as he did. He took out the two men with the children, and then began speaking to the children very fast in French. He told them to run into the jungle with him.

Kaz fired his rifle and took out two more of the soldiers. The others, believing they were surrounded, didn't bother to fire back. They ran.

I threw more fireballs as fast as I could, pulling energy from the nature around me so I wouldn't deplete my own power. Kaz and Ezeoha took care of the rest.

The soldiers had to die. I knew from the quick trips I'd taken into their brains the atrocities they had committed. Kind and wonderful people populate most of Africa, but these guys were not among them.

Shoving my hands out, I used my powers to push one of the men against a tree. Sending my mind through his, I saw my brother blindfolded, his hands tied behind his back.

I stepped over some of the dead bodies to reach him. "Where is my family?" I demanded. The anger burned within me. "I know you have them. Where are they?"

The man shook his head, and I realized he didn't understand English. I had a feeling that if he did, he would have answered me. A wet spot spread in the front of his pants. He was afraid of me.

Good.

I sent my mind into his. I rewound it a few days and saw how he and the other men had snuck into the medical tents and had taken my father and brother. They had moved them to a cave not far from here, maybe another two-and-a-half days' walk. But they had used transports, which got them there in a matter of hours.

I opened my eyes and Kaz stood with a gun pointed at the soldier's head. "Tie him up. He knows where my father and brother are."

Kaz did as I asked. Ezeoha motioned to me from the edge of the clearing.

"What do we do with zee children?" There were about six of them, huddled together. Buttoning my shirt, I smiled as I walked toward them.

Sending a healing-of-the-spirit spell, I knelt before them. "You are safe."

Ezeoha stood beside me and repeated the words in French.

"I won't let anyone else hurt you. This nice man," I said as I pointed to Ezeoha, "is going to take you to a place where you will be safe."

One little girl who couldn't have been more than three scooted toward me, and then threw her arms around my neck.

The other children followed, and soon I was flat on my butt with all six of them wrapped around me. I hugged them back, and it suddenly dawned on me why my brother couldn't leave this place. Things like this happened to the children here every day. It was wrong, and he had to stop it.

By the time we made it back into the clearing, Kaz had moved all the bodies out of sight and had left the lone soldier tied to a tree.

We loaded the children into one of the boats. "I do not like to leave you," Ezeoha said as he ushered the last of the children in. His heavy French accent had grown on me. He'd been very brave—well, he and Kaz—and there was no way I could ever possibly thank him enough.

"Thank you for everything, Ezeoha, but we can make it from here. You are a good man."

"You are a fearsome but kind witch. I wish you well on your journey." He handed Kaz the maps. "In case the prisoner tries to take you in the wrong direction, I have marked the trail we were to follow."

Kaz took the maps. "Be safe, my friend."

"And you," Ezeoha said as he held up a hand to wave good-bye.

We traveled for a couple more hours, stopping when it grew dark.

Kaz wants me to sleep in a tree tonight, but after the run-in with that Black Mamba, I'd rather sleep by the fire. Kaz had promised that he checked the tree and shook every branch, but I'm not buying it.

Oh my god.

"What the hell is *that*?" I pointed to what looked like a large black plate moving across the ground about fifteen feet from us.

"Spider." Kaz shrugged.

Crap. That tree doesn't look so bad after all.

Sixteen

Pungent witches: 1
Pissed-off leopards: 1

I don't like it when leopards eat people. It's gross.

Last night we'd tied our prisoner to the tree. Kaz did it so the guy could rest, but not get away. It seemed, at the time, more humane than the guy actually deserved—I mean, considering on what he planned to do to those poor children.

Anyhoo, I fell asleep in the tree. Don't ask me how. I didn't think I'd ever be able to do it. The next thing I know, I hear this low growl. The prisoner below screams, and it sounds like something is ripping him to bits. Low, guttural moans, and then silence.

Honestly, the last thing I wanted to do was climb down to see what had happened. It was pitch black. Kaz had doused the fire before climbing up on his own branch earlier in the evening.

I sent Kaz a mental message. *"What do we do?"*

"Don't move or speak." Kaz's words were strong, even though he didn't say them out loud.

We waited in silence for what seemed like hours. As the sun rose, the jungle lightened and I had my first peek at the carnage below.

A hand, still tied to the rope, was all that was left. It held a small pistol. The sight made my stomach roll, and I took a deep breath.

"Where did he get a gun?"

Shaking his head, Kaz motioned toward the other side of the tree. "I do not know. I feel the leopard favors us, but we shouldn't tempt fate. We must move quickly, down the other side of the tree. You do not want the blood of the prey on you." Kaz was already moving behind me. I carefully followed him across the branches of the huge tree until we reached the other side.

The lowest branch was still about ten feet off the ground, so he jumped off and then reached up to help me down.

As my feet touched the ground, we heard a roar. It sounded far away, but the jungle can be deceptive.

"The camp where your brother works is nearby, a few hours' walk." Kaz loaded his pack onto his back, and I did the same. "We'll stop there and see if we can get any more information as to where your father and brother are."

I nodded. With the lone remaining soldier dead, we'd lost our guide. I knew the camp was probably crude, but I prayed there might at least be a place I could take a quick bath. There are at least twelve layers of insect repellant on my skin, and I've surpassed my personal best with the body odor.

We've stopped to have a quick bite to eat and to rest. Kaz believes we are only about two hours away. *Please, let him be right.* It feels like someone is watching us, but every time I send my mind out, I don't see a thing.

The jungle is getting to me. I'm going mad, I tell you, mad!

Geez. I really do need a shower and a Diet Coke.

Camp Maharas
9 p.m.
Zonked witches: 1

Compared to where I've spent the last few days, Camp Maharas is the Ritz. It's basically a medical facility my brother set up to help the Rwandan refugees. It consists of five large tents, with a well for water and more children than I've ever seen in my life.

When we first walked into the camp it was silent, and I wondered if it had been abandoned. I called out, "Hello? Is anyone here? I'm Bronwyn, Brett's sister."

"Yes?" A beautiful African woman poked her head out of a tent with the huge red cross on it. "You are Doctor Brett's sister?"

I nodded and tried to smile. I say "tried," because at that moment exhaustion had overtaken me—it was all I could do to stand. I said a quick energy spell, and it helped some.

Wearing a long white coat over denim shorts and an olive tank, she rushed out to meet me. "I'm Doctor Sarah Umbarto. We are so happy you are here." She took my hands. "Your brother speaks highly of you." Her bright eyes were so green they looked like glass marbles.

I seriously doubted my brother ever said a kind word, but I appreciated her attempt at being friendly. "Thank you." I motioned beside me. "This is Kaz. He's been helping me get through the jungle the last few days."

She nodded toward him and he gave a slight bow in her direction. I could hear whispering from the tents.

"Children, it's safe."

There was a rush of giggles and suddenly we were surrounded by chattering children. They didn't seem to mind the fact that I smelled of bug repellant and sweat. They patted and pawed me until Dr. Umbarto shooed them away.

"You must be stern with them or they'll pester you for as long as you let them." She smiled and shook her head as she spoke. "Off to school, now." She pointed to one of the larger tents.

"Where do they all come from?" I followed her into the medical tent.

"Many are refugees, others are orphans who have lost their parents to AIDS." She waved to a nurse and another doctor. "This"— she pointed to the nurse—"is Tiana. She assists us with everything from surgery to physicals and probably knows more than all of us put together."

Another woman walked up beside Tiana. "This is Doctor Carmen González, who has been with us for the past eight months."

Carmen held out her hand. "I'm so sorry about Brett. I've worked with him on and off for many years, and we've never had anything like this happen. And your father, well, it's too much." She had beautiful olive skin, light brown eyes, and a figure that runway models would die for.

Something about her name seemed familiar. I wondered if she might be the same Carmen he dated in med school.

I shook her hand. "Thank you. Are you the same Carmen from college?"

Her smile turned shy and she looked away. "Yes." She sighed. "Have you heard any more news?" Her hopeful plea made me cringe.

"No. But I've been in the jungle the last few days, so if any came, I wouldn't know it."

Carmen walked over to a computer with a satellite hookup. "If you want to check here you can. We can also make calls through an Internet link." She held up a headset.

"Thanks." It suddenly dawned on me that we'd lost Kaz somewhere along the way.

I called out, "Kaz?" No answer. "Did you see where he went?"

Dr. Umbarto shrugged.

I stepped back outside the tent. "Kaz?"

"I'm here, Bronwyn." He stood at the edge of the camp. "They have no guards, guns, or protection." The worried look on his face told me loads.

"You know you don't need guns when I'm around." I smiled to ease his worry. "I'll put a protection spell up for the entire camp, and I'll make charms in a bit so we'll know when an enemy approaches."

Kaz put his rifle back into the shoulder holster. "There should be men here to protect the children."

"I know. That's probably why my brother has refused to leave all this time. He's been here for two years straight and hasn't so much as taken a weekend away. Well, until now. And I have a feeling wherever he is, it isn't much of a vacation."

My brother felt so drawn to this place and now I understood why. These people needed him. That's why he'd given up his cushy practice at home and stayed. Never in a million years would I admit it, but we have that in common—when our friends need us, we're there.

Brett had come here two years ago as part of the Doctors Across

Borders program and never went home. His two-week trip had turned into two years.

I have to find him. These children need him.

11 p.m.
I'm going to kill Sam and Azir. I mean it. The idiots followed me here after I begged them not to, and now I can't sense them.

Sam had sent an e-mail.

> *Bron,*
> *Azir and I are headed your way.*
> *Taking the river so we can catch up with you.*
> *Love,*
> *Sam*

Idiots. I just sent my mind out to check on them, but I can't find anything. It's as if they've disappeared, which is never a good thing. Usually even if Sam blocks me I at least know he's around, but not this time. When I find him I'm going to cause him extreme physical harm for putting me through this. Then I'll attack him like a horny tiger, but only after I hurt him bad.

Cole had also e-mailed—no word on Garnout, which really pisses me off. I can't believe the huge spook brigade can't find one wizard. It's nuts.

They did find some interesting information about Jason. His family has disowned him, which is a good thing in my book. Turns out he killed one of his cousins after he escaped the Institute, and that didn't sit well with his folks. The family has promised to assist the spook investigators in whatever way possible.

The prime minister is furious with me. I received a snippy e-mail from Miles about how unprofessional I've been, and that I've abused Dr. Zocando's kindness.

Bite me. As far as I can see, Zocando still hasn't done anything to find my dad or brother. The prime minister said they were heading this way in the next few days. Geez, my family could be dead by then.

Throughout this whole escapade I've been second-guessing myself and wondering if I've made the right decision. Now I know. I can't sleep, even though I'm exhausted. I'm so worried, and we're supposed to leave at first light tomorrow.

I guess I'll at least make good use of the time and put together some protection charms for the camp.

11 a.m.
The jungle
Eerified witches: 1

The whole time we've been in the jungle it's been noisy, until today. I've heard the occasional bird, but most of the time it's gunfire that interrupts the silence. It's eerie because there's no way of knowing where it comes from or how far away it is.

We left the camp around seven this morning, a little later than expected. Kaz had a tough time waking me up, probably because I'd only fallen asleep three hours before.

"Here—you should eat these to keep up your strength." Carmen handed me a dozen protein bars. She'd been waiting outside my sleeping tent. I knew the bars had to have come from her personal stash, and I waved them away.

"No, I know how precious these things are out here. We have food."

"Please, take them," she begged. "It's the one thing I can do to feel like I'm helping to find Brett." Her voice caught. She looked at me and I noticed her eyes were shiny.

I don't know what made me do it, but I took the bars and hugged her. "I'm going to find him." I patted her back, wondering if my brother had any idea how much she was in love with him.

"I can't imagine why you care so much about him. He's such a pig-headed jerk." I pulled away from the hug.

She wiped her eyes with her hand. "I know," Carmen sniffled, "but I love him anyway." She smiled. "Of course he probably doesn't have a clue. He's so wrapped up in this place he barely notices I'm around."

I had a hard time believing that. Carmen was beautiful, with her shiny black hair and perfect figure, and I had a feeling she had no idea how gorgeous she was. My brother was stubborn, but he wasn't stupid.

"I'll have him back here soon. No worries."

It took fifteen minutes to say our good-byes to the rest of the staff and the children. We'd been walking for the last three-and-a-half hours through the jungle. The farther we moved away from the camp, the quieter it became. Then about an hour ago we began to hear the gunfire. The jungle is tense with the sound of it.

From what Kaz whispered earlier, it may be good news—we might be close to where they are holding my family. I hope so.

We stopped a few minutes ago to rest and eat a light lunch.

I'm so sick of all this crap that if those rebels find us now they are dead meat. There's nothing I'd like more right now than to blow someone up.

Well, a hot bubble bath would be nice, too. Oh, and Lulu's fried chicken and chocolate pie. Hell, right now I'd settle for a turkey sandwich, potato chips, and a big glass of iced tea. My throat aches with the thought of it.

Damn. Kaz is doing that twitchy thing with his head, which means it's time to move on. I shouldn't complain. Every step we take is bringing me closer to my family . . . and to the rebels who kidnapped them.

I'm soaking up all the nature I can, and I've been building my power for days. When the time comes, I'll be at full capacity and very, very dangerous to any foe.

✩✩✩ Seventeen

The Congo
8 p.m.
Witches who need tranquilizer darts: 1 (If they don't work on the big cat,
maybe I can use them on myself.)
Scary leopards: 1

"When faced with a leopard, do not run," Kaz told me when we stopped because of the darkness. Once the sun dips it's like walking into a black hole. Of course, Kaz shares his leopard advice just as the darkness falls, and it totally creeps me out.

No chance for a fire. Kaz worried the rebels might see the smoke.

He left me in a small clearing to search for a "sleeping tree." I was propped with my back against a tree trunk, my lantern next to me, eating one of the protein bars.

Something sent alarming goose bumps down my arms and back.

If they could speak, the bumps would say, "Danger, Bron, danger!" The problem was, at first I couldn't tell what was going on.

Then I sensed it.

I was being watched again. I sent my mind out and soon discovered whatever was watching me wasn't human. I stood up and stared out into the darkness. Sliding my pack up my back, I slipped it over my shoulders.

"Do not run," Kaz whispered behind me.

At the edge of the clearing I saw her—a leopard. It was large, lithe, and golden, with a khaki spot in the middle of bigger black ones. Her eyes glinted in the shadow where she sat. She was beautiful, in a scary kind of way. I've always loved big cats. Well, until that moment.

"Um, is she going to eat us?" I kept my eyes on her. I didn't really know if she *was* a girl, but right then I wished I'd paid more attention to the Discovery Channel.

The leopard sat down on her hindquarters. She turned her head to the right, and left. Then she did the weirdest thing: she stood again and sat down, but this time with her back to us.

"Shouldn't we run now?" I whispered.

Kaz didn't move. "Get in the tree."

"But—she's giving us a head start."

He shoved me toward a massive trunk. "No. If she wanted us, we would already be dead. She's guarding us. This is her way of offering us her protection. This tree will do." He pointed upward.

"Kaz, I can't sleep with a leopard staring at me all night."

He sighed. "She's not staring, she's guarding. If we run she will only follow. Please, I am tired. Get in the tree."

"Kaz, how do you know she's guarding us? Maybe she's staking us out for a meal later."

"For the last twenty-four hours she's been following us through the jungle. When we went into the camp she stationed herself outside of it. She didn't try to eat the children or anyone else. I believe she is a magical creature sent to help us on our journey."

He said the words so earnestly, I couldn't argue. *A magic leopard?* Hell, I'd come across stranger things.

I had serious doubts I would get any sleep, but I crawled up onto the highest branch I could reach. Leopards like to hang out in trees, too, but for some reason being high up made me feel better. I stared out into the darkness for a long time.

"What the hell is that?" A distorted male voice cut through the fog. I tried to open my eyes. They wouldn't budge. Something cold and wet covered my body.

I'm dreaming. My last thought had been to send myself out to search for the missing men using astral projection, while I tried to sleep in the stupid tree—the safest place to doze in the jungle, Kaz, my guide, had told me. This after a run-in with a leopard that made me feel like a T-bone on a platter. I can't believe I actually fell asleep with those eerie cat eyes staring at me all night.

"Jesus! It's Bronwyn." That voice I knew. Sam was in my dream. No surprises there. I'd been tramping through this godforsaken African jungle for days trying to find my hunka burnin' love.

"Is she alive?" That was Azir, my favorite sheik. I could almost smell his sandalwood scent in the air. It all seemed so real. "Where did *she* come from?"

Two fingers brushed my neck and a hand pushed the hair from my forehead. "Her pulse is weak, but her breathing is steady." Sam again. "Bronwyn, can you hear me?"

Wow. This might be a really good dream. Both Sam and the sheik.

It was weird, though; I couldn't take control of my dream like I usually did. I wanted to talk with them, to tell them I was on my way, but my mouth wouldn't work.

"Bronwyn. It's Dad. I need you to try to open your eyes." My dad had his doctor's voice on. Stern but kind. "Come on, honey, you can do it." Um, yuck. What was my *dad* doing in the middle of my sexy dream?

I took a deep breath and the effort caused me to cough.

"There's fluid in her lungs." That came from my dork-faced brother. I hadn't seen in him in two years, and he sounded older, worried, and as annoying as ever. "Turn her over on her side."

Bite a big one, Brett. Dad was a top-notch surgeon before Brett had been a zygote. Leave it to my brother to get all bossy. I sure as hell didn't understand why he would be in my dream.

They turned me over on my side, and that was when I realized it wasn't a dream. Their hands poked and prodded. I felt it all. I was with them, but I had no idea how I'd done it. Had I accidentally astrally projected my body? No, I couldn't have. I didn't have that power yet. My brain felt like it had been sucked through some kind of vacuum and I couldn't get my thoughts to gel.

Then I felt an evil presence, strong and malevolent. The stench of sulfur filled my sense. *Crap.* I had to wake up. I had to protect them. I reached out and connected with Sam's strong arm. I'd know those hard biceps anywhere.

"Talk to me, Bron." He squeezed my hand. "She's fading, how the hell is she doing that? Baby, say something." I heard the worry in his voice. He loved me so much.

Straining to speak caused something weird to happen in my head. As I slid back into the darkness, I whispered, "Evil's coming."

* * *

The next thing I knew, Kaz was shaking my shoulder. It had rained, and my body trembled with the drop in temperature.

"We must move. The rebels come," he whispered.

It took me a minute to realize where I was and that I must have dreamed about finding Sam and my family. I was so angry with Sam for being captured, too. He and Azir had put their lives in danger for no reason. That meant I had to save four of the most important men in my life. I had no idea how they'd gotten ahead of me, unless they'd been traveling the river or roads. That's the only way they could move faster.

I was furious with all four men.

The leopard growled, low and guttural.

I raised an eyebrow at him.

"She has been guarding us through the night." Kaz helped me down out of the tree. "She does not wish us harm."

As my feet hit the ground, I saw the gorgeous creature with her black spots at the edge of the clearing. She moved her head as if to say, "Hurry up."

I didn't need to be told twice. I lifted my pack onto my shoulders and followed Kaz into the cover of the jungle. I heard gunfire to the east of us and wondered how close the rebels were. At least now I had a point of reference for where they were. Earlier, it sounded like they were all around us.

When I turned to look back, I noticed the leopard followed us.

"Um, we seem to have picked up a traveling companion."

"Yes, I heard her." Kaz kept moving.

It was still raining and I constantly had to push curling wisps of hair off my face and out of my eyes. My boots sloshed in the mud. I figured, at least my calves were getting a good workout.

"Why doesn't she try to eat us? Is she saving us for later?"

Kaz put a finger to his lips to shush me. I was about to protest when I heard them: men's voices, one barking orders.

Pushing me back behind a tree, Kaz whispered in my ear, "Diamond mine. We can't let them see us. The men who work here do not appreciate visitors."

I must admit, at the word *diamonds* I'm quite certain my eyes grew a tad wider. I'm kind of fond of all things sparkly, but Kaz was right. This wasn't the time to go ring shopping. I'd read stories about what the miners did to trespassers. Beheadings were the norm.

My hair is a big, wild mess, but I kind of like my head, so I followed him and did my best to be stealthy. Men yelled and I could hear a truck grinding gears. I wondered if maybe they were stuck in mud. The rain continued and everything and everyone was drenched.

We'd just made it past the large opening of the tunnel when there was a tug at my heart. It's hard to describe. It was like something was pulling me back into the open mouth of the mountain. I stopped and closed my eyes.

I could feel the tiny tendrils of a protection spell—one of my spells, the one I'd sent to my brother.

We were still in the trees and Kaz had moved several feet in front of me. I opened my eyes and stared into the tunnel, sending a message with my mind to Sam, my brother, and my dad. "I'm here."

I closed and opened my eyes again and saw the magic protecting the cave. It was dark and knotted. Black magic.

That happens to be something I know a little bit about, so I began unraveling the knots, one by one. The black ropes dissipated into the air. Every time I conquered one, I could feel Sam a little closer.

Kaz had come back and he touched my shoulder.

I pointed to the cave. "They're in there."

He nodded and readied his gun. Our friendly leopard suddenly looked on guard, and Kaz yanked me back behind one of the trees.

One of the rebels walked past, his machine gun slung across his shoulders. If he stepped any closer he would have heard us breathe, but he was preoccupied with taking a pee.

This is the part in the movies where the good guys quietly take out the bad guys by knocking them on the head, or by using their bare hands to pop necks. But Kaz had a different script.

He let the guy do his business and then go.

"Why didn't you do something?" I whispered.

"He's a sentry. If he doesn't answer back they'll be suspicious. We can't risk them knowing we are here until we have a plan."

I rolled my eyes. "I have a plan. I'm going in there and saving my family."

"Bronwyn, it is surrounded by rebels. And the miners in the cave are just as bad. They will kill you."

I sighed. "Not if they can't see me. I've been pulling power from this jungle of yours for days. I'll cloak myself so no one can see me, then I can shield them until we make it out of the cave.

"All I need you to do is have one of those trucks ready so we can get the hell out of here." It sounded like a great plan to me, especially since I'd come up with it on the fly.

He shook his head. "I will do what you ask, but how will you find them? They could be anywhere in the mine, and the mountain is huge."

I shrugged. "I have my ways. I can already sense them. Once I finish releasing the magic surrounding the tunnel, I'll be able to hone in with my mind and find them."

"At least wait until it grows dark." Kaz shoved his pack up into a tree, and took mine from my shoulders and did the same. "The miners leave at dusk and then only a few guards will be left."

That made sense, and so I agreed. Besides, it would take me a while to undo the rest of the black magic. We climbed up into the tree and waited.

7 p.m.
Charms: 6

I'm getting ready to make my way inside. Kaz was right about all of the miners. They left in three big trucks about a half hour ago. He expects there will be a shift change for the guards in a few minutes, and that will be my best bet to slip inside undetected.

Once I released all of the magic protecting the mountain, I was able to get a message to Sam.

"I'm here. Are you okay?" I sent my mind in search of Sam, Azir, and my family and found them all inside a small room with a large wooden door. It had been carved into the mountain and there was nothing in there except rock.

"Bron? Where are you?" Sam looked up as if he could see me in the ceiling. I noticed his cheek was puffy and he had a black eye.

"I'm outside the cave, baby. What did they do to you?"

He waved a hand. "Don't worry about it. Are you okay? We were worried last night and couldn't figure out where you had gone."

Last night?

Oh my god. I really *had* been in the cave, with no idea of how I'd done it. I thought it had been a dream. Somehow I'd been able to astrally project my body. I wished I could do it again.

Sam was still talking. "Be careful, this place is crawling with rebels. Tell me you have backup."

I looked over at Kaz, who was watching the mouth of the cave intently.

"Absolutely," I lied. Well, technically, I did have Kaz. He was more backup than I usually had in tough spots like this. "Listen, I'm coming that way in a few minutes, so tell everyone to keep their shields down so I can find you."

Azir, my dad, and my brother all stared at Sam as if he'd lost his mind. They circled him.

"Um, you might want to inform the gang that you're talking to me."

He looked away and smiled. The effort hurt his swollen mouth and he touched it with his hands. I didn't know who had done that to him, but whoever did would pay. Since Sam wasn't blocking me I took a quick tour of his brain and discovered he and Azir had been captured on the river, almost at the same place where we had saved the children. The rebels had probably been looking for their comrades. The two guides had been murdered, and Azir and Sam had fought bravely. Well, stupidly, really. They could have been killed.

Then Azir and Sam had been blindfolded and brought to the cave, probably while we were making our way from the camp. My guess is those were the guns I'd heard that night in the jungle.

"It's Bron. She's outside. She wants us to keep our shields open so she can find us." He looked at my father. "She says she has backup."

My dad stared up at the ceiling with one eyebrow raised. "She damn well better have help. If she gets herself killed trying to get in here, her mother will never forgive me."

I could have sent myself into my dad's mind to reassure him, but I have a really hard time lying to him.

"Tell him I really do have help this time." Well, I did have Kaz, and I think the leopard is on my side. She hasn't eaten me yet and I'm taking that as a good sign.

Sam turned his face back to the ceiling. "You know I love you." He reached out as if to touch my cheek.

I almost blubbered, but I kept it together.

"I love you, too. I'll see you in a few." I smiled, but I knew my eyes were shiny. I pulled away before he heard me sniffle.

The sun had gone down and the jungle was black once again.

"Kaz, I'm putting a protection charm on you and on our leopard friend." I pulled a charm out of my backpack that I'd made back at my brother's camp. "This burns inside your pocket if someone tries to harm you, and puts up a shield to protect you. It doesn't last long, so move fast once it begins."

He took the charm from me and put it in his pocket.

I moved toward the leopard, seriously doubting my sanity as I did so. She had been protecting us, I was certain of it now. The night she'd eaten the soldier, I have a feeling she was protecting us from his gun. Kaz was right about her being a magical creature.

There was no telling how wild things were about to get, and I didn't want the leopard hurt. Whispering, I spoke to her. "I'd like to put this around your neck for protection." I took a few steps and stopped. The leopard watched me curiously and then moved majestically, muscles flexing, until she was a foot in front of me, and I had to remember to breathe. I said a quick prayer that she didn't swallow me whole and then bent down to wrap the leather necklace with the amber amulet around her neck.

I've been using amber this trip because it amplifies whatever spell or charm it's given.

When I finished, she moved away to the edge of a clearing.

As I walked back past Kaz, he grabbed my hand.

"Be safe, my friend." He squeezed my fingers tight and let go.

"You, too." I squeezed back, then, "Kaz, you are an amazing man and no matter what happens, please know I will always be grateful."

"It has been an honor to assist one so powerful." He gave a slight bow.

I gave him a tiny salute, then faced the cave opening with determination. It was time to save the goofy men of my life.

Eighteen

Sweet, Texas
2 p.m.
Witches with bipolar cats: 1
Dead guys: I lost count. Again.
Spells: 10

Casper, the crazy cat, has decided she can never be more than two feet away from me while I'm home. Maybe it's because I was gone so long this last time, but I'm not sure.

The weird thing is, she hates me. From the day she showed up on my doorstep in New York and insisted on coming in, she's detested my every move. While we lived in the bigger cities, like Paris, London, and New York City, she never left the apartment. She's always been my guard cat, and has let me know more than once when a warlock was trying to get past my wards. But she's never wanted to be petted or to curl up in my lap. There is always disdain in her eyes, like she barely tolerates me.

When we moved to Sweet, it was a whole different story. From that first month, I was lucky if I saw her once a week—until now. I came home from Africa, and she's been stuck to me like glaze on a sugar bun.

I'm out in the conservatory taking a rest and admiring my handiwork. I transplanted thirty different herbs from pots to the ground this morning. I've pruned, plucked, and have just about everything in order.

After the chaos in Africa, it feels good to do something that feels so normal.

I thought I knew what I was walking into that night when I made my way through the cave, but I didn't have a clue.

Kaz had been right about the guard change. There was about a ten-minute window for me to slip in while they changed shifts.

I used the cloaking spell to get inside, just in case there was someone on the mountain we hadn't seen.

There were several large trucks at the entryway and just inside the cave. Some held heavy machinery, and the others were transport. I'd seen several of the miners climb into one an hour or so ago.

One thing I hadn't expected was how large the inside of the cave was. There were a couple of offices on the right and three tunnels off to the left.

Concentrating, I tried to hone in on where Sam and the others were. He opened his mind to me immediately and I followed the link to the tunnel on the far left.

I had just made it around the corner when I saw two guards headed my way. Sinking back against the wall, I waited as they passed. Taking a breath, I moved farther down the tunnel, sticking close to the wall. Every once in a while, there would be a door. The first two were locked, but I opened the third. There were about fifteen small mats on the floor. The room had been hollowed out of the rock and I wondered if maybe the guards or the miners used it to rest.

After another few minutes I came to a passage that had two entrances. I opened my mind to Sam again and moved to the right.

That's when I heard them—not my family, but children. A baby cried, and I heard another child scream. I moved faster. The door had a window, and I peeked inside. There were five children, from the baby to what looked like an eight-year-old boy. The older children were sitting on the edge of their mats with their legs crossed.

What the hell are children *doing in a mine?*

A woman, dressed in the same blue uniform the rebels wore, held a syringe and the baby in her arms. She handed the child to the oldest boy, but he didn't want to take her. He shook his head and a tear fell to his cheek.

She forced the child into his arms. Then she took the baby's thigh and was about to plunge the long needle in.

I shoved open the door and threw my hands out. I used my power to push her into the wall and hold her there.

"What the hell are you doing to them?" I screamed at her. Realizing someone might hear, I used one hand to shut the door while holding her with the other.

She stared at me, first in shock, then in anger. Her mouth moved into a straight line.

The children jumped up and ran to the other side of the room, as far away as they could get from both of us.

"Look, lady. You better answer me." I pushed my mind into hers just in case she didn't speak English.

Her chin jutted out and she spit at me.

I really hate it when people do that.

"Hey, chick, keep your saliva to yourself." Using my power, I probed her mind. She was doing experiments on the children. Something to do with AIDS, but it definitely wasn't a good thing.

I watched her memories as she took blood and poked the children with needles. She enjoyed her job a bit too much. It was disgusting. I gave her a mental pop, and I meant to knock her out. But she fell to the floor and she wasn't breathing. *"Oops."*

The children gasped behind me, and the baby cried again. I turned to them and smiled. "I won't hurt you. Do any of you speak English?"

A young girl who couldn't have been more than five raised a shaky hand. "Yes."

"Good girl. Can you tell your friends that I'm going to get you out of here, but first I must find my friends? I'll be back in just a minute. I know this seems scary, but I promise everything is going to be okay." I smiled and sent a calming spell to them.

She spoke to the other children. They gave me a cautious glance, then nodded.

"I'm going to put something on the door so that the bad people can't get in. Then I'll be back for you. Okay?"

The young girl nodded. "Yes."

I was about to go when it dawned on me that it probably wasn't a good idea to leave a dead chick with the poor kids.

Grabbing the woman by the collar, I tugged her through the door. I couldn't leave her out in the hall, so I kept trying doors as I walked down. She wasn't light and dragging her was wearing me out. I was about to shove her into one of the small holes when I heard someone say my name.

It came from a door just a few steps down. "Bron. In here."

Relief washed over me. It was Sam. I left the woman on the floor and tried the door. Locked. "Move back." I flicked my wrist and the door popped open.

Sam rushed out and grabbed me. I wrapped my arms around him and kissed him hard.

"I'm really mad at you." I pushed him away and hugged my dad and brother, then gave a quick wave to the sheik, who smiled. "All of you. Getting captured by rebels. I swear."

My dad patted my arm. His hair seemed grayer and he had a few more wrinkles around the eyes than the last time I'd seen him. "Bronwyn, dear. You can scold us later. Let's get the hell out of here."

I rolled my eyes. "Fine. But first, stick Broom Hilda into your deluxe accommodations. We have some children to save."

They gave me a strange look, but did what I asked.

When we found the children, my brother let out a cry.

"Tambana, oh my god." He rushed in and picked up the little five-year-old who had been speaking to me.

"Dr. Brett, you find me. Very good. Very good." She sobbed the words as she patted his cheek.

It was such a precious sight I had to look away, or I would have cried.

I motioned for the oldest boy to hand my dad the baby. If we had any trouble, I'd need both my hands.

Azir took the other little girl by the hand and Sam held the two remaining boys' hands.

"Okay. This could get a little crazy. The guards have already done their shift change, so there's a good chance they can show up at any time. I have someone waiting for us outside, but we have a long way to go."

When I'd come up with my sort-of plan, I hadn't known about the children. We'd have to move slower, but everything pretty much stayed the same. "Try to be invisible," I added.

The children seemed to understand the gravity of the situation, even the baby, who had stopped crying as soon as my dad held her.

Walking slowly, we made it to the tunnel where it forked, but this time, there were guards stationed on both sides.

Crap.

Making a silent motion to Sam, I held up two fingers. He nodded, and then shielded the eyes of the two boys. I looked and all of the men had covered the children's eyes.

I couldn't risk the two guards screaming, so their deaths had to be fast. I threw two big fireballs from behind that consumed them instantly. All that was left were two piles of ash, and a tiny bit of smoke.

We moved forward again and made it all the way to the big, open cavern, when the real trouble hit. Someone must have noticed the guards were missing, or had found the dead woman. An alarm went off and lights flashed. Twenty guards poured out of the offices and headed our way.

Well, hell.

"I'm going to do what I can. Pick up the kids and run like hell!" I screamed over the noise. "Azir, Kaz is out there with a truck, but I have no idea which one."

Azir helped Sam lift one of the children onto his back. "Do not worry, Bronwyn."

I nodded.

Gathering strength, I prepared for battle. All of a sudden the guards, who I noticed wore the blue rebel uniform, had turned their attention to the entrance and away from us.

There was gunfire and then they ran toward the cave opening.

"What the—hey." There was a hand on my back. My dad was pushing me forward. "Your friends are giving us the distraction we need. Don't just stand there."

The cavern was now empty, except for the trucks. Dad was right. I put a protective shield around all of us, then told everyone to run. We made it to the back side of one of the transports, and I peeked around the hood. The guards were firing into the jungle. I could hear the growl of not one, but *several* animals.

"Good girl, Shanasa," my brother whispered.

At the time I had no idea what he was talking about, but I later discovered the leopard who had followed me was his protector. In much the same way Casper is mine, only a whole lot bigger and deadlier. She'd shown up in the middle of the jungle one day and had protected him and the children at the tiny camp from the rebels. Brett figured she'd felt guilty for going on a hunt when he was captured. That's why she'd been following me, to make sure I made it to him.

We were at the mouth of the cave but I wasn't sure how we were going to get through the guards to find Kaz.

Azir touched my arm and pointed to a truck a few yards ahead. It was one of the smaller transports and I saw a figure move slightly. Kaz sat behind the wheel.

Staying behind the cover of the other vehicles, we made our way to the truck at the front of the cave. One by one we loaded the children in, and each of the men grabbed a gun from the pile Kaz had stashed in the back.

Sliding into the cab with Kaz, I sat next to him.

"Give me a minute," I whispered.

Chanting a protection spell, I created a bubble around the truck, but I wasn't sure how long I could sustain it.

"Go." I held my hands out against the dash. Pulling as much as I could from the jungle around me, I continued the chant.

Once the truck engine turned, the guards moved their attention to us. At first they were shocked. As the truck lurched forward they opened fire.

I chanted louder, and I could hear Sam and my brother doing the same. They are both warlocks who do not use their powers, but they understood what I was doing. Not long after, Kaz and the children also chanted, though I'm not sure what language it was in. It didn't hurt to have our collective power protecting everyone.

"They are loading the trucks!" Azir yelled.

I looked in the rearview mirror. The guards were piling into the two remaining transports just inside the cave.

"Can you outrun them?" I asked Kaz.

He frowned.

There was no way I could use my firepower and protect us at the same time. "Put the children flat on the floor. I have to release the shields for a moment." I could hear them moving in the back.

Focusing on the gas tank of the first truck, I threw a fireball with my mind. It exploded and caught the other truck on fire. The ground rumbled and I threw another fireball at the mouth of the cave. Rocks slid down a few pebbles at a time, and then the entire thing collapsed. Smoke billowed out and more explosions followed. Whatever I had done had set off a chain reaction inside the cave.

We were on a rough road at the base of the mountain and Kaz swerved to dodge boulders sliding down and smashing into the ground.

Throwing up the protection spell, I began the chant again and heard the men and children doing the same. Except for Azir, who was barking orders into his cell phone.

Tired, I was so tired, and I could feel the nausea from overextending my powers.

"Azir, tell me you have friends close." I focused hard on keeping the truck protected from the falling debris.

"Two miles!" Azir yelled through the window in the rear of the cab.

Two miles could be an eternity in the jungle, but I held tight. When the helicopters came into view in the clearing, I finally let myself take a breath, and that's the last thing I remembered until waking up in my brother's camp with Sam on one side of the bed and my dad at the other.

"Welcome back, my dear." My father put his hand on my arm. "Did you rest well?"

I snorted. "What day is it?" I squeezed Sam's hand, which was holding mine.

"Same day. You've only been out a couple of hours." Sam kissed my knuckles. "How do you feel?"

I sat up on the cot, and noticed I was in a private tent. "Where are we?"

"In your brother's tent." Sam smiled. "He insisted."

My brother could be bossy.

"Are the children okay?" I coughed, and Sam handed me a cup of water. My throat felt like I'd been swallowing glass. "And Kaz?" The man had risked his life to save my family and I needed to know he was okay.

"Everyone is fine. Azir is working on transport to move the children to a safer location. In fact, he's moving the entire camp." My dad walked around to take my other hand and he checked my pulse.

"The whole camp?" I frowned. "Why?"

"Whoever was running the mine did not have permission from

the government," Sam added. "The area is too unstable, and Dr. Zocando feels it would be safer if the camp moves about ten miles down the river.

"Dr. Zocando?" For some reason the mention of his name made me uncomfortable. I don't know, maybe because I'd totally gone against his wishes and struck out on my own last week.

"Yes, he's helping with the relief effort. He, Azir, and the prime minister have already found a place for the new camp." Sam frowned. "Why?"

My dad had stepped out of the tent.

I reached across and wrapped my arms around Sam. He felt so good against me. I never wanted to let go. "No reason. I just can't get a read on Zocando, and that always makes me cautious."

"I missed you," Sam whispered across my cheek. He still sounded congested and his lip was twice its normal size on one side.

Touching it, I sent a healing spell. "I'm still mad at you for coming out here. You could have been killed." I kissed his neck to take the sting out of my words.

"You know I'm not a very good listener. Especially when my favorite witch is in trouble."

I love it when he calls me "witch." I don't know why. When other people say it, it sounds like a dirty word. But when he says it, it makes me feel sexy.

"I don't suppose we could . . ."

He laughed. "Bron, we have no privacy here. But as soon as we get home, we can do whatever you want. I promise."

Before we left the camp, I had a chance to tell Tambana and the other children good-bye. She hugged me hard for such a little girl. Each of them is so precious, and it hurts my heart that they live such difficult lives.

I was feeling so melancholy that I even hugged my brother. "Don't get captured again, idiot. This place is murder on my hair."

He squeezed me back, and not the tepid hugs we usually dole out at the holidays. "For a runt, you pack a punch." Stepping back, he stared at me. "I'm not so sure I could have made it out of this one on my own." His voice caught. "Thanks."

"Golly, Brett. Don't go gettin' all soft on me. I might have to like you or something." I grinned. "You take care of these babies." I pointed to the children. "Anytime you need anything, call me. And don't be a stubborn butthead about it."

He laughed.

When we made it back to Sweet, Sam was true to his word about letting me do whatever I wanted. I jumped him over and over again the night we finally made it home, and he never complained once.

We even tried out the new shower for two, which was mighty delightful.

Argh! Is that the time?

I need to get cleaned up. We're meeting the coven tonight to discuss my Jason problem.

I checked with Cole and there's still no word on Garnout. He's just disappeared off planet Earth.

The trouble just never seems to end.

Nineteen

I'm one lucky witch. Sure, I have a nasty ex-boyfriend who is trying to assassinate me, but I'm equally lucky to have a perfectly lovely boyfriend now who loves and adores me.

Last night Sam devised a new game called "How Do I Worship Bronwyn." I must say it's a delightful game, where I am the prize. It's my absolute favorite way to pass the time.

Usually Sam finishes at the office early on Fridays, but there was a problem with one of the patients at the nursing home and he was running late.

I'd been working with plants and potions all day, and I finally had my potion stock back up to where it needed to be. I was sticky from ingredients and sweating from working out in the September heat, so I decided to take a hot, soaking bath.

A few weeks before I'd left for London, I had a big new tub installed. It looks like a giant soup tureen and it has jets that come from every angle.

I lit a few candles, threw in my favorite vanilla and cinnamon oil, and turned on some old-school Joss Stone. The tension of the day melted away in a matter of seconds once the pulsating jets beat a calming rhythm into my neck and shoulders.

My mind wandered over the past few weeks and all the craziness, from Jason to Africa. I forced my mind to let go of of it all and I concentrated on finding peace, staring at the candle's flame.

I must have dozed off, because at some point my dead Irish ancestor Darcy came to visit. She usually shows up in my dreams when she wants to chat. I'd helped to reunite her with her lost love a while back, and she's been visiting me since.

"Good evening, young witch." I opened my eyes to see Darcy standing there. She was dressed in a lacy white dress and her long blond curls were piled on top of her head.

I smiled. "How are you?" The first time I met her she'd possessed Sheik Azir, which was beyond weird. She usually shows up with sage advice when something big is about to happen. Sometimes I'm smart and follow it; other times, not so much.

She sighed, but it was a happy one. "Lovely, my dear. I'm perfectly lovely. I have a message for you from Garnout."

That made me sit up, and I wrapped an arm around my chest. "What?"

"He's fine, and he says not to worry, all will be well."

A crushing thought entered my mind. "Is he dead?"

She laughed. "No, darling child, but he does want you to let go and concentrate on your troubles here."

"Why did he just disappear like that? I've been worried sick. Did that sorceress Calinda kidnap him? Who is she? If you can talk to him, why can't I?" My mind raced with questions.

Darcy smoothed an errant curl off her forehead. "Who can say?"

Have I mentioned that my ancestor isn't always straight with the answers?

I didn't understand how he could get a message to Darcy but not to me. It didn't make sense.

"I see your mind is turning fast. He didn't want to cause you worry. He's conserving energy and it was easier for him to contact me than you. I'm not someone *she* can harm."

I wondered if the "she" was the sorceress. "He's really okay?" It dawned on me that I was sitting naked in the water, but it didn't seem to bother Darcy. After all, she was family.

"Yes. Now, on to the real business of my visit." Darcy pointed at me. "You must find a way to defeat the past, and the only way to do that is to grasp on tight to the future."

Geez, I hate when she talks in riddles like this. "Darcy, if you have something to say, just do it." I rolled my eyes.

She gave me a smart look. "I did, young witch. You know we must be careful when discussing future events. Keep your wits about you and strengthen your powers."

She looked at the door. "Ah, that is lovely. I must go now."

A few seconds later I woke up when Sam slid a finger between my breasts. Then he reached down and kissed me hard.

I wanted to pull him into the water with me, tie, shirt, shoes, and all, but he backed away.

"You look like a goddess." He stood and grabbed a fluffy towel from the rack. Then he reached down and pushed the button to turn off the jets and pulled the lever to drain the tub.

"Really?"

"Yes." He pulled me to a standing position. The cool air on my wet skin made my body tingle and my nipples turn into tight peaks.

Beginning with one breast and then the other, he moved the towel in slow, sensual circles, drying me off inch by inch. Moving to my arms, he slid the towel down to my hands then took my fingers and kissed each one.

I couldn't breathe, and my body warmed under his touch as he moved the towel under my breasts and down my belly.

"Lift your leg." That sexy voice of his made me want to pounce, but I enjoyed the game and wanted it to continue. I raised my foot to the edge as he asked, and he slid the towel from my thigh to my ankle.

"The other one," he demanded.

I shifted and put the other leg up this time and when he reached my ankle, he went back up and slid his fingers inside me. I almost collapsed and knocked him to the floor. He dropped the towel and pulled me to him as his fingers slid in and out.

Holding me close, he picked me up out of the tub, and moved me to the bathroom counter. When he found the tiny nub between my legs and rubbed it, my body exploded.

"Sam."

"Yes, my goddess."

"I want you." The words were difficult to say because I was in the middle of another orgasm. "Please."

"As you wish." I heard his zipper, then his pants fell. I leaned back on my hands, giving him full access. When he pushed himself inside me, I wrapped my legs around him tight. At first, his thrusts were slow and agonizing.

"Sam." I growled.

He shifted and pulled me toward him, shoving his tongue into my mouth as he pounded me harder and harder. I moved my hands into his hair and then slid them down to his back. I know I had to have left marks as I came again and again. My mind was a blur and I thought of nothing but him and our bodies being together.

When he finally came, something happened with our auras, a flash of gold and then tiny shimmers of silver. I'd never seen anything like it, but in that moment my heart was so filled with love for the man, I can't explain it. Not because he'd just played my body to perfection, but because he'd opened my heart and I think I finally, really, let him in.

He must have realized it, too. He stayed inside of me, but pulled back a little to look at my face. Taking my chin in his hand, he kissed me softly.

"I love you, Bron."

I kissed him back. "I love you, too."

For a moment we stared at each other, and then we smiled.

"Kind of cool." I was a little embarrassed and I didn't know what to say. I knew I loved the guy, but this was something more.

He chuckled. "Very cool." Reaching over he grabbed another towel and wrapped it around me. Then he hugged me, and suddenly I felt filled with love. I know it sounds so damn corny when I try to explain it, but I've just never had such an intense feeling. We stayed like that for a few minutes.

"I have another surprise for you." He pulled away and wrapped a towel from the rack around his waist.

I laughed. "Whew. I'm not sure I can handle another surprise right away." Well, I could have, but I was curious about what he had in store.

"I stopped at Lulu's on the way home."

That made me perk up. "And?"

"There's chicken-fried steak, fried okra, and mashed potatoes downstairs on the table."

I gently shoved him to the side, and tucked the towel more firmly around me. "Why the hell didn't you say so? My god, man. What were you thinking?"

He faked a hurt look. "I was thinking it might not be such a bad idea to get a little exercise before we clogged our arteries."

I giggled. "True. You are forgiven. But now the goddess really needs to eat." I took off in a run downstairs with him close on my heels.

In that moment I felt such complete joy, and I savored it along with the food.

Later in the night, when we made love again, I felt the same thing as before. It made me wonder if this is what Darcy had been talking about—if Sam was my future that I needed to hold on to in order to defeat my past.

One thing is for sure, I'm not letting go of this guy anytime soon.

Sunday
Noon

We're headed to the Methodist Men's social at the church this afternoon. The guys cook hamburgers, tell really bad jokes, and the men's choir sings. It's hokey fun, and I love that kind of stuff. It's one of the best things about living in a small town.

Kira, Caleb, Margie, and Billy will be there, and it should be interesting. Billy still hasn't asked Margie to marry him, even though Kira and I both know he has the ring.

Awkward? Perhaps.

Interesting? Absolutely. It's like having our own little soap opera right here in Sweet.

The only person I'm not looking forward to seeing is the head of the coven, Peggy. She still isn't happy about the extra protection they've had to put on the town because of Jason. So far no one has tried to get in.

I would have thought this would be the first place he'd show up. In a way he's already working magic against me because he's made me paranoid in my own home—I keep waiting for something to happen. It's sort of like what happens with terrorism, part of the way terrorists get to you is mentally.

After I looked out the window for the thirtieth time, I made myself stop. There was no way that puny warlock could get past my wards, and if he *did* show up the coven would be aware immediately.

The last time Blackstock, the badass warlock who tried to kill me a few months ago showed up, the coven knew before I did. Again, that's another great thing about living in a town that's flush with cool witches and warlocks.

Unfortunately, I think there's trouble brewing in Sweet. When I met with the coven the other night, something didn't feel right. I'm not sure, but I think Sheriff Mike, Peggy's son, may have had enough of his mom holding the town's every move in her tight fist. Much like my own mother, she tends to only be happy when things are going the way she wants.

When I walked into the meeting at the community center Peggy and Mike were arguing in the corner. No one said anything, but it all felt very uncomfortable.

She was whispering something through gritted teeth, but I couldn't tell what she was saying. Whatever it was, it made him angry and he stomped out.

She conducted the meeting and was as polite and cordial as ever, but I could tell she was still angry. She asked me to lead some protection spells that were strengthened by all of us working together.

After it was over she thanked me and then said she had to run.

Nosy me wanted to ask if maybe I could do something to help, but I've got enough going on right now between trying to find Garnout and keeping on top of Jason's whereabouts.

If Peggy needs me, she knows where to find me. Which isn't always a good thing.

Twenty

I never did get to find out about the drama between Peggy and her son. They didn't show up at the picnic. But that's okay because I seem to be able to create my own little dramas out of complete nothingness.

There must be some kind of karma ruler in the cosmos that keeps people from being too happy. Or maybe I should learn to keep my mouth shut.

Like that's going to happen.

The Methodist Men's social was fun. The guys set everything up picnic-style under a huge tent to save us from the hot West Texas sun. The burgers were delicious, and I'd just discovered a vat of banana pudding that I was certain would make my day, when the trouble started.

Billy and Margie were ahead of me, arguing over some of Ms. Johnnie's chocolate icebox pie.

"You two sound like an old married couple." I joked, and smiled knowingly at Billy.

"As if I'd ever marry him." Margie frowned. "The man would choose banana pudding over chocolate pie. That's just crazy."

It was the stricken look on Billy's face that almost made me drop my plate. "Margie, don't be an idiot." The instant I said the words I knew I'd screwed up. They'd come out much harsher than I'd planned. Actually, there was no planning involved, which was part of my problem. "I mean, it's just, um, dessert. I like them all." I smiled.

"Idiot?" Margie shoved her plate at Billy, her voice rising. "What would make you say something like that, Bronwyn, and take his side? I thought you were *my* friend!" Suddenly, the music stopped as well as the conversations.

If only I had the power to stop time and reverse it. "Margie, please. I didn't mean it like that. Really."

Her chin jutted out and her hands went to her hips. "Well, miss high-and-mighty *witch*—oh, I'm sorry, did I offend you?"

Okay, so I have a bad temper. It pisses me off when people do that. Make "witch" sound like "bitch." Margie's my friend, but I didn't care for her tone.

That's when my mouth went into overdrive. "I meant that if you start hen-pecking the guy now over something as stupid as dessert, he'll never ask you to marry him." See, it's my mouth. It never stops.

It was about this time that Kira walked up and grabbed my arm. "Margie, I think Bron's had some kind of sun stroke or something.

She hasn't been herself since she came home from Africa. Maybe it's malaria."

Margie crossed her arms in front of her chest. "Huh. That would explain a lot."

I opened my mouth, but Kira's hand flew up and covered it. "Bron, just leave it alone." Then she proceeded to drag me out of the tent.

"What the hell was that about?" She continued pushing me toward the parking lot.

"I don't know, and stop shoving me. Did you see Billy's face when she said she wouldn't marry him? He looked like his dog had just died, and he really loves his dog." My head hurt, probably from the tension.

"You called her an idiot. You know how sensitive Margie is about that kind of thing. She's brought herself up from difficult circumstances and made a good life for herself. She even put herself through nursing school. What you said was cruel."

I rubbed my head with my hand. The pain was searing. "Geez. I'm sorry. I wasn't thinking." That's when I started sliding down the side of the big red truck we'd been leaning against.

"Bron?" Kira's annoyed tone turned to worry.

I tried to open my eyes, but I couldn't. Someone had left a burning match in my brain. "Kira, get Sam." The words came out garbled, but she understood.

She screamed for him. I have no idea where he was during all the commotion, but he came running.

By the time he put a hand on my head the pain had lessened, but my vision was blurry and my stomach felt like someone had taken a sledgehammer to it.

"Bron, honey, can you hear me?" He snapped his fingers. I wanted to answer but I couldn't get my mouth to work. Then I blacked out.

I woke up in the hospital, one of the places I hate most. I felt fine, except for a wicked case of cramps. I told everyone who would listen that I could go home, but Sam insisted I stay overnight for observation. He can be so bossy sometimes.

They CAT-scanned my brain and ran all kinds of tests while I was out. So far, nothing has shown up.

Margie stopped by a few minutes ago. She peeked her head in the doorway. "So I hear they found a brain in that head of yours. Surprise, surprise." Her southern twang made me smile. She wasn't dressed in her nursing gear, so I knew she was here to see me.

"Have you forgiven me for being a jerk?" I motioned her to come in the room. My arm was still hooked to the IV, and I pushed the button on the bed so I could sit up. "I'm so sorry. Obviously I was having some kind of brain hemorrhage."

She paused for a moment and stared at me thoughtfully. When she walked into the room, she smiled. "Hey, don't joke about that. Sam was worried you really had picked up something in the jungle. You had us all scared." She sat down on the edge of the bed. "And of course I've forgiven you."

I reached my arm out and she grabbed my hand. "You know I'd never do anything to hurt you, Margie." I still felt the need to explain myself, and I prayed I didn't offend her this time. "Whatever happened to my head made me stupid. Well, more stupid than usual. I think Billy's really serious about you, and he looked so hurt when you said you wouldn't marry him."

She squeezed my hand. "You don't have to talk around it. Kira told me everything. I know about the ring." She shrugged. "I'd sort of given up on the whole idea of marriage. Figured maybe it wasn't in the cards for me. I love Billy so much. I hope I haven't screwed it all to hell."

Smiling, I patted her hand. "Nah. Billy won't give up. He's a tough guy, and he'll only see this as a setback. I bet you guys will be married by the end of the year. That is, if that's what you want. Margie, you are an amazing chick and any man would be blessed to have you." I chewed on my bottom lip.

She let go of my hand and stood up. "Have you ever wanted something so much that you were afraid to think about it for fear of jinxing it?"

I chuckled. "Absolutely." There had been many times in my life when I'd felt that way, most recently with Sam. I'd never thought about the future with him because it seemed like too much to wish for, and I worried that I'd mess it up.

"That's the way I feel about Billy. I hope you're right about him not giving up. I have some serious making-up to do with him." She moved toward the head of the bed and straightened my pillows.

"Well, why don't you stop by and see him on the way home?" I pulled the blanket up under my arms.

"I may just do that." She smiled. "I wonder if I can find some banana pudding this late at night."

As she left, I asked her to find Sam for me, but he still hasn't shown up. I've backtracked through my day trying to see if maybe I did something to bring this all on. I don't know. Before Margie arrived I did a quick once-over of myself trying to see if maybe someone had spelled me, but I didn't find anything.

Sam knows how much I hate hospitals and that I heal better at home.

So where the hell is he?

Monday 11 a.m.

New York

Bad witches who are in trouble: 1

My cell phone started ringing about one this morning. I must have dozed off waiting for Sam. I was sound asleep and dreamed my ears were ringing. That's when it dawned on me that it was my phone. I pulled open the bedside table and dug my hand into my purse.

I was groggy when I flipped open the phone and didn't bother to check the caller ID. "Yes?"

"Bron?"

"Yeah." For a few seconds I couldn't place the voice then I realized it was Cole. "What's up?"

"We have a trace on some magic in Budapest. It's the same as what we found in Amsterdam." Cole sounded tired.

The news made me sit up. "Is it Jason?"

"Possibly. We found two witches who had been tortured. Their powers were stripped just before they were murdered. The magic belonged to your ex. We've been able to pinpoint it exactly, thanks to the help of his family. So it's definitely him."

My stomach made a funky noise and bile rose in my throat. I knew I'd been right about him in the first place.

"Are you in Budapest?" I moved my legs to the side of the bed and carefully pulled the IV out of my arm. Sam had insisted on hydrating me intravenously. I found gauze in the drawer and held it against my arm to stop the bleeding. Moving fast made me dizzy and it took a few seconds for me to find my feet.

Cole sighed. "I'm in London right now, but I'm headed that way." I could hear his shoes clicking on the floor.

"Are you with the PM?"

"No. I've been here on personal business." He said it in a way that suggested he had no plans to tell me the nature of that business.

"Okay. I'll meet you in Budapest tomorrow."

"That's not necessary, Bron. We can handle this."

I slipped the pair of jeans that Kira and Caleb had brought by earlier over my hips. "Cole, if it's Jason—and I know it is—I need to be there."

"It's a police matter." Even as he said the words he had to know they didn't mean crap to me.

I snorted. "And I'll give you my full cooperation. I'll be more than happy to tell you where I've left the pile of ashes when I'm done."

Cole laughed. "Okay. Call me when you get there and we'll get to work immediately."

There was no way I could fly myself, just in case my brain really was self-destructing. I punched some numbers on my cell and called Caleb. He and Kira had been at the hospital until about eleven, when I made them go home. She was worried she had caused my headache, and it took forever to convince her not to feel guilty.

He picked up on the second ring. "Bron, what's wrong?"

I cleared my throat. "Nothing. I need you to come pick me up."

"Did they release you?"

Caleb always knows when I'm lying so I didn't bother. "Not exactly."

I heard him sigh. "Where's Sam?"

"I don't know, but I've got a job and I really need to leave. Now."

"I'm not getting my ass kicked by your boyfriend because I broke you out of the hospital. Besides, what if your head explodes? Then what will you do?"

"If my head explodes it won't be my problem, it'll be someone else's. Come on. I need you to come get me and then fly me to Dallas."

He coughed. "Are you serious?"

"I know it's late, but just in case my brain *does* decide to do something crazy I don't want to be the one flying the plane. I need to get to Dallas so I can get the first flight to Hungary in the morning. It's important, Caleb. Trust me, I'm not being dramatic when I tell you lives are at stake." That wasn't a lie. Jason was stripping the powers of these witches to build his own power, and he wouldn't stop—at least, not on his own.

I searched for my shoes while I talked to Caleb. I figured I had another ten minutes or so before one of the nurses came in to check on me. They were pretty regular about that sort of thing.

"Meet me on the side of the building close to the nursing home."

"I'm not coming to get you, Bronwyn. You blacked out this afternoon, and if Sam thought you were better, he would have released you."

I slid on my Keds that had been tucked away in the closet and pulled the orange T-shirt I'd been wearing earlier over my shoulders, moving the phone as necessary. "Caleb, if you don't do it, I'll just ask someone else. Please. I wouldn't ask if it weren't important." I had to go, and I really would do whatever it took.

I heard him whisper something to Kira. "If you tell her, she'll call Sam."

"She already knows it's you. Okay. We'll be there in five minutes."

Sweet's hospital is small, and it shares the building with the nursing home. My only big problem was getting past the front desk. I was just about to leave my room but I stopped to write Sam a quick note.

> *Heading to Budapest. Feel fine. Sorry.*
> *Love you,*
> *Bron*

I snuck out of the hospital, and I knew Sam was going to kill me when he saw me.

It was awful to leave without telling him good-bye, but I didn't have time for the drama. I still had to go home, pack, and put my bag o' magic supplies together. And grab a suitcase full of tampons, pads, and anticramp herbs to deal with the worst period of my life. In fact, I was certain that's why I had passed out today and been so grumpy.

Kira and Caleb lectured me the entire time I packed, *and* during our flight to Dallas.

I had to turn my phone off. Sam started calling about twenty minutes after we left the hospital. I'm not sure, but just as we were taking off I think I saw his truck pull into the hangar.

I have a feeling he's really, really pissed and hurt. That's the worst part for me. I can't stand the idea that I've disappointed him. I haven't had the courage to listen to the seven voicemails he left.

Maybe later.

Twenty-one

Budapest
Tuesday
2 a.m.
Travel-weary witches: 1

Whatever happened to me yesterday wiped me out. It's a good thing I didn't try to fly myself anywhere. I slept almost the whole way to Budapest and I feel way better than I did yesterday.

I love it here, and I try to visit as often as possible. I'm fairly certain that back in the day when they were writing fairy tales about princesses in castles they were totally thinking about Budapest. Everywhere you look it's like a giant, picture-perfect postcard, castles against blue sky. It's beautiful.

They also have these really great spas all over the place with water that is supposed to be both magical and medicinal. All I know is that after an hour in the water, I feel rockin' good.

Cole met me at the airport in a big sedan. He was standing just outside in jeans and a dark blue button-down. Sometimes I forget how handsome he is with his curly blond hair and Caribbean blue eyes. "I just received a call from your boyfriend." He smirked.

I shrugged. "Figured he'd track me down eventually. Did you have a pleasant conversation?"

Cole chuckled. "Not exactly. He wants you to call him as soon as you get in."

He opened the car door for me and I sat down on the leather seat. "I'll call him later." Sam must really have been upset to call here, and right now it was just easier to avoid him. The guilt slid uneasily into my belly.

Cole stared at me for a minute. "Your funeral."

"Yeah. I know. So what have you found out so far?"

We pulled out into the traffic. "There's been a series of murders, all of them related to magic in some way. Most of the victims have been tortured, all of them had their powers stripped."

I bit the inside of my lip. Why hadn't I killed the bastard when I had the chance? More people had died and it was my fault. "Have you been able to track him yet?" The view outside was filled with historic buildings and the Danube. Everything seemed so serene; the exact opposite of the turmoil inside of me.

"No. We still aren't certain it's Jason." He paused. "But whoever it is, he is using some dark magic. The same kind we found in Paris where we had that run-in with Calinda. If she really is involved here—well, you saw what can happen."

Rubbing my head, I tried to think. "It doesn't make any sense.

Why would she be working with someone like Jason? He's just your run-of-the-mill dumbass warlock." I looked at Cole. "Sorry, no offense."

He waved it away. "None taken. If Jason is mixed up with her, well, it could be bad for all of us."

"I don't get it, Cole. Jason hates women with a capital H and he wouldn't work with anyone more powerful than him."

Cole shrugged. "I don't know what to tell you, but the magic definitely matches. It's the same thing we saw in Amsterdam, Paris, and now here."

Great. "So what do we do?"

"For now we're going to get you checked in to the hotel. Then I'll take you to headquarters so you can view the evidence we found."

"Any chance I can see the witches?" We'd turned the corner and the hotel came into view. It looked like a giant castle.

"Not a good idea." Cole checked his rearview mirror and frowned. He moved the car into the other lane. "They were brutally tortured and left in rough shape."

I sighed. "I need to see them."

He glanced at me. "Okay, but I've warned you."

I've seen some pretty nasty stuff over the past few years. Sometimes even by my own hands—blowing up evil warlocks may be necessary, but it can be gross. I've also seen some disgusting things done by true evil. That's never fun.

"Someone must have spotted you. We've caught a tail." Cole was looking in the mirror. "I'm going to skip the hotel and go straight to headquarters." He pushed a button on the dash.

"Yes, Cole?" A feminine voice came through the speaker.

"Amy, I need you to check these plates." He gave her the number.

It took a few seconds. "They aren't registered."

Cole took a big breath. "Okay, tell Marcus we're coming in and I want him to set up a three-car tail."

Amy had a high-pitched voice and I wondered if she might be a fairy. They were good with all kinds of communication. "Should I notify the locals?" Amy tapped on a keyboard.

"No. Don't need the attention. Let them think we haven't spotted them."

"Okay, boss. What's your ETA?"

I tried not to be obvious, but I glanced into the side mirror. The car following us was a black sedan, much like the one we were in. I was just about to send my mind out again when Cole grabbed my hand.

"No, Bron. If they sense you know about them, we'll lose them. They're probably tracking your magic, so you don't want to clue them in that you know they are there."

I opened my eyes. "Okay. But when we do find these bastards, promise me I can kill Jason."

Cole frowned. "I'm a cop, Bron. I can't give you permission to kill someone." He squeezed my hand. "But after what he did to those witches, and to you, I have no problem with you doing whatever you need to in self-defense. In fact I'll help you if I can."

I nodded.

We were nearing a beautiful castle that looked like something you might see in fairy tale, only it was very real. The large iron gate opened as we approached, and Cole pulled into the circular driveway at the front entrance. The sedan continued on, but we heard the other spook squad members as they took off to follow our tail.

The gates clanged behind us. I jumped a little when the car door suddenly opened. A beefy man with a gun stood there. I hadn't even seen him approach.

"Ma'am." He held out a hand to help me out of the car.

I grabbed my bag of supplies and stepped onto the drive. The car had been surrounded by security guards, which appeared out of nowhere.

One of them handed Cole an earpiece. He motioned to me to follow him. We climbed the large marble steps to the entrance. Two large iron doors opened into one of the grandest foyers I'd ever seen.

A chandelier with millions of little crystals shone above and gave everything a beautiful glow. There were paintings and tapestries all the way up the walls of the three-story entrance.

I followed Cole toward the side of the massive stairway and to a door. It was a closet under the stairs.

He was busy talking to whoever was on the other end of the earpiece so he didn't notice my surprise. He stood inside the small room, which was empty except for a light on the ceiling above.

"What are you doing?" I wasn't going into a closet with Cole. It was weird.

He didn't answer, but he grabbed my hand and tugged me inside. As the door shut behind me, the floor shifted and moved. I almost fell down and Cole grabbed my elbow.

It was an elevator and we were heading down.

I turned to Cole. "Very James Bond."

He smiled and nodded. Then he frowned. "Marcus, what happened?"

The door opened again and we were in a large laboratory. There were computers on long metal tables and a variety of magical creatures sat at them. Two gnomes were arguing over something on one of the screens. Most gnomes, like gargoyles, are actually guardians and are really great at security. People always underestimate them because of their size, but you don't want to get into a fight with one. People look at me strangely when I pass gnomes in a garden, because I always say hi. Trust me when I tell you it is smart to be on their good side.

A fairy, about fifteen inches tall with blond curly hair and green eyes flitted around another monitor and waved a wand. She was dressed in a red top and jeans. Except for her height, translucent wings, and pointed ears, she could have been any woman on the street. Not many fairies chose to live in this dimension because of the pollution of the planet, so it was a surprise to see her. When I heard her speak, I realized it was Amy.

I'd never been to a magical investigator's headquarters, and for a witch, this is a good thing. If you wind up here you've usually done something really bad. Sometimes I even forget how many magical beings we have on Earth, but here they had a very eclectic group.

"Crap. They couldn't have just evaporated!" Cole yelled into the earpiece.

He obviously didn't like the answer and yanked the earpiece out. "They lost the tail about two miles from here."

"You said they disappeared." We were walking through a long hallway with offices. Everything was concrete, metal, and glass, but there was art, sculpture, and plants everywhere. I wondered how they kept the green stuff alive in the concrete bunker.

Cole paused outside a door. "Yes. Marcus says the car evaporated into thin air. They're checking the area to see if maybe there was a portal used. If so, there will be trace magic around."

He stopped outside some stainless steel doors. "Okay. This is the morgue. I'm warning you, it's bad." He pushed a button and the metal door slid open. I'd been in a few morgues and they are always the same. Dead people on tables, and an antiseptic smell that never does a good job of covering the stench of death.

"Rolf, I need seven and eight." Cole moved inside the doors.

Rolf reminded me of that scientist on *The Muppets*: round wire glasses and bald, with a shock of hair right in the middle. Plus he didn't have any feet.

"You have a ghost for a medical examiner?" The room was chilly and I rubbed my arms with my hands.

"He's the best, and he wanted to continue his work when he crossed over. Who better to look after the dead than the dead?" Cole helped Rolf pull a rolling table out of one of the bays.

I didn't really follow his logic. I was a little distracted by the two women in the corner. They were both witches and I could feel the magic rolling off them. Their hands were joined over a cauldron and they chanted.

"Who's that?" I asked Cole.

"Bernice and Chowana." He moved the table in front of me. "They are tracing the magic from some of the evidence we found in the witches' homes. Are you sure you want to do this?"

I stared at the sheet covering the body on the metal table. *No.* "Yes."

He slid the sheet back and I bit the inside of my lip to keep from throwing up. The perfect skin and beautiful auburn hair were at odds with the black holes where her eyes used to be, and the enormous slit that began at her throat, separating her perfectly round breasts, and stopped where her belly button used to be. At some point her wrist had been bound and the bruises there were still swollen and blue.

I sent a spell of healing to her soul and hoped that she had been able to move to the other side in peace. That asshole Jason would have done the same to me if I'd given him the chance. I wished I could go into her mind, but it's difficult with the dead. The soul usually takes the memories with it. Still, I thought it was worth taking the chance.

Placing my hands over her body, I concentrated. Her life force had been gone for hours, but I probed her brain. There was nothing but darkness. The brutality of what Jason had done tore at my heart. I would kill him. I would do it for this poor woman.

"Do you sense anything?" Cole pulled the sheet back up when I moved my hands.

"No." I circled my head to pop my neck, easing the tension. "Can I see the other woman now?"

"The injuries are exactly the same." Cole pushed the table to Rolf, who slid it back into the metal bay.

"I don't care. I need to see her." My voice caught. I blamed myself for all of this. These women had died because of me.

Cole was right about the other witch. She had been attacked in much the same way, but I sensed magic coming off her, which gave me some hope.

I moved my hands over her. At first there was nothing but blackness. I was about to give up when a tiny light appeared. A flash of a memory moved through me. She was tied to the bedposts crying. She'd been drugged and her brain was foggy, but she knew her life was in danger.

A dark figure stood at the end of the bed, chanting. The witch's body arched as the golden aura of her powers flowed out of her and into the other person. I could feel her terror and her pain.

Her body was weak, and yet she fought. Pulling against the ropes on her wrists, she screamed.

"I like it when you scream." Jason's face came into focus. He was older, with lines around his eyes, his cheeks thinner, and his hair stylish but shaggier.

The nasty warlock was a vicious as ever.

Something glinted in his hand, and I saw the athame. It was double-bladed with a black hilt.

Terror filled the witch, but she said a small prayer of peace as Jason moved to the side of the bed. She closed her eyes, and then there was darkness.

I opened my eyes and stared at the ceiling. Cole was chanting a healing spell. I must have fainted.

"What the hell?"

Rolf moved beside him, holding a glass of water. I sat up and took it. "Did I pass out?"

Cole nodded. "Rolf caught you before you hit the floor."

I looked up at the ghost. "Thank you."

My head hurt. Not as bad as the day before, but painful just the same. I rubbed my temples with my fingertips.

"Let's get you to the med facility. Do you think you can walk?" Cole reached down a hand.

"Yes, I can walk, but I don't need a doctor. Cole—it's Jason. I saw him kill her." I grabbed his hand and stood up. I was a little woozy. "We have to find him."

"We will. Maybe you need to eat or something." I saw the concern in his eyes.

I thought about it for a minute. It *had* been a really long time since I'd eaten. "Food would be good."

Cole pushed the button that opened the door. I started to follow him, then turned back. "Be at peace." I waved my hand over the second witch's body. I prayed that she did find solace.

The guilt of both of their deaths fell heavy upon me. I sighed. I would avenge them. I would find Jason and burn his rotten soul to hell.

Twenty-two

Tuesday

2 p.m.

Witches with really angry boyfriends: 1

Spells: 2

Potions: 3

It's kind of sad, but food is often my greatest solace during troubled times. Seriously, give me a piece of chocolate cake and I can deal with the fact that my ex-boyfriend is a serial-killing maniac, and that my current love is ready to hang me by my toes.

Cole thought it best I stay here at headquarters for now, until we are able to locate Jason. They've given me a small room the size of a walk-in closet. Okay, it's a little bigger than that, but it looks like something on a spaceship in one of those bad horror films. It has a small bunk that folds out of the wall, a metal rack to hang clothes, a two-drawer dresser below, and quite possibly the tiniest bathroom I've ever seen. You actually shower next to the toilet. No curtain or anything.

"The room isn't meant for anything long-term," Cole told me as he showed me around. We'd just eaten in the commissary and I was feeling loads better about life after having eaten the chocolate cake I mentioned before. "A place for those of us who have to work extra-long shifts and need to catch some sleep now and then."

For the foreseeable future it's my new digs. I'd probably be fine in a hotel with some protection wards, but if Jason and his people do attack I'd be risking the lives of innocents all around me.

With a full stomach I thought I'd be able to pass out, but no such luck. I just spent the last twenty minutes listening to Sam become more and more irate on my voicemail.

"Bronwyn, I can't believe you did this!" He growled into the phone. "You actually passed out today. Did you forget that? Jesus, what could have been so important that you had to run off?"

The next few messages were about the same, and then came the last one.

"Bron, please call me. I need to know you're okay. There's something about your test results and I need to talk to you about it. I promise I won't yell. Well, not much anyway. Just call." His voice was sad, which instantly made me wonder if I was about to die.

I held my cell phone for several minutes trying to gather the courage to call. When it vibrated in my hand I almost dropped it. I checked the number. It was Sam.

"Hey, please don't be mad at me. I'm really sorry." My words came out in a rush.

There was a pause. "I'm not mad." He cleared his throat. "Well, not really, anyway." He sounded more tired than anything. "Why didn't you just tell me what was going on? I thought we were working on trusting each other. That's hard to do when you sneak away."

Issues with trust in relationships were something we both had to deal with, and there had been several times in the last few months when I thought we wouldn't make it.

I sighed. "Honestly, I wasn't thinking straight. It's not an excuse and it was kind of dumb. But when Cole called and said they had a trace on Jason, all I could think about was getting here and blowing him up. I was afraid if I told you what was going on, you wouldn't let me leave the hospital."

"That's probably true, because you don't need to be running around the world right now. You should be resting." This time his voice did catch.

I didn't want to ask the question. My mind instantly flipped through the past few months. I'd survived multiple hits of black magic and almost died a couple of times. And I'd been in the jungle for all that time and I could have picked something up there. I was fairly certain I'd seen the monkey from that movie *Outbreak*, and we know what happened to the people who came into contact with *that* guy.

Maybe I'd done something irreparable to my body. I felt sick again. I reached into my bag for the herb capsules I'd made that helped to relieve cramps, and took some with a gulp of bottled water. "So, you said something about the tests."

"Yeah, I did. Look, there isn't an easy way to say this and I wish I could tell you in person." He paused again and my chest tightened. "We ran a series of blood tests, most of which came back normal. Your white count is slightly elevated, which is a sign of an infection. But—it's the . . ."

He cleared his throat. "Babe, your pregnancy test came back positive."

I can't really explain what went through my mind right then. Shock and, well, shock.

"That's not possible. I'm on my period now. The tests were wrong." I sat on the bunk and leaned back against the wall. Besides, we take more than one precaution to make sure that there are no babies in my immediate future.

"They weren't wrong. Bron, you had a miscarriage. From what I can tell you were about six weeks along. Had you noticed your cycle was late?"

I put a hand against my forehead. I felt hot, but my hands were clammy. "No. I've never been terribly regular. Are you sure?" I thought about how much I'd been eating the last few weeks and the fact that some of my jeans wouldn't fit. And how inexplicably tired I've been. It all sort of made sense now.

"Yes, I'm certain. You're losing a lot of blood and we need to fight this infection. I've already sent antibiotics, and some medicine that will help with the cramps. When you get back we're going to have to make sure all the tissue is gone." He coughed. "I'm sorry that sounded cold, but you'll need a full pelvic exam when you get back."

I'd had a baby inside of me and I hadn't even known. That's when I began wondering if I'd done something to cause the miscarriage. I'd had the occasional drink, and had been running all over the world fighting bad guys. I'd like to think that if I knew I'd been carrying a child, I would have done things differently.

"Sam, I didn't want a baby, but I'm feeling really sad." The words sort of tumbled out of my mouth. "I've been doing everything exactly the same; I don't understand how this could have happened. I mean, with the birth control. We've both been so careful."

"No birth control is one hundred percent effective. And miscarriages can happen for a variety of reasons. Most of the time it's because the fetus isn't healthy, and the body rejects it."

He sounded so professional. "Sam, don't be a doctor right now. Be my boyfriend." I started crying. "I'm sorry. I feel stupid because I don't even know why I'm crying."

"I'm going to sound like a doctor again, but your hormones are going to be a mess for a while. It's normal to be overly emotional. For the record, you aren't the only one who is sad. I wasn't looking to be a dad anytime soon, but for a moment there, I didn't mind the possibility. I love you, Bronwyn, and we'll get through this together."

His words made me cry harder. "I love you, too." I blew out a breath and found a box of tissues on the small table next to the bed. "Every time I use magic, I pass out. I was afraid someone had hexed me, but do you think this is why it's happening?" I dabbed my nose with the tissue.

"It's possible. Your body has been through a lot the past few months. That's why I think you should be resting. It's the same advice I'd give any of my patients going through something like this."

I suddenly felt really tired. So much so I could barely keep my eyes open. "I can't come home right now, Sam. We're close, and we have to get this guy before he kills someone else."

"Do me a favor and try to rest whenever you can. Take the medicine when it arrives today, and drink a bottle of your blue potion every six hours or so."

"I will. I'm sorry I ran away." I sniffled.

"It's okay." He didn't sound very convincing, but I chose to believe him.

When we hung up I curled into a ball on the bed, pulled the lightweight blanket over me, and fell asleep. Cole woke me up with the buzzer at the door. I pushed the button to let him in.

"Are you okay?" He looked at me funny, and I realized I'd fallen asleep in my clothes and I'm sure my makeup and hair were a mess. "This came for you a few moments ago."

He handed me a FedEx package. I opened it and found two prescriptions and a note that read:

> *Bronwyn, I love you so much. Please take care of yourself and come home to me. —Sam*

The words were so sweet and I couldn't control the tears as they fell in big, fat drops down my cheek. I sat down on the edge of the bed.

"What is it?" Cole sat down next to me, and took the note from my hands. He read it. "I don't understand."

I don't know Cole that well, but he's a good guy. And right then, I just needed to talk to someone. I told him everything. When I finished, he shook his head and hugged me. I cried for another five or six minutes until there were no tears left.

"I'm a mess. I'm sorry. Sam says it's hormones."

"Well, I don't know much about this kind of thing, but it's understandable you'd be a little emotional." He and I smiled over the "little" comment. "Maybe you should go home and get some real rest."

I pulled away from him. "Cole, I can't do that." I took a deep, cleansing breath and sent myself a healing spell. I had to be strong. "We're close to finding Jason, and I have to do this. Have you heard any news? Did they find traces of a portal?"

He leaned back on his arms. "There was something. If it was a portal, they've closed it, but there was magic."

"The thing is, Jason isn't strong enough to do something like that." I stood up and paced in the tiny room. "Even if he's been drawing powers from others for a while, he wouldn't be able to create a portal like that. I mean, that's something only a wizard or—oh, wow. Do you think he really *is* working with the sorceress?" I paused and looked at him.

Cole shrugged. "Yes, but why would she bother with someone like him? It doesn't make sense."

I pursed my lips and thought for a moment. Then it dawned on me: "What if he's the one who brought her back? You said she'd been banished to another dimension. If he conjured her up, then she'd be more inclined to work with him. She hasn't been a part of this world for several centuries, and she'd need someone to help her acclimate.

"Why are they in Budapest? That's what we need to find out. He'd sent the killer to assassinate me and the prime minister in Amsterdam. He didn't do it himself, but he did commit the murders of those witches. So, why are they here?"

Cole jumped up. "Time to do some research. I'll see if maybe she had favorite haunts here back in the day. This city has been rebuilt several times by different conquerors, and she loved war. There's a good chance she considers this home base."

I nodded. "Give me twenty minutes and I'll help." I looked down at my clothes. "I need to get cleaned up."

"Take your time. Grab something to eat and come to lab A when you are done. I'll put a team together and meet you there."

He started to walk out the door and turned back. He took me in his arms and hugged me hard. "This sucks, what's going on with you right now. But it's going to be okay."

His kindness was my undoing and the tears flowed again. I'd been certain I didn't have any left.

I pushed him away. "Oh, stop being so sweet. I'll never be able to get ready." I shooed him out the door.

After he left, I took a quick shower. By the time I'd eaten and made my way to the lab, I was back to my old self. Well, not quite, but close enough.

I meant what I said before—it was time to be strong. If I needed to grieve over what had happened, I would, but later—much later.

Twenty-three

Manhattan
Thursday
9 p.m.
Dead guys: 10
Spells: 20

I've never really suffered from PMS, but I think I get it now. I've read stories about women who shoot their husbands because they are suffering from a wicked case of hormones. My friend Simone says she slays more demons the week before her cycle begins than she usually does the rest of the month. Until now, I always thought PMS was a copout.

My body has gone berserk. There's no other word for it. One minute I'm crying, the next I'm blowing someone up. No one who doesn't deserve it, but it has been easier than ever to do what was necessary over the last few days.

Cole and his team found three locations where they felt the sorceress Calinda and her minions might be hiding.

It was me who suggested doing a drive-by to see if I could sense some of her or Jason's magic.

The first place, which was a residence that had been around for a few centuries, was a bust. We headed out of town to an old Turkish bathhouse just on the outskirts of Budapest. The place was gorgeous, with huge spires and mosaics that took my breath away.

We'd stopped to take a quick look around the grounds. It seemed deserted, but when I first stepped into the building, I had a feeling.

I touched Cole's shoulder. "There's something here. Do you sense it?"

He nodded, and we continued to search the building with the rest of the crew. We'd brought along six security agents, LaRie, a witch who had worked with Cole on several cases, and a shapeshifter, Logan, whom I was told could turn into any animal. He was a big man who looked more like he belonged on the cover of one of Ms. Helen's erotic romances, but I knew he had to be talented or Cole wouldn't have called him.

There weren't any wards I could see on the premises. I'd checked as we entered the building, but I didn't immediately see any magic inside.

If they were here, Calinda hadn't done a very good job of protecting the place.

The team, which had gone in a half-dozen different directions when we arrived, all returned.

"I sense it, too," Logan told Cole. "But I haven't seen anything."

I was standing in the middle of the large foyer. It had a huge circle of mosaics in an array of patterns that all made sense in the big picture, but could drive you insane if you stared at it for too long.

It was when I closed my eyes and sent my mind out that I heard a familiar voice.

"Bronwyn." He was weak, but I'd know Garnout's voice anywhere. "Danger."

"Are you okay?" I searched to see if I could spot him, and I did. He was underground, in a glass coffin. Nasty black magic surrounded him. The magical knots were so tight they looked like braids. He wasn't okay.

Calinda was sucking the life force from him.

I reached out for someone, and opened my eyes to see Logan's enormous bicep. He'd been holding on to me as if he were afraid I'd fall.

"You look like you're going to faint." Logan held my hand in his. He had a German accent and his words were strong and clipped.

"Damn. My strength isn't what it needs to be. They're here, underground. There's a friend of mine down there and we have to save him. Calinda's trying to kill him."

Logan touched his earpiece and told Cole what was going on. He'd left us to search the grounds again with the rest of the crew.

Moving around the room, I pushed on the various wall panels. "There have to be tunnels, or some way to get down there. What I don't understand is why they haven't attacked yet. She has to know we are here."

Logan shrugged, but pulled out a nasty-looking dagger, readying himself for battle.

Cole and the others came up behind us. "There has to be a way down to the basement. Did anyone see a stairwell?"

They shook their heads.

"The water has to come into the bath from somewhere. They had to have a way to fix pipes and that sort of thing." I was talking to the group and trying to keep my mind on Garnout. He grew weaker by the moment. I looked around the room where they had him and couldn't see anyone else.

"Where are they?" I sent the question to Garnout.

He shook his head as if he didn't know.

"Garnout, stay with me. We are coming to get you."

He raised his head and stared at the ceiling. "Be careful young witch, she's set a trap. She's clever, that one."

I assumed he was talking about the sorceress. It's funny—in a way, Garnout seemed to like her, even though she was the bitch zapping his powers.

"Good news is Garnout's alive. Bad news is he says we are walking into a trap." I moved toward the back of the building. I had a sense of where I needed to go.

"Bronwyn, let me call for more backup." Cole tugged on my arm.

"There isn't time. She's draining his powers. If we wait, he'll be a pile of nothingness. That's the worst thing that can happen for a wizard." I pulled myself out of his grasp.

He spoke into the microphone of his earpiece, ordering backup. At the very least there would be someone to clean up the dead if we didn't make it.

In the far left corner of the building I found it: a large closet with a trap door in the floor.

Before Logan reached down to open it, I sent a protection spell to the team. Then I grabbed a small vial of blue juice and chugged it down, and sent myself a strengthening spell.

I would survive this, and when I found Jason he would pay for helping that bitch hurt Garnout and for killing those poor, innocent witches.

The trap door opened with a creak right out of a Hollywood horror flick. It was a giant black hole until Logan pointed his flashlight inside. There were steep steps leading down into nothingness.

Cole moved to begin the descent and I followed him. Normally I'd take the lead, but this way I could focus more on the magic we were walking into.

The steps seemed to go forever, with walls on both sides. Two of the agents had stayed at the opening of the trap door to keep us from being, well, trapped. The last thing we needed was an attack from behind.

Halfway down, the stairs began to curve and I realized this was much more than a basement. The walls, made of wood, were intricately carved. I couldn't really see the patterns but I felt them with my hands. We were walking into a temple. I grabbed Cole's shoulder and whispered in his ear.

"Give me a minute." I sent my mind ahead and I could see a large room with an altar. Candles lined the stone structure and there were sconces lit around the room. At first I didn't see anyone, but then there was a tiny flash of a blue streak. Magic. Concentrating, I saw more movement against the columns beside the entrance and by the doorways leading out of the room.

A small army had been hidden by magic.

I told Cole, who relayed the message to the rest of the team.

Garnout hadn't been wrong. We were most definitely walking into a trap.

As we rounded the last curve, I saw the large altar. There were two people guarding the entryway. I sent a small burn to them both, and their screams created the diversion we needed. Once the others moved forward I could see the magic surrounding all of the people.

"Reveal!" I screamed and threw a spell at them. The cloaking fell away and the craziness began. A tiger—I assumed it was our shape-shifting friend Logan—leaped into the middle of the group headed for us.

Cole and his team used a combination of magic and weapons to fight the witches and warlocks surrounding us. We'd already decided that my job was to find Garnout. I knew he was near; I could feel him. I kept close to the wall and sent protection spells to our team.

I made my way to the large doorway on the right and ran into a wall of man. He was huge, at least seven feet tall, and was dressed in a dark robe. His fist reared back as if he was going to hit me. "I don't think so," I said, and threw out my hand, tossing him to the side, conveniently cracking his head against the wall. He slid down into a giant lump, his jaw still wide with surprise.

The door to the entryway was locked, and protected by a ward. I worked fast to undo it and made my way inside.

Garnout was in the coffin, but it was so covered in knots I didn't know how I would ever release him. He raised his head and moved his eyes to the corner. Someone was there. I threw up a shield just as a giant ball of green slime headed my way.

The stench of it made my nose burn. I knew that magic. Jason.

"I knew you'd try to save him, you stupid bitch. Didn't even see the trap we set for you. You always were easy to fool." I couldn't see him, but his voice was venomous and evil.

I hated him. Every horrible, nasty emotion I'd experienced after his betrayal filled my body. I sent a burn toward the voice.

"Oh, no. The witch is trying to burn me." His cruel laugh filled the room.

He came out from behind a column and I saw him for the first time in years. Dressed in an old T-shirt and jeans, he looked the same as he had in college. His sandy-colored hair was longer and tucked behind his ears, and his shoulders were broader. But it was the same asshole from five years ago. The burn I'd thrown had landed on his arm but it was no more than a tiny flame.

Taking a deep breath, he blew it out and smiled. "You aren't looking so good, Bron. You look almost as pale as your friend, there." He waved a hand to Garnout.

I shrugged. "Never been one to tan." As I spoke I continued to unwrap the knots surrounding Garnout. Jason was strong and I thought about those poor witches in the morgue. They hadn't been the only ones. Obviously he'd been stealing powers for a while. The shield protecting him would deflect most anything I threw at him. I had to get him to take it down.

"Oh, Jason. I have so much to thank you for." I smiled.

He raised an eyebrow.

"No, really, I do. It's because of you that I learned not to trust people. Especially warlocks. Through the years, the lessons I learned from you have helped me survive." Of course, I didn't mention that it's also played hell with my love life.

"There was a time when I loved you so much, I would have done anything for you. If you'd just asked, I probably would have even shared my power. You didn't have to try to kill me." I stayed calm, even though my insides were a boiling mass of anger.

I had to do something to distract him to get him to put down those shields. I'd almost finished with the magic surrounding Garnout, but I couldn't get the last few knots untied. My power waned, but I refused to give up.

"But killing you, Bronwyn, will be the sweetest part of all of it." He put up his hands as if readying for battle. "And I can't wait to finish the work I began so long ago."

He threw another whoosh of slime, but this time it grew as it neared, becoming a huge ball that crashed down on my shields. I backed up against the wall and felt my power lessen.

When the slime cleared, Jason was right in front of me. His hand wrapped around my neck and the force of it made my eyes bulge.

Oh crap.

I tried to focus, to send even the tiniest of flames into his brain, but it was a struggle to breathe. I'd already been weak and I could feel my life force slipping away. My eyes darted to the right and I saw Garnout struggling in the box. He was gaining strength.

At least I'd done one thing right.

There were spots in front of my eyes and suddenly I heard Simone's voice. *"Do the unexpected."* Using the little strength I had left I brought both arms up and shoved my thumbs in his eyes. The attack surprised him and he dropped his hold on my neck.

Air rushed into me and I slid down the wall. He'd reached up to grab his face where his eyes were bleeding. His crotch was in my line of vision and I threw a flame right at it.

Jason howled and backed farther away. His screams gave me strength. I could have thrown another fireball to burn him instantly, but I wanted him to suffer.

He threw some slime but he couldn't see, and it went far to the right. Evidently his jeans weren't fire-resistant and he screamed again, falling to the ground as he did.

"Now, this is fun. I *so* should have done this with more force the first time you tried to kill me." I moved around so that if he tried to throw something toward the sound of my voice, he'd have a hard time finding me.

The flames had reached his shirt and were heading to his face. He was paralyzed with pain and couldn't move. I saw his expression of terror and hatred.

"I'll die today, witch, but you'll never be happy. The one closest to you will destroy you. And I take the knowledge with me that I killed your child."

I had a sharp intake of breath.

"That's right." He half laughed, then screamed his final words. "Consider it my final gift to you!"

This time it was me who yelled. "Aggghh!" I threw a fireball so large he disintegrated on the spot. I stared at the ashes for a moment, and then turned my attention to Garnout.

He'd managed to get out of his box, and he moved toward me. Wrapping his arms around me, he hugged hard. "All will be well." His words sent instant comfort.

Usually I pass out after a fight like that, but this time I stayed on my feet. I wasn't exactly feeling like the Energizer Bunny, but Garnout and I managed to make it to the main hall.

Cole's chest was bleeding through his shirt, but he was still standing.

Logan had taken a hit to the hindquarters. He'd shifted into human form and sat on the floor, trying to stop the bleeding with his rolled-up shirt. He was beautifully naked, but he didn't seem to care. Both men were surrounded by dead bodies.

"Where's the rest of the team?" I coughed from the stench of death. These men had fought to the end to save my friend and I wouldn't forget it.

"Chasing down a couple of the warlocks who ran away." Cole swayed a bit as he spoke and I sent a healing spell his way. The effort made me even weaker, but I was determined to walk out of there.

We'd made it to the steps when there was a loud *pop* and wind *whooshed* around the room. For a second I thought a tornado had touched down in the center of the room and then I saw her: it was the blonde sorceress, Calinda, who had been with Sphere in Paris.

She threw her hands out and pulled Garnout to her. Her flowing blood red robes whipped around her. "Oh, but my dear, we have so many more games to play." I could see him trying to resist, but her magic was strong.

I tried to hit her with a fireball, but she tossed it aside and slammed me into the wall.

"Little witch, he's mine, and you can have him back when I'm finished—*if* he survives." Cackling, her beautiful face twisted into a cruel smile.

I would not let that bitch take my friend.

Once before, when I was in dire need, Garnout had shared his power. Now I would return the favor. Thrusting my hands outward, I sent everything I had to the wizard. As I did so, I could see Cole doing the same thing. The energy charged through the wizard, arching his back. Garnout's feet hit the ground and it shook.

"No more!" he bellowed. "This stops today, Calinda." Waving his hands, he shoved her against the wall. She struggled, but he was too strong. "I banished you, my love, even though you held my heart in those wicked hands of yours. I prayed, as only a wizard can, that you would learn your lesson."

Calinda wiggled and twisted, but she couldn't move. Her eyes shot darts of fury toward Garnout. "You banished me to Hell, wizard. What lessons would I learn there? My hate only grew, and I knew one day I would be back to destroy you."

Garnout shook his head. "I am weary of your temper, sorceress. I banish thee. I banish thee—"

"No!" Calinda screamed. "I will not go back to purgatory. Stop, please. Garnout." She paused for a moment. "Please, my love." When she spoke this time, it was soft. "I know I've done so many bad things. I was angry, so very angry." The regret was heavy in her voice, and for a moment I believed her.

"I banish thee." Garnout finished the spell.

Her face twisted into an angry scowl and her eyes burned red. "I'll be back, wizard, and next time you and your precious witch won't be allowed to live so long!" She screamed the last word as a wall of flames swallowed her.

The room was silent as we sat there, stunned. For a minute Garnout stared at the wall where Calinda had been, before turning to me.

"It is time to go home, witch." He reached out a hand and pulled me up. Then he did the same for Cole. After restoring our powers, he just disappeared without a word.

I couldn't say I blamed him. He'd been through total crap the last few weeks and he needed to heal. I was kind of looking forward to going home, too.

Twenty-four

Sweet

Saturday

9 a.m.

Potions: 8

Something weird is going on, but I can't figure it out. Sam has been nothing but kind to me since I came home. He took me to Lulu's on the way home from the hangar, where I loaded up on ribs, corn fritters, and blackberry cobbler.

Then he brought me home and fixed me tea while I took a hot shower. Afterward, I returned downstairs to find him on the couch watching a football game.

"Feel better? Do you want to watch a movie or something?" He smiled.

"Nah. This is fine." All I really wanted to do was go to bed and have him hold me. The miscarriage would keep us from doing anything more fun than that for at least the next few weeks. "Sam, are we going to talk about what happened?" Through dinner, every time there was any kind of pause in the conversation, he'd fill it with some inane bit of gossip or news about medical findings. I can spot avoidance a mile away, but I didn't want this thing to eat away at us.

He didn't look at me, but he grabbed my hand. "I think *Master and Commander* is on." He pushed the button on the remote. "I know how much you like that old movie."

Sam was dressed in jeans and a white and green striped buttondown. He must have visited the barber recently because his hair was cut above his ears, where I kissed him.

"*You* are the one who likes that movie, but I never have a problem looking at Russell Crowe." The truth is, Russell's not really my type, but I was trying to get a rise out of Sam. He didn't take the bait.

"Okay, well, we could watch that home and garden channel you like."

"Jesus, Sam. What the hell is going on?" The words came out stronger than I'd meant. "I'm sorry, I didn't mean to say it like that. It's, just . . . Why can't we talk about what happened?"

"What is it you want to discuss, Bronwyn?" He turned to me. "You had a miscarriage; neither of us knew you were pregnant. It was all for the best."

Gah! *All for the best?* Well it was, but it sounded so coldhearted when he said it. Tears formed in my eyes and my nose itched.

"I'm sorry the idea of having a baby with me seems so appalling to you." I jumped up from the couch. "I'm tired and I really want to go to bed." *And blubber like a . . . No!* I was tired of crying. I bit the inside of my lip to stem the tears.

"Damn. That's not what I meant at all, Bron." He reached up, but I shook him off.

I threw up my hands. "Maybe it's the hormones, but I feel unsettled, and I wanted to talk about this but you are acting like a big jerk."

He looked away for a moment and then back. "I'm not going to say it's hormones. I've been a doctor long enough to know that's not a smart thing to tell a woman, but feeling unsettled after what you've been through isn't unusual. And I'm sorry I was a jerk. I was trying to comfort you, and of course it came out all wrong."

I knew something wasn't right with me because right then I wanted to hug him and kick his ass at the same time. Suddenly I needed to be alone. I didn't want to deal with this. Didn't make any sense, I know—I was the one who started it all—but that's just how I felt.

"Sam, I'm sorry, but I'd like you to go." The words came out harsh. I needed him to leave before I said something really stupid. "I just want to crash. I shouldn't have brought this up tonight. I'm too hormonal to talk about it." *And if you say the wrong thing again, I might have to kill you.*

Whoa. He really had to go.

Sam didn't move from the couch. "Let me help you, Bron." He looked at me funny.

I shook my head. "I don't need help, I just want to be alone right now." Geez, how many times did I have to tell him to get the hell out?

Finally, he moved. He hugged me, but I couldn't seem to move my arms around him. He stopped at the door and it was his parting phrase that was my undoing.

"I wished for that baby. I wanted it so bad it's not funny." He turned and stared at me, his face a sad mask. "It's selfish of me, but I thought that if you were pregnant, then you would stop trying to get yourself killed. And maybe, just maybe I'd be able to convince you to marry me. I knew you were taking the pill, but I still had hope, and when I saw the results of that test . . ." He turned back to face me. "I love you more than anything. Call me if you need me." The door slammed, and I was alone.

I sank down onto the couch and cried for a long time, and that's where I woke up this morning. I'm a little embarrassed about my tantrum and I haven't had the courage to call him. He wanted the baby and he loves me so much. And the idea of a baby with him wasn't the worst thing I could think of, but I wondered how he would react if he knew my ex-boyfriend killed our child.

That seems like such a weird thing to say. I didn't even know I was pregnant, barely so, and I'm calling it "our child." I really am losing it.

To keep my mind off things, I've been making potions.

Twice this morning I've checked my eyes for a weird orange glow. I felt possessed last night, and I remembered when that happened to Sam. He'd tried to kill me when he'd been taken over by that nasty warlock Blackstock.

I also said several cleansing spells. One thing is for certain: Losing the baby was sad, but I'm nowhere close to wanting babies. But if I did, I'd want them with Sam.

I guess I need to tell him that.

Be a big girl and dial the phone, Bron. Argh. Being a grown-up really sucks.

Noon
I finally called Sam. He was so cautious about every word he said, it made me laugh. I told him to get his ass over to the house, that I was over my tantrum, and that he'd better bring food.

I've been sifting through my e-mails and boy, had they piled up. I hadn't checked anything since I came back from Africa. Craziness. Zane sent me some gorgeous pictures from Zoë's birthday party. She's such a beautiful child. He has his hands full now, but wait until she hits her teens. Knowing Zane he'll probably hire a private security force to keep the boys away.

Miles sent an agenda for some meetings next Tuesday. I guess I'm headed to Fiji. A girl could do worse. Hopefully the meetings won't run too long and I can catch some rays on the beach.

Oh crap. It's been weeks since I've checked in with Simone. I just realized that. I'll have to call her later. I hear Sam's car. Time to go make nice with my hunky man.

11 p.m.
I'm alone again. Sam had to go up to the nursing home. One of his patients is being moved into Hospice and he wants to check on him. We had a good chat that pretty much went like this.

"Sorry I was a bitch. None of this is your fault."

"It's okay, Bron. You know I love you."

"Yes, and I love you."

Kiss, kiss, and then lunch. I wish I could say it's all better, but it's not, really. I feel like there's a space between us. That sort of thing happens when couples fight, but this felt like something that wouldn't be such an easy fix.

Simone called. I'd left her a message earlier in the day.

About two minutes into our conversation I told her everything that had happened, including the miscarriage.

"Shit, Bron. That's heavy-duty." She had me on speakerphone and I could hear her doing sit-ups. She's dedicated that way—always working out. I guess when you slay demons on a daily basis it's a good idea to keep in shape. She paused for a moment when she realized what I'd said.

"Yep. I'm not really sure how it happened—well, I know *how*, but I was protected." I was in my office and had pulled out my Book of Shadows and was thumbing through it. I'd been writing sticky notes with spells for months and needed to write them in. "So, what's been going on with you?"

She laughed, but it was a frustrated sound. "Well, I've been celibate five days, twenty hours, and three minutes."

I choked. "Excuse me."

"You heard me. Shaman Roy told me that if I turned my sexual needs inward, I might become even more powerful."

I knew Shaman Roy. Well, not really. He'd brought me back from the dead when some warlocks did their best to kill me on my last trip to Los Angeles. The shaman saved my life, but I never had a chance to meet him. "Sounds to me like maybe he wants to get in your pants."

"What?" Simone laughed, this time for real. "Roy? I don't think so. He has no interest in me that way. No." She snorted. "He's been studying up on demon slayers and says that sex is a big part of what makes us tick. But we can learn to use that power in a different way. I've been bored lately. I've only killed three demons this week. So I thought what the hell, I'll give abstinence a try."

This time I chuckled. *Simone without sex? What is going on with the world?* "Well, I feel sorry for whatever guy is around if you happen to fall off the wagon."

Her breathing intensified and I heard a motor running. She was probably on the treadmill. "You've got that right. Any chance you'll be out for a visit?"

"Nah. Not anytime soon. Want to come to Fiji with me next week?"

"No can do, my friend. I'm teaching a fall class and I've got to whip these ignorant puppies into shape."

I feel sorry for the students in her class. If you think she's tough on demons, you should see what happens when you forget your homework. And her tests have sent grown men home in tears.

We chatted for a while longer and then hung up.

I noticed something weird during our conversation. Garnout had left me several notes about sorcery and its power in my Book of Shadows. I have no idea when he did this. The last time he was at the house was months ago. He couldn't possibly have known that he'd be kidnapped by Calinda. Or maybe he did. Garnout usually knows the future, or at least when big things are about to happen.

There were also notes about combining my power to increase strength. Maybe he'd known about Calinda and had tried to warn me. I'd have to ask him about it later. In the meantime, I decided I wanted to know how to defeat an evil sorceress, should I ever come across another one. I had a feeling that someday Calinda would be back, and she would be even tougher to take down after a second visit to Hell.

Twenty-five

Somewhere over the Pacific on the PM's jet
Witches with great friends: 1
Charms: 5
Spells: 15

I'm headed to Fiji to help the prime minister, but man, it's been a wild couple of days. Cole called from Tibet to say he finally had some info on Calinda, and why she wanted Garnout as her boy toy. I have no idea what he was doing in Tibet, and he wouldn't say.

"They've been married for several hundred years," Cole said. "One of our people discovered that in the fourteenth century he'd been married to a witch named Calinda. She was powerful, but when they consummated their relationship, something happened and her power increased a hundredfold."

Here's the thing. Wizards and sorceresses are usually born that way, kind of like high witches. It is possible for one's power to increase over time and become one or the other. But I'd never heard of a high witch becoming a sorceress overnight. It just wasn't done.

"Holy crap! She must have been one of the most powerful high witches on the planet," I said.

"Some people who knew her back then believe she planned the whole thing and used Garnout," Cole continued, "but there's no proof of that. They seemed to get on well for a couple of hundred years and then something happened. Her penchant for war created chaos and more than ten thousand people died. Garnout doesn't reference what conflict that might have been, but he had to banish her in order to return the magical balance to Earth."

I was in my office trying to make sense of Garnout's notes. "So she definitely has a grudge." If Sam had tried to banish me, well, it wouldn't be pretty. Still, I felt sorry for the wizard. It was obvious he loved her, and it must have killed him to banish her again.

"I'd say so."

"Any chance she can get out of Hell again?"

Cole coughed. "This altitude is killing me. It's possible. She's powerful enough, but I don't see her doing it anytime soon. It took her several hundred years the last time."

I didn't know about that. She'd seemed pretty determined to get back at Garnout right before she'd disappeared into that wall of flames.

"By the way, your ex is the one who conjured her back into existence. We found Jason's place where he had the altar and he's definitely the one who brought her back. He used the souls of more than fifty witches and warlocks to do it."

The idea of all those people losing their lives for his malice made me ill. It was just more thing to hate Jason for. Then again, he's already dead, so it's all good.

"Do you think Garnout is really okay? Is he safe?"

Cole was panting now. "Yes. Bron, he's my friend, too. I haven't known him as long as you have but I want him protected. He's one of the wizards who keeps this place, and by that I mean our world, in balance."

I realized how selfish I'd been. I wanted my favorite wizard back because he was my dearest friend and I miss him. But the rest of the world needed him, too.

I sighed. "I forgot to say thank you for what you did in Budapest. If we hadn't shared our powers there's no telling what that bitch would have done."

"It was the only way I could see to save our lives. I was certain she would kill us." He blew out a breath.

"Are you okay? You sound like you are having trouble breathing."

"It's Tibet, Bron. It's kind of high up and I've been climbing a damn mountain while we talked."

A mountain? "Geez, you could have called me back."

"Nah, keeps my mind off the terrain below. I'm not a big fan of heights."

That made me laugh. Big cop man was scared of heights. "Then why the hell are you scaling mountainsides?"

"Work. Trust me, I'd rather be at the dentist getting a root canal."

Yikes. He really was out of his element.

"Oh—whoa. Hey, I'm getting to a part where I really need to concentrate. I'll call you back later."

I sent him a protection spell just in case he decided to go tumbling down the side of the mountain.

I didn't want to bring my spell book out of the protection of my home, but I did make copies of all the notes Garnout left. I'm using my time during the flight to see if I can figure out what the hell he was trying to tell me about combining my powers.

I tried to ask him the few times I've spied on him over the last couple of days, but he ignores me and then shuts down his shields.

I hate puzzles. I'm a smart girl, but my brain just doesn't work that way. Maybe he knows something is going to happen, but he's not exactly sure what. The notes aren't spells. They are more like history lessons in witchcraft and wizardry.

The entries are about the true origins of the craft and why there are different levels of magic and how one goes from being a warlock to a wizard. I'd always thought you were born a wizard, but that isn't necessarily so. In literature we begin to hear about wizards around the eleventh century, but they were around long before that.

There's not a darn thing in here about how to kill a sorceress. But I do have Kira working on that one. She's the queen of the research and totally rocks when it comes to finding the tough answers. And now she has another crack research staff on the other side. Dead people really like to talk.

Last night, before I packed for Fiji, I met her up at the library. That's where I made copies and I left a set for her, too. In addition to being a rockin' lawyer and Queen of the Books, she has a love for the history of magic.

"There's an archive in Budapest. It's too bad you didn't know about all of this while you were there." She flipped on the lights in the front part of the building. The fluorescent bulbs hummed to life like a hive of bees. "The archive at the library there has more magical texts than anywhere else in the world. Next time you go, I'm traveling with you. I think that's where we can find some real answers. But I have some other sources, too."

Suddenly there was a chill and it wasn't from the air conditioning. "Um, Kira . . . who else is here?" The temperature had dropped another twenty degrees. Now I knew why she always wore sweaters even when it was one hundred degrees outside.

She looked around the room. "Arnie's here. He always hangs out in the section for gardening books. It's kind of sad because he hasn't quite mastered picking up the books, but he's working on it. Rosalee is here, she always shows up when you are around. She likes your spunk." She waved. "Mr. Carmichael's over in the World War Two books again, and Jerry is in the romance section. That man can't get enough of romance authors Nora Roberts and Jodi Thomas. He cracks me up."

I watched her as she talked about the dead and she looked more at ease than she had in a long time. "So it doesn't bother you that you are never alone anymore?"

She shrugged. "I've learned to tell them to get lost when I need my space and for the most part they give it to me. Here." She handed me a book. "This is a journal from a J. K. Stone. He was a wizard in the eighteenth century. Take it with you on your trip. I've ordered another copy for the library. He doesn't have much to say about sorceresses, but he did have to fight some pretty nasty wizards who turned to the dark side. No specific spells, but some definite strategy in there. Also," she said as she opened a drawer in her desk, "I ordered this one off the Internet for you a couple of weeks ago. It's the *Black Magic Handbook for Ghouls*. Though I can't imagine any ghoul being bright enough to read."

I laughed. She really was into all of this and had come a long way over the last year. When I first met her she was just getting used to the idea that witches and warlocks were real. She'd known about witches, but she'd never worked with a high witch until she met me. She's become one of my dearest friends and it made my heart happy that she was so determined to find a way to help.

Like I said, I have great friends. If Calinda ever showed up again, we would be ready.

I'm not sure where Sam and I stand right now. Things are still kind of weird. There's no anger or anything. In fact, he's being overly nice. It's like we experienced this big thing that neither of us was really ready for, and now we don't know how to deal with it.

It's weird when you think about it, because he's died a couple of times and so have I, and it would seem that would be a much bigger deal.

Maybe it's just one of those things that takes time. I hope so. We'd hit a really good place in our relationship and it's pissy we have to go through something like this right now.

Oh, well, whining about it isn't helping anything. Time to get back to work.

Fiji
9 p.m.
Charms: 5
Spells: 3

We're in a private residence on the Coral Coast and it's gorgeous. The house belongs to one of Dr. Zocando's friends. Everyone is here to talk about human rights.

They couldn't have picked a more beautiful site. It's more like a compound with one large home and then several smaller ones around it. I'm in a small house that has a thatched roof and opens right onto the beach overlooking the beautiful blue-green water.

It's all very isolated so security isn't as big a concern as we usually have. Still, I made some new protection charms for the prime minister, one to keep in his pocket at all times, the other for under his pillow.

Azir is here, too. I saw him walking on the beach about an hour ago. It was a surprise since he wasn't in my file folder of politicos. I hadn't seen him since Africa.

I was perched on the edge of a beach chair watching the waves, but I sensed his presence before he even came into view.

Dressed in his suit pants with his white shirt unbuttoned at the neck and rolled at the sleeves, he had the total casual *GQ* vibe going. He wasn't wearing shoes and the legs of his pants had also been rolled. Very yummy.

"Did the prime minister call you in?" I leaned back in the chair so I could look up at him.

"Yes. They are discussing the trouble in the Philippines and he wanted some firsthand accounts. How are you, Bronwyn?" He smiled.

"Good. It's hard not to be, in a place like this." I waved a hand toward the ocean.

The sun had just gone down and lanterns had been lit around the beach. Azir stood beside the chair for a minute and then plopped down by me on the ground, never worrying about what the sand might do to his pants. He lives in a desert, so I guess sand is a part of life for him.

We sat in silence for a few moments, both of us staring out at the waves.

"How are your mom and sister? Did Shera go back to school?" Azir's sister, Shera, is a total brain and she's also beautiful. I'd met his family when I had to protect him from some evil dudes a few months back. His family changed the way I viewed the incredibly wealthy. Oh, they have their problems, but for the most part they are loving.

"Both of them are well. Shera's heading to California and in fact, she will be doing her dissertation at the same university where your friend Simone runs her research project. It was Simone who convinced her to go out there."

Well, Simone and I were going to have a talk. I had no idea she was conversing with the Sheik and his sister. She hadn't said a word when I spoke with her last week. "Well, at least she'll know someone, even if it is a demon slayer."

Azir laughed. "I know she'll be safe if Simone is around. There isn't much that gets past her."

"True. Is your mom running the foundation?" I was wearing a long, slinky skirt and a white tank, which had been fine when the sun was still up. Now my arms were a little chilly, and I rubbed them.

"Yes. She's traveling a great deal. We're working on an initiative to open one hundred new safehouses for women and children around the world in the next four years. It's a big project, but so far she's doing well."

I whistled. "Wow! That *is* impressive."

He clasped his hands over his knees. "It's never enough." I couldn't see his face, but he sounded sad.

I touched his shoulder. I always forget about the chemistry between us and I was startled by the tiny spark of energy that sizzled in my hand. "You don't get to feel bad about what you do, Azir. You help so many. Countless women and children owe their lives to you."

"How are things at your home?" He crossed his legs in the sand.

I had a feeling he was asking about Sam. Azir always seems to sense when my emotional state isn't perfect. But I wasn't about to tell him about the miscarriage and my worry that Sam and I weren't as close as we had been.

"Well, everything's just peachy back home." I threw in a little southern drawl for fun. "We did have a run-in with a sorceress, who tried to kill me and Garnout."

Azir's head snapped around. "Are you okay? Is there anything I can do?"

The sheik is such a caring man. He carries the weight of the world on his shoulders. If he's your friend, and even though we have our differences, he's mine. The man will do anything for a friend.

"That's sweet of you. I've had the misfortune to meet her up-close and personal. I'm fine, and so is the wizard."

I stopped talking. Something made my skin tingle. I stood up and looked around.

"What is it?" Azir jumped up and moved next to me.

"Someone protected by black magic is near." As fast as the feeling came, it evaporated. I sent my mind out to see who it was, but didn't see anything. They must have spotted me and immediately masked their power. "Huh. That's interesting."

"Did you find them?"

"No, but I will. The island isn't that big and there are less than thirty people at the compound. I'll find them." I stretched my arms out and tried to see if I sensed anything else, but there was nothing.

I moved toward the little house where I'd been staying. "Hold on a minute. I want to get something for you." I went to my room and picked up a couple of the protection charms I'd made.

When I came back out, Azir was standing in the doorway.

"Here." I handed him the charms. "Put one of these in your pocket at all times, and don't forget to switch out when you change. And put this one under your pillow."

He sniffed it and wrinkled his nose. "It's very feminine."

I laughed. "Well, a big macho man like you can handle it."

"Thank you." He put the charms in his pocket. He started to walk down the path and then he stopped, still facing away from me. "I miss talking to you." Then he continued on his way.

I missed talking to him, too, but I didn't have a chance to tell him. He was halfway down the beach before I found my tongue.

I don't really have much time to think about what it all might mean. I need to find who it was with all that black magic.

Twenty-six

Fiji
Wednesday
10 a.m.
Slightly tanned witches: 1 (Okay, so it's not a real
tan. It's pink, but it counts.)
Spells: 7
Charms: 2

Lucky for me, no one around here seems to be in a hurry to do business. Some guy from Greece and another from Moscow aren't here yet, so the meetings have been postponed until tomorrow.

That's all good with me because I was up all night trying to figure out who my magical visitor was. After several spells and a trek around the compound, I came up with absolutely nothing.

I've put wards on the prime minister's quarters and insisted he carry a charm with him at all times.

The PM and I had breakfast this morning out on his veranda. We'd been planning our strategy and I'd discovered there were several people he wanted me to read, including Dr. Zocando. This surprised me since I thought they were the best of friends.

I'd just swallowed some juice when he mentioned the African diplomat, and I almost choked. "I thought you two were close."

The PM has a distinct tell when he has to discuss something unpleasant. He always looks down at his fingers and then away. "We are friends, but I witnessed some things in Africa that made me uncomfortable. I don't know if he had anything to do with it, but I can't be sure. I just want you to check him out."

I'd met the doctor a few months ago and tried to read him with no luck. And I tried again at his camp in Africa. Then it dawned on me: he might be my black magic dude. Of course, I had no proof, so it wouldn't do any good to mention that to the prime minister. But at least I had a target.

"Could you at least give me some idea of what kinds of things made you suspicious?"

The PM looked down at his files. "I thought I saw the plans for a diamond mine. The one where your family was taken, but I can't be certain. He gathered the papers too quickly for me to see."

Of all the ignorant . . . Okay, the PM's not ignorant. Quite the opposite, and he's never been one to jump to conclusions. "Sir, don't you think it might have been a good idea to share your thoughts while we were still in Africa?"

He cocked an eyebrow. "You'd already left when I saw the

papers, and as I said, it was brief." His tone was biting. "Had I any *real* proof, I would have contacted you."

"I apologize, sir. But if he did have anything to do with my brother and father being kidnapped, I'm going to have to kill him."

The PM studied me for a moment. "Hence the reason I waited to tell you. Please don't do anything rash until we are certain."

I nodded in agreement.

We were finishing up our chat and preparing to leave for the meeting when Miles came in.

He was dressed in a ridiculous pinstriped suit and tie that was absurd on the island. Even the PM had gone without his requisite tie. Miles was mopping tiny beads of sweat on his brow as he came out onto the porch. It was hard for me to believe that he'd almost died a few weeks ago.

"They've delayed the meetings until tomorrow morning." He sneered when he saw me.

I smiled sweetly.

"Several of the guests were caught in bad weather. The earliest they can be here is eleven tomorrow." He said the words a tad bit snarkily and his head sort of bobbled like it was too big for his neck.

I'm not sure I've ever met a more annoying man, and I keep saving his life. I have to stop doing that.

"Make certain the rest of our guests are comfortable. Check with Dr. Zocando, perhaps we could take a boat out and do some diving." The prime minister turned to me. "Would you like to join us?"

I didn't answer his question, but the answer was hell, no! I don't know why the idea of plummeting to the bottom of the ocean with a tiny mask and tank scares the hell out of me, but it does. "You said that you need to check with Dr. Zocando. Why?"

"Did you read the bloody files?" Miles was thumbing through

the papers in his hand. "This is Dr. Zocando's property. He was kind enough to let us use it for the conference."

I did read the file several times last night but didn't see anything about that. I thought it belonged to one of the doctor's friends.

Turning away from Miles, I faced the prime minister. "I wasn't going to say anything, but I sensed dark magic last night when I was out on the beach. I searched for hours but couldn't find who it was. I don't think it would be a good idea for you to be out in the middle of the ocean with a bunch of people you don't know."

There were a few seconds of silence. He frowned. "You felt it here?"

"Yes, but only for a few seconds. Whoever it was spotted me and quickly masked their magic."

He handed some files to Miles. "Perhaps our guests would enjoy some snorkeling. Does that meet with your approval, Bronwyn?"

I walked toward the doorway where Miles stood. "Yes, but don't go out too far and keep your charm with you at all times."

I took another charm out of my pocket. "You, too." I handed it to Miles. "And get out of that ridiculous suit. You look like a moron."

When I left the PM's room, I went in search of Dr. Zocando. I wasn't exactly sure what I'd do when I found him. It didn't matter. His assistant said he'd be out for the rest of the afternoon. I went back to my room and sent my mind out for the doctor magically, but I couldn't get a sense of him. It doesn't happen often. I mean, most times I can pinpoint an ordinary person across the world and shove my way into their brain, but occasionally I get stumped.

The few times I'd been around him, I never sensed any magic. Very strange.

I've been skulking around the island trying to see if I can find a secret hideout or something, but no luck. I did get some color on my pasty skin, so it wasn't all bad. I'm calling Cole to see if he can do a little digging on Dr. Zocando for me.

I wonder if he ever made it off that mountain.

4 p.m.

I fell asleep. Right in the big middle of trying to find Zocando, I zonked out on the bed. Probably has something to do with the fact that I hadn't slept since I arrived. Anyway, I feel loads better.

I left a message for Cole, but I haven't heard back from him. My cell service is a little iffy here, but I also left a message for Sam, to let him know all is well.

When I woke up from my nap I had this sudden urge to talk to him, to make certain that everything was right between the two of us. I'd had the most luscious dream about him giving me a massage. He'd made me strip and lay on the bed. Then he rubbed hot jasmine-scented oil on my shoulders. Pure heaven. His hands were sliding down my back when something woke me up.

I was very disappointed.

This part of the beach is pretty isolated, but some of the guests were outside snorkeling around the reef.

I sent a quick mental nudge out to see if I could find Dr. Zocando, but I didn't see anything. I'd just about decided to go out and get some sun when my cell rang.

"Bron, it's Kira."

"Hey. Is everything okay?" I was searching through my things for something to wear.

"Oh, yeah. Well, um, Margie and Billy eloped."

I dropped the pair of shorts I had in my hand. "Whoa. That's so cool. When?"

"Last night. She called me from Vegas. They hopped on a plane and did it. We didn't have time for details. They were going to eat lobster, but she wanted me to call you. She said, 'Tell Bron that love always finds a way.' Which, if you ask me, is a little corny, but it's sweet. She sounded so happy." Kira's tone was wistful. She might be a barracuda of a lawyer and a stern librarian, but she was a romantic all the way.

"Oh, I'm so happy for her." I really was. I'd been worried that our little argument at the picnic had done a lot of harm. "I guess she finally convinced him to give her the ring."

Kira giggled. "Yep. I had a feeling when I saw them at Lulu's the other night. He'd walked her out to the car and you couldn't fit a penny between them while he was kissing her good-bye."

I smiled. "When they come back we should throw them a party." I picked up the shorts I'd dropped and threw them back in the drawer. Thirsty, I grabbed a bottle of water and twisted off the top.

"I'm already on it. They both took off for a few days but will be back on Saturday. Margie said sooner, if their money didn't hold out."

That wasn't likely to happen. While Billy acted the good old boy routine with his beat-up pickup truck and cowboy hat, he owned one of the larger ranches in Sweet. He had an enormous house all to himself. It would be a big change for Margie, who, up until a year ago, had shared a double-wide trailer with her sister. When her sister married, Margie had moved into a small apartment in town, right on the square.

We might have had our differences in the past few weeks, but I had a lot of respect for the woman. She'd put herself through nursing school and had carved out a life for herself that she was proud of. Her friendship meant a lot to me.

"Well, let me know what you need and be sure to pull Ms. Johnnie and Ms. Helen in for the food. If we don't let them do the catering, they'll ground us both."

"You aren't lying. Listen, I've been doing a lot of research on the sorceress thing. Like you, they draw their power from different elements. But there's no way of knowing what provides Calinda's main source. Once you find that out, then you have to get her away from it, and then about six high witches, like you, need to gather and spell her to death. See? Easy."

I snorted. "Well, since there are only about seven high witches on the planet, and there's not a chance in hell we're all going to be together in the same place at the same time, I think we need a new plan."

We, all of the high witches, are aware of one another, but seldom meet. It's too dangerous for us and for anyone around us. As constant targets for warlocks who want more power, to kill two high witches at once . . . well, it wouldn't be pretty.

I have a tentative friendship with one of the witches, Callie, but she stays in Australia most of the time. She did help me with the PM a few months ago, when I'd gone down for the count.

Kira sighed. "I know we need a new plan. A wizard would be good, but then look at what she did to Garnout. I mean, he's okay now, but if she was that tricky once, she could be again. I've been e-mailing back and forth with a librarian in Budapest. He's been really helpful. Maybe he'll come across something."

"Cole and his crew are on it, too." I chewed on my lip. "Do you mind if I give him your number? I'm kind of busy trying to deal with something here, but I don't want you guys to stop looking for a way to defeat her if she comes back."

"We won't. And sure, give him my number. Is everything okay there?" She sounded worried.

"It's all good. Nothing I can't handle."

I meant what I said. I can handle whatever comes my way. There hasn't been any trouble so far on the island, but I'm ready for some action. My body must be getting back on track because I feel better than I have in weeks.

Someone's knocking on the door. Hmmm . . .

Twenty-seven

Fiji

8 p.m.

Bad witches with sexy thoughts: 1

Is it cheating if you think about doing the nasty with another man? I hope not. I wouldn't do it in a million and two years. I'm totally devoted to Sam, but *whoa*—that Azir is some powerful stuff.

While I'd been talking to Kira I'd put on my new one-piece bathing suit with tiny red and white flowers all over it. I was still really bloated, but I didn't care. It was hot and I wanted some time in the ocean.

When I heard the knock, I just wrapped a towel around me and went to the door.

There stood Azir, in board shorts and nothing else. His body was as ripped as they get. The sight of him was enough to turn a good witch bad. Then he smiled and my knees went hooblie-booblie. I had to lean against the door for support. Don't get me wrong. I'm a solid, one-man woman these days, and Sam's my man. But it's hard not to appreciate a hottie like Azir.

I smiled back. There was something about seeing one of the wealthiest and most powerful men in the world in a pair of blue and white surfer-dude board shorts.

"Out for a swim?" Lame, but it was the only thing I could think of to say. In my mind I was running my hand up and down his washboard abs.

He held up two masks. "I thought you might like to do some snorkeling. Some of the other guests say this side of the reef is teeming with fish."

"I can't. I'm working." The words came out in a rush. There was no way I could tell him that hanging out with him half naked wasn't good for my sanity.

He looked down at my body wrapped in the towel and one of his eyebrows rose.

"Well . . . I was going to work." The last thing I needed to do was swim next to a guy who'd just give me cardiac arrest with his smile.

Crossing his arms against his chest, he leaned on the door.

"Fine. I'll go snorkeling with you." I smiled to take the bite out of my words.

I *should* say I had a terrible time, but it was a blast. He didn't lie about the reef; there was an amazing array of fish. The water was really shallow on the side where we were and it was as if the entire ocean had come to sunbathe. We saw stingrays, puffer fish, and a zillion others I couldn't possibly name.

We swam next to each other and would point whenever we saw something amazing, which was often. I wasn't sure how long we'd been out, but my backside was feeling warm. I motioned to Azir that I was going to the shore and he followed me in.

There were two large chaises just outside the door of my little house and we plopped down.

"I can't wait to tell Zoë that I saw Nemo." I used the towel to dry off my arms and legs. "She's going to be very jealous." Zoë had a fascination with all things Disney. Her rooms at Zane's various homes were filled with stuffed animals and she carried a small pack of DVDs and her own little player, so she could watch them whenever she wanted.

He laughed. "I haven't seen the film, is that the small clown fish?" Azir didn't bother drying off; he just leaned back and let the sun do its business.

"Yep. He gets lost and his dad has to go find him. It's one of those movies made for kids and adults. It's old, but Zoë loves it."

"How is Zane? Any more trouble?" Azir stretched out the length of the chair.

"As far as I know, things have been quiet for him. They did a short tour after the concert in Los Angeles, and now he's back home for a bit. Zoë wants to attend a regular school. She is already tired of the tutor, and she misses having other kids around."

We sat in silence for a few minutes. At first I wasn't sure what I was hearing; then I realized it was Azir's light snoring. I didn't know if I should be offended that he was so bored with me, or delighted because he felt so comfortable hanging out that he could fall asleep. I chose to believe the latter.

While he rested, I decided to change. I felt antsy and wanted to see if I could get my laptop to work. Much like my cell phone service, the satellite link on my computer is hit-and-miss here.

After throwing on some shorts and a tank, I grabbed my laptop and took it outside. Azir continued to sleep. I still didn't have a signal, but I studied the notes I'd gathered before I left.

Yikes! Magic, I feel it covering the island. Someone is up to something. I'd better check it out.

11 p.m.

Well, that was interesting. By the time I made it to the door, the magic had disappeared. My body still tingled with it, so I knew it hadn't been my imagination. I sent my mind out several times through the evening, but didn't find a damn thing.

I don't know who it is playing games. At dinner, Azir and the prime minister went through the entire list of attendees at this minisummit. No one on this island is supposed to have any kind of magical security, except me, which means someone really is up to no good.

Dr. Zocando returned to the island during our meal, but "retired to his room." At least that's what his assistant told us. I don't believe him.

Speaking of assistants, are there sharks in Fiji? I'm seriously considering turning Miles into fishbait. The idiot is driving me and everyone here insane.

Throughout the meal tonight he kept coming in with phone calls for the prime minister, to the point where the PM told him to hold them all, he'd return them later.

"My god, man. Unless the Queen has died, I'd prefer not to be interrupted again." The PM is the poster boy for patience and it takes a lot to get to him.

Miles had this hurt look on his face, like the PM had slapped him. I know it's awful, but I had to bite the inside of my lip and look down at my plate to keep from laughing.

The way I see it, this is Miles's first trip back since the shooting and he's trying to make up for lost time. Miles is so in love with the PM it's ridiculous, but the feeling isn't mutual. The PM appreciates Miles's organizational skills, but that's about it.

Miles was a nasty little mosquito looking for blood tonight and he had to be swatted down. I should say I didn't enjoy the dressing down of the snitty Brit, but I totally dug it.

I digress.

What I'd really like to know right now is how Zocando is able to block me. I couldn't get a fix on him all day, and now he's back and I still can't get a lock. The weird thing is, I don't detect any magic protecting him.

I pretended to get lost a little earlier in the evening. I'd excused myself to the ladies' room and snuck up the stairs to the long hallway where I'd seen the doctor's assistant the day before.

There was an armed guard stationed outside his door. I thought about cloaking and slipping past, but he was right in front of it. There was no way to open the door without him seeing me, and I wanted to be a little more prepared. I'll wait a few hours, and then see what I can do.

First I'm going to take one last stroll on the beach. After our meetings tomorrow morning we're headed home.

I'm missing Sam big-time. I hope all the weirdness between us will be gone when I get home. I should have asked him to come to

Fiji with me, but since Azir's here that probably wouldn't have been the brightest of ideas.

For some reason I'm feeling wistful. I thought my body was back on track, but maybe I'm not as together as I'd like to think.

Perhaps a stroll will help me clear my head. I need to devise some solid plans on what to do about the black magic on this island.

Twenty-eight

Sweet, Texas
Friday
9 p.m.
Dead guys: 3 (But I only killed one)
Spells: 4

Trust your instincts. I keep telling myself that over and over so it will finally sink in. I knew the first time I met Dr. Zocando there was something wrong with the guy.

I wasn't mistaken.

My last stroll on the sand was a bit more exciting than I'd planned.

A full moon hung above the dark water and the stars seemed even closer than they do in Sweet on a clear summer night. I'd walked halfway down the beach when I saw Azir standing behind a tree staring out onto the water. I almost turned to walk the other way, but he looked so sad and intense.

"There's a corny saying about a penny for your thoughts. How much would yours be worth?" It seemed funny to offer pennies to one of the wealthiest guys in the world. Smiling, I moved beside him and turned toward the ocean.

He didn't say anything at first. Leaning back against the palm tree, he stuck his hands in his pockets. "I'm afraid my thoughts aren't worth much." There was a strange look in his eyes, almost like he was angry.

I laughed, trying to lighten the mood. "I seriously doubt that, Azir. What has you, of all people, looking wistful tonight? Are you worried about the meetings tomorrow? Everyone here is on your side. It's more about who will pony up the big bucks to help set up these programs."

He grunted.

"What? Is there something you and the PM haven't told me?" I cocked my head and stared at him.

"It's nothing to do with work." He turned to walk away.

I grabbed his arm and sparks sizzled in my hand. He tried to shake it off, but I held tight. I didn't understand why he was acting this way. We'd had such a wonderful day.

"Azir, you know you can tell me anything."

Using his other hand he pried my fingers from his arm. "No, Bronwyn. Not this time. I need to go."

I knew something was really wrong, but I couldn't figure out what had happened between dinner and now. The three of us—the PM, Azir, and myself—had talked and set up a plan to investigate Dr. Z. In hushed tones we discussed strategies about what we could do. Everything had ended on a positive note.

Now this.

Azir took a few steps away and turned. He shook his head in an exasperated way and waved his arm. "I don't know what's wrong."

There was a long pause. I'd taken a step back at the gruffness in his voice.

"In my country . . . men don't discuss feelings or troubles. We do what must be done, and we move on."

"That's the way men are in every country, Azir. What feelings are you talking about? Did I say something to make you or the prime minister angry?"

He frowned. "No, it has nothing to do with you."

I knew whatever it was weighed heavy on him. For once I kept my mouth shut and didn't push.

"My mother—" he began the sentence, but stopped. "With my father's death, my mother is now free to do as she pleases."

"Is she okay?" I adored his mother and sister. They were head-strong, wonderful women.

He shrugged. "She is fine. She wishes to take a lover, or so my sister tells me." He shook the cell phone in his hand. "Why do they insist on informing me of these things? I do not need to know."

Suddenly it all clicked. Sherah must have just called him with the news. Azir had been incredibly loyal to his father, even when he thought the man might be trying to kill him. Turned out his dad was a really good guy.

But I could just imagine how Azir might see his mother wanting a new boyfriend as a bad thing. I wanted to point out that before he died, Azir's father had been seeing another woman while still married to Azir's mother, but this didn't seem like the right time.

"Is there some kind of mourning period or something she has to go through before she can date?" I had no idea what kind of traditions he had in his religion. Back home, I have friends who started dating long before their divorces were final. And if there was a death, all bets were off. Mr. Mackey started dating Ms. Johnnie two *weeks* after his wife died, and no one said a word.

"She and my father were estranged, but she observed *iddah*, the four months and ten day mourning period that is our tradition."

This time it was me who shrugged. "I'm sorry, but I don't understand why this upsets you. I mean, I do in general, but she's a big girl and she should be able to move on with her life."

"In my head I know what you say is true." Azir pointed to his forehead. "But here"—he put a hand to his heart—"it is difficult for me to imagine my mother with someone new. Would it not bother you, if your mother began dating a new man?"

That made me think. "I see what you mean. Yes, it would bug me big-time." I made a funny face. "Yuck, I totally get it." The idea of my mom with someone else was downright repulsive.

He smiled. "You see, I can say nothing, but I don't have to like it."

Azir turned away for a second, as if he heard something in the dense jungle behind us.

There was a tiny whistling sound, and then he grabbed his neck and fell onto his side. As I was reaching down to check on him, I heard the sound again. Something stung my neck. I touched the point of entry. *Poison darts? Who knew?* I passed out.

When I woke up I was strapped to a hospital bed. Freaking out shot to the top of my list when I wiggled and discovered my legs had also been tied.

I like some pretty crazy stuff, but being strapped to a hospital bed is not on my fantasy list. The room was dark, and I couldn't see anything. There was the smell of antiseptic.

Using my magic I concentrated on the straps. Nothing happened. Thinking maybe I was tired, I did it again. Zippo.

Great. Where the hell am I? My powers had been bound by powerful magic. I tried to see the knots of a spell, but I couldn't quite make it all out.

Crying was a valid option in that particular moment, but I made myself pull it together. I couldn't be a baby, at least not then. *I can have a total nervous breakdown later.*

My brain hurt, but I pushed myself to remember what had happened. I'd been on the beach with Azir. We had had been talking about his troubles with his mother.

Azir had gone down and when I reached for him . . . *The dart in my neck—they'd poisoned us both!* I prayed he was still alive.

"Azir?" My throat was tight and I needed a drink of water.

Silence.

I tried again. "Azir?"

There was a groan to my left. No way to tell if it was male or female. I sent my mind out again to see if I could detect anything but all I saw was darkness.

I heard something creak and a light shone through the crack of the door, making me blink. Two figures came in and the room flooded with light.

I squeezed my eyes shut, then opened them slowly. I was in a small, hospital-like room, only the walls were rock. I wasn't sure but it looked like a cave, much like the rooms I'd seen in Africa when I'd found Sam and the children.

"I see the witch is awake. Good. We may proceed." My eyes still wouldn't focus, probably because of the drug on the dart, but I knew the voice.

Dr. Zocando.

A woman walked closer; she seemed familiar. It took me a minute, but I realized she looked exactly like the nurse I'd seen taking the blood from the children. I'd killed her. I'd been certain of it, and if I hadn't, the blast from the explosion would have.

From the dour look on her face, she didn't seem at all happy to see me. She held something in her right hand and rolled it toward the bed. Just as I realized it was an IV pole, she jammed a needle in my arm.

"Hey! What the hell?"

She sneered and put tape on my arm to hold the needle in place.

"You've met Melini. She wasn't at all happy when you killed her sister." Dr. Zocando came into view. "To answer your question: I am saving my country."

The nurse pushed a button, and I looked down to see my blood shushing through the plastic tubing.

"I gave at the office." I tried to keep my voice light. I didn't want him to know I was scared crapless.

He *tsk*ed. I hate when people do that.

The fear was replaced by anger.

"Well, the least you could do before you kill me is explain to me how taking my blood will save your country."

"Your blood has healing properties and is only part of an experiment. No, it's your *powers* that will help me save Africa from the plague it suffers."

Power vibrated in the room and for the first time I saw Dr. Zocando for what he really was. A warlock.

"How?"

He walked around to the other side of the bed. "How did I mask my powers from you?" Grinning, he waved his hand over himself. "Like this." The energy dissipated from the room.

"I had to learn as a boy to hide my power from the elders in the village. There hadn't been a warlock born there in hundreds of years. They were suspicious of me because I seemed to learn everything so much faster than the other children. In the end I had to kill them all. A pity. I loved my mother, but even *she* had begun to eye me with fear.

"Ah, but you do not need a history. You only want to know the future. You will die, witch. Once I have your powers for my own, I can do so much more. See, I only have the power to destroy, but you can heal."

My mind whirled. I had to get the hell out of there and I didn't have a clue how to do it. I looked to the left and saw Azir tied to the bed. He was asleep, but his face was contorted in pain.

"What have you done to him? You don't need him. Let him go!"

Dr. Zocando gave me a fake frown and pursed his lips. "He's only dreaming. I've made his worst fears a reality. He's going to watch his family die over and over again. The stress of the constant fear will drive him mad." Zocando said it in a singsong voice, like "whoop-de-doo, going to drive the Sheik crazy, it's such a wonderful day. La-de-da."

The cruelty ate at me.

"Too bad he was spending time with the wrong witch at the wrong time." The doctor smiled, but it wasn't a happy look.

I must have blanched. *Azir was here, and being tortured because of me.*

"None of that matters now, because you won't be around to worry about it much longer."

This insane creep's babbling was getting on my nerves in a big way.

Think, Bronwyn.

My mind was still heavy with the drug he'd given me and I was losing blood fast.

I've been in this position many times. There was Jason in college. But I'd also been attacked by a group of warlocks a few years ago. After they bound my powers, they tied me to a spit. Then there was . . .

Dr. Zocando was right. This was no time to think about the past. It only weakened me more. I wanted to see Sam again, and even my snotty cat, Casper. I wanted to eat Lulu's fried chicken and throw a huge party for Margie and Billy.

I don't know what happened, but I must have passed out again while thinking my happy thoughts. I drifted back to Sweet in search of Sam. I found him in his office. "Sam?"

He looked up. "Bronwyn? What's wrong? You're doing that fading thing again."

I stared down at my hands and I could see right through them. That idiot Dr. Zocando hadn't known about my newest power. Hell, *I* hadn't known I could really send my form through astral projection until that night in the jungle. I'd been able to send my *image* for years, but not my body. It was such a dumb thing to forget. So much had happened since Africa, I hadn't thought about it much.

"I need help. We're in Fiji in a cave somewhere. Call the prime minister. Tell him Dr. Zocando also has Azir. I love you." The effort to speak drained the last of my powers. "I'm dying, baby. I'm sorry. I love you so much."

"No!" Sam jumped up from behind his desk and ran toward me, but I could feel myself pulling away. He disappeared. As I slid back into the blackness I wondered if Sam had really heard me or if it had all been a dream. . . .

Twenty-nine

Sweet, Texas
Saturday
9 a.m.
Ready-to-go witches: 1

Oh, jeez. I did it again. I keep falling asleep in the middle of writing in my journal. It's been a busy forty-eight hours.

The last thing I'd written was about seeing my hunky love.

Saying good-bye to Sam had been tough. I felt like I'd disappointed him, Garnout, Azir, and everyone else I cared about.

Something funny, a clicking sound in my head, made me think time really *was* up.

After that, well, quite honestly, I thought I was dead. I couldn't really wrap my mind around anything. There was only darkness, but I was alert. Then there was this terrible pain in my chest and fire burned through my body.

Dr. Zocando stood over me with a large syringe. "You can't die yet, witch. I'm not finished."

The fire burned through my brain and every sense went on high alert. He must have shot me with adrenaline. My arms and legs twitched, needing to move.

I twisted my head around and saw Azir still tied to his bed. But I noticed a sliver of one brown eye just below his lashes. He was awake. I didn't know if he could really see me, but I winked at him. Don't ask me why. I just wasn't ready to give up on either one of us.

The idiot doctor had given me a second chance and he didn't even know it. Oh, my powers were still bound, but my mind was as clear as the ocean water Azir and I had gone snorkeling in earlier that day.

The crazed Dr. Zocando would try to take my powers, but I'd be ready for him.

The blood still flowed from my arm. I looked down at the tubing. "If you want to take my powers, you might want to think twice about draining me of all my blood. You can't take something like that from a dead person." I smirked.

The sudden attitude shocked him and he frowned. He pointed to my arm. "You were only supposed to take a pint!" He screamed at the nurse.

She hurriedly slipped the IV from my arm. She did it too fast and blood spurted up and landed on all three of us.

Something about the blood really sent him over the crazy cliff. "Idiot!" He barked. "She could be tainted!" Moving around to the other side of the bed, he grabbed her by the throat.

I should have been insulted that he thought I might have tainted blood, but I was enthralled by the drama playing out before me.

The fear in the nurse's eyes almost made me feel sorry for her. Well, not really. Lifting her with one hand, he slammed her into the cave wall. I had to contort my neck to see what was going on, but it wasn't pretty. Her eyes grew wider and then the life force slid out of her as he slammed her head into the wall again.

I turned back to see Azir was watching the whole thing. Dr. Zocando was too busy beating the crap out of the nurse to pay attention to either one of us.

"Can you move?" I mouthed the words.

He shook his head and showed me his restraints. Then he shut his eyes.

Dr. Zocando came back to the bed. "I detest ignorance. Her sister was equally stupid. I told her to kill the children once she'd taken their blood. Her ignorance killed her. Stupid women."

Of course I wanted to say something snarky, but it wasn't the time. I watched as he moved to a table near the wall. There was a crash cart and several trays of medical instruments. I had a feeling these were all considered torture toys to the doc? There was no telling what kind of evil experiments he'd carried out here.

The man had to be stopped.

This time, when he came over to the bed he had a spell book. He dribbled something on me that smelled like rubbing alcohol with a mustier scent.

"I'm happy to be rid of you. Once I'm finished here, I will destroy your brother. The both of you cost me millions when you shut down my diamond mine. And your brother has always meddled, getting in the way of my men, endearing himself to my people. The only reason I'd kept him alive was because your family or his friends always paid the ransom. But I don't need their money anymore. I will enjoy killing him, almost as much as I will you. Time to die, witch."

I snorted. "I swear. You guys are so predictable. Just once, I'd like to hear a warlock use an original phrase. You goin' down bee-yatch." I did my best impression of someone from the hood. It was horrible, but I didn't imagine Dr. Zocando spent much time watching bad American movies with terrible stereotypes.

"Or maybe. Death be not . . . well, hell. I can't remember, but it's Shakespeare or one of those guys. It would still be better than 'You will *die now*.'" I lowered my voice for that "Luke, I am your father" kind of drama.

There was a noise out in the hall and Dr. Zocando glanced at the door. He moved his hand and the bolt slid into place. "I must hurry."

He began to chant and for a split-second I panicked. The power swirled around the room and I could feel mine building.

Someone banged on the door and Zocando faltered, turning toward the door. It only took that split-second for me to make my move. To take my powers he had to unbind them first. I used my mind to toss the book from his hands.

He was powerful so I had to move fast. I didn't have time to pull through the restraints so I pointed a finger and whispered, "Burn, baby, burn."

I sent the fire to his brain.

He screamed and grabbed his head. "No! No!" He kept hitting the top of his head like a manic monkey.

I sent a quick burn through the right wristband, and with one hand free I tossed everything I had at him. It was the combination of fire and force that slammed him into the cave wall. His eyes were wild and his screams bloodcurdling.

Then there was nothing left but a pile of ash.

"Die, warlock." I spat out the sarcasm.

I heard Azir snicker behind me.

I laughed with him. "Well, I didn't say *I* had to be original."

There was a gunshot and the prime minister and Miles busted through the door both holding small pistols. They looked more like the Apple Dumpling Gang than Wyatt Earp, but I was so happy to see them.

"About time you guys showed up." The PM rushed to the bed and undid the restraints on my feet while I let loose the one on my left wrist. "How did you know where we were?"

"Sam called Cole, and then they both called us. It was Cole's team who helped us locate you."

"Well, yay, team!" I scooted to the side of the bed.

Azir was released from his bindings and jumped up. We both stood at the same time. My legs were a bit more wobbly than his and he rushed over to help the PM keep me upright.

"Who's the bloody pile of ashes?" Miles quipped. He now had on bright yellow Bermuda shorts, boat shoes, and a T-shirt that said, "You've been boned at Bones Bar." The guy's a total weirdo, but I was grateful he was there.

"Dr. Zocando." Azir lifted my arm and wrapped it around him. "Our Bronwyn dispensed with him rather cleverly. She is an amazing woman."

"I'm sorry, Prime Minister, but I really had no choice but to kill him."

"That's quite evident, my girl. Any idea what the bloke was up to?" he asked as we passed by the ashes.

"Well, he was a warlock." I coughed a little. I needed a glass of water. "He used those poor children in Africa to try to come up with some kind of AIDS cure—the bastard. He thought if he mixed my blood with the children who had survived the disease that he would come up with some kind of vaccine. That, or if he had my power he could heal the country. He was friggin' insane so it's really hard to decipher his thought process. All I know is that he wanted me dead, and I wasn't about to let that happen."

We'd made it to the doorway. Miles still had his gun pointed. "Miles, put that thing down before you hurt someone," I said.

"Like hell," the snippy Brit shot back. "See that bloke?" He pointed to a dead guard in the hallway. "He tried to attack us. I'm not taking any chances." He pulled the gun up in a stance that would make Clint Eastwood proud.

I laughed. "Are you telling me you shot a man to save me, Miles?"

He shrugged. "Not really. The prime minister killed him, but I was his backup."

I paused and turned to the PM. My eyes watered. "Sir, thank you."

He shook his head. "No need for that, my dear. You've saved us all more than once."

We made it to a long stairway. "I'm good, guys. I can take it from here."

Azir and the PM wouldn't let go.

I was serious. I didn't need the help, but I held on. It seemed to make them both feel better.

Once we made it up the hallway I had expected to be somewhere in the tropical forest, but we weren't. We were inside Dr. Zocando's house.

There was some commotion in the big room as we entered and we saw several people running toward us. The PM had sent word and these people were rushing to help. Of course, I didn't know that at the time. It was a mob and I pushed the PM and Azir behind me as I put up a shield.

"No, Bronwyn!" the prime minister yelled as he stumbled to the floor. "They are here to help."

I immediately put my hand down and scrunched up my face. "Um. Oops. Sorry about that."

Azir belly-laughed.

I shot him my most evil glare, but he only smiled wider.

I finally made it home on Thursday and Sam was waiting at the hangar with a bag filled with Lulu's strawberry shortcake.

I love that man. We still couldn't make love because my body is continuing to heal, but we did everything else we could. And we are a very creative couple. The weirdness that was there before I left is gone, and I'm not going to question where it went.

Time to get ready. We're throwing a party at the new community center to celebrate Margie and Billy's engagement. The whole town is invited. Kira and I are decorating and Ms. Helen and Ms. Johnnie are providing the "vittles," as Ms. Johnnie calls them. She must be watching *The Beverly Hillbillies* on Nick at Nite again.

Anyhoo, I need to get my butt in gear and pick up the supplies from the Piggly Wiggly.

Well, hell. Someone is at the door. Who could that be?

Thirty

Sweet, Texas

3 a.m.

Optimistic, slightly drunk witches: 1

ow, *that* was a party. I wasn't kidding about the whole town being invited. Billy's friend Joseph owns the liquor store and he brought five kegs. Everyone contributed food, bottles of wine, and whiskey. There were bowls of punch for the kids and some great music.

Ms. Johnnie had her new boyfriend, Hawk, who is only 50 (but we aren't going to dwell on that), bring his jukebox up. It was loaded with all kinds of music, even some of Zane's tunes.

Caleb picked Margie and Billy up in Dallas and flew them to Sweet. They had no idea we were throwing a party for them. He told them there was a town meeting and everyone wanted to kick me out of Sweet, so they needed their votes. Of course they came with him. They are both as loyal as it gets.

We didn't want to do crepe paper streamers, so we took all of the white twinkle lights we use at Christmas and put them on every plant in the Civic Center. Kira had ordered tons of flowers and we had tiny votives in little colored glass holders on all the tables. It created a very warm and romantic atmosphere.

Old Mr. Coleman waited at the door to let us know when the couple arrived.

When they walked in we all yelled, "Congratulations!" Margie busted out in happy tears, and I saw Billy wipe a few off his face, too. Those two are so in love. They danced all night long, never straying far from each other.

Sam and I were able to dance to a few slow numbers. Wrapped in his arms, tight against his chest and swaying to the music, is just about the best feeling there is. But midway through the party he was called away to the hospital. That's what happens when you hook up with a doctor. He's still there, which is one of the reasons I'm up writing at three in the morning.

The knock on the door earlier had been from FedEx. They had a package from Azir. I opened it when I got home after the party.

With Azir it could be a check for a million dollars, or the title to a fleet of Bentleys. He's insanely generous.

We'd left on a good note in Fiji. I'd gone with him to the airport, but before we boarded our different jets, we had a quick chat in the car.

"Azir. Are you okay?" I was checking my purse to make sure I had all my papers. I'd packed in a hurry and was worried I'd left my passport behind.

"What do you mean?" Azir asked.

I sighed. "About all of this crap. If it hadn't been for me, you wouldn't have been kidnapped and driven half mad."

He smiled. "We are good, my friend." He reached over and squeezed my hand.

"Cool."

And that's how we left it.

When I opened the package, my breath caught for just a moment. Inside a bubble-wrapped package was a small, glass clown fish.

The note read:

"Thank you for being my friend.—A."

The simple gift was so precious that it brought tears to my eyes. Of course, I seem to be overly sentimental about everything these days.

My mind keeps churning through everything that has happened the last few weeks.

Garnout's disappearance was the toughest thing for me. Every time I think about him I get teary-eyed. I'm so grateful he's home. Last night I couldn't resist doing a mental check on him.

"Hello, witch." Garnout said without looking up. He sat at the counter of his shop perusing a large book. "Spying on me?"

What could I say? "Yes. Is everything okay?"

He shook his head, but smiled. "I am well. Are you continuing your training? It is of the utmost importance. You will have a grave responsibility soon, and you must be up to the task."

"What kind of responsibility?" Much like Darcy, Garnout always talked in riddles when it came to the future.

"There is an imbalance now, and when that happens, evil moves fast. You are stronger than you know, and you must train over the next few weeks and discover how to combine your powers. And you must always be aware. *Always.*"

This was the third time in three days I had the same lecture. I didn't roll my eyes, but I wanted to. To be honest, I hadn't done a lot of training, but I would. I knew what Calinda could do if she showed up, and the wizard was right—I had to be ready for anything.

He waved a hand at me. "Away with you and stop wasting your powers spying on me." The words were said in a harsh manner, but he smiled.

"Whatever. Geez, I only wanted to make sure you were okay." *And that the wicked sorceress hadn't kidnapped you . . . again.* Of course I didn't say that part. I said good-bye and tried to relax.

In addition to wondering where Calinda will pop up next, I also have stupid Jason's words rolling around in my head.

"The one closest will destroy you." The words had been spoken when he knew he was about to die. He probably wanted to mess with my brain. At least, I keep telling myself that.

The one closest to me is Sam, and if he has a secret that is going to destroy me, I don't want to know. Really. Well, I don't want to know today. Things are so good for us right now; our relationship is stronger than ever.

I love him so much, and I'm not ready to let that go. I refuse to let Jason's words make even one day I have with Sam an unhappy one. I'm moving forward with my life, and with the man I love.

Candace (Candy) Havens is a veteran entertainment journalist. In addition to her columns seen in newspapers throughout the country, she is the entertainment critic for 96.3 KSCS. She is the author of *Charmed & Dangerous*, *Charmed & Ready*, and the nonfiction biography *Joss Whedon: The Genius Behind Buffy*, as well as several published essays. You can visit her at www. candacehavens.com or for the real crazy stuff at http://candyhavens.livejournal.com.